A FIELD GUIDE TO
DEAD
BIRDWATCHERS

other books by Gary Alexander

Harry Saves The World
A Field Guide to Armageddon
Pigeon Blood
Unfunny Money
Deadly Drought
Kiet and the Opium War
Kiet and the Golden Peacock
Kiet Goes West
Blood Sacrifice
Dead Dinosaurs
Dragon Lady
Disappeared
Zillionaire
Interlock
Loot
Gold
A Book of Facts a novel
Father's Day
Damn Near Broke
Bad Elements
Humpty Dumpty Goes Kersplat
Numerous short stories

A FIELD GUIDE TO
DEAD
BIRDWATCHERS

A Ted Snowe Fable

GARY ALEXANDER

Encircle Publications, LLC
Farmington, Maine U.S.A.

Editor: Cynthia Brackett-Vincent
Book design: Eddie Vincent
Cover design by Deirdre Wait
Cover photographs © Getty Images

Published by: Encircle Publications, LLC
PO Box 187
Farmington, ME 04938

Visit: http://encirclepub.com

Sign up for Encircle Publications newsletter and specials
http://eepurl.com/cs8taP

Printed in U.S.A.

It is not only fine feathers that make fine birds.
—Aesop

I wish I had eight pairs of hands,
and another body to shoot the specimens.
— John James Audubon

Prologue

Birdwatcher Bob

"M r. Chance, this is your exit interview," Ted Snowe said. Mr. Chance turned to Snowe and said, "I beg your pardon?"

The field trip had ended and Bob Chance, the leader, was breaking down his scope, a Carl Zeiss 20-75X DiaScope, and putting away the Leica 10 x 42 Ultravid HP waterproof binoculars around his neck. Over $5000 worth of top-notch German glass.

The attendees were walking from the boardwalk to the parking lot. The majority were senior citizens who were climbing into the small bus that would take them back to the retirement home, their excitement done for the week. Chance and Snowe had a little privacy.

"To exit from your present life to a future life of my making. Or the dreaded alternative."

Bob Chance stared at a lean and supple man of roughly forty, who appeared to be smiling even though he wasn't, a natural smart-aleck. He was good-looking without being handsome or pretty, the type Bob had hated and envied for as long as he could remember. He was the star athlete who always got the girl. He aced any class he took if he felt like it. He'd be the boy next door, a Joe College big-man-on-campus look to him when he was eighty years old.

Worst of all, he was probably a nice guy who as a kid could whip

1

Chance's ass with one hand tied behind his back. But he wouldn't intentionally humiliate a porky kid with two left feet. Chance had hate *hated* him at first sight, suspicious as to why he was along today. He was different from the others, by himself and obviously bored.

"I am not understanding and I don't think I caught your name. I'd been wondering about you. You're not on my sign-up printout."

"You will understand, Bob, and I'm not pitching my name," Ted Snowe said. "You're a CPA and comptroller for South Seattle Industries, an aerospace subcontractor. They export titanium or import it or make widgets out of it in the back room or some damn thing. Or they don't. I hit a solid titanium firewall when I searched for fine details on them. Aerospace is a stab in the dark because titanium is widely used in aircraft, even if South Seattle Industries has never sold an ounce of it to an airplane maker."

"Uh, well, yes. Yes it is. Yes I am."

"What is it they do there? Specifically."

"I can't answer that."

"Because you don't want to or you don't know?"

"Yes."

"Great answer. Know what I think, Bob? The general contractor hiding in the background may have government contracts front and center, real or more likely a shell, with waste taken for granted. There's indifference and inefficiency galore, lose money piled in every direction for the general and the subs and employees. Hogs at the trough. You've been considerately and considerably tidying up crumbs. The unpleasant people who hired me know you have, but don't know how. You're good, Bob. Damn good."

Bob Chance did not acknowledge the compliment. He was in his mid-forties, moon-faced and rumpled. His thick glasses were smudged, his graying hair wispy. He was soft, plump and had boy tits. Chance was shaking his head in denial of what he knew was coming, but his ruddy complexion had turned a shade paler, not an unusual reaction when Ted Snowe prepared to pose his offer.

"There's a third party in the shadows who's unknown to you, a land mine you've been so close to stepping on. I'm here to lead you safely out of the minefield."

Chance said nothing.

"This is too complex to explain in detail in the short time we have, but there are Russians with vested interests," Snowe lied. "Russians who make Uncle Joe Stalin seem like a teddy bear in comparison."

"Impossible."

"That's what I'd think too, but they're the ones who hired me," Ted Snowe said.

"Hired you?"

"Stop playing dumb. The money you embezzled was money they laundered in South Seattle Industries. Money from robbery, extortion, murder for hire, and the other things they do to earn a tainted buck. It's too convoluted for me to analyze, lacking accounting expertise, but it must be substantial for them to take these measures. You should've let your preservation instincts overrule greed, man. Titanium? I'm willing to guess that the only titanium you've seen lately is your tripod."

"It's aluminum."

"Pricey, though," Ted said.

"Do you hear that?" Bob Chance said.

"The highway noise?"

"No. Listen. A bird. *Wichy*."

"I heard a bird too. Many of them that you pointed out and described. You really know your stuff."

This was a man who didn't know a crow from a goldfinch, Chance thought. "Thank you. It's a common yellowthroat. They're abundant in the Pacific Northwest during the summer in moist and grassy areas such as this. Colorful birds are a treat at this latitude. We saw a red-shafted flicker too, you know. The closer to the equator, the more colorful the birds are. Did you know that?"

"I do now."

Bob Chance swept a hand behind him. "This riparian habitat is one of the best in the area and was a gold mine for birders this morning. We saw forty-one species."

"I didn't keep a tally, but I knew it was up there. You were stopping every thirty seconds to zero in on a bird," Ted Snowe said. "A fun outing too. Fresh air, exercise, bright companions. You may have hooked me as a birdwatcher."

"Not birdwatcher. We prefer to be called birders."

Saying *birdwatcher* as if it were an obscenity. "Okay. Birders."

"We saw a varied thrush, an evening grosbeak, a common merganser, a Barrow's goldeneye, a belted kingfisher."

"You're not having a bad dream, Mr. Chance," Ted interrupted. "This is real. I am real."

Backdropped by an inlet and brushy tide flats under the boardwalk, hand on a corner of the railing for support, Chance looked at Mr. Nameless.

"We can do this the old-fashioned way, how they're paying me to do it," Ted said casually, hand moving inside his jacket as if touching a firearm. "A week from now they'll find you in the trunk of a stolen Cadillac in the airport garage. Wrapped with duct tape. In the fetal position. A bullet hole in the chest. A coup de grace, a nine-mil round in the head, how us pros do it."

"Please, sir. There's been a horrible mistake."

"There has been a mistake, Bob, and you made it by reaching into the cookie jar with both paws."

"Please."

Chance was unsteady, gripping the railing hard. Ted was poised to rush to the birdwatcher and prop him upright, all part of his disappearing service. The bus was pulling away, some of the oldsters watching them.

"Jesus, don't faint on me, Bob. Let me finish. We can do it another way. My way."

Chance couldn't muster a word. It was a cool autumn morning, but he was beginning to perspire as if it were the hottest day of July.

Snowe removed his backpack, unzipped it, and took out three thick manila envelopes.

"Get rid of that optical gear, Bob. You won't be needing it any longer, not for awhile as you adjust to a new life," he said, handing him the envelopes. "Inside is your new identity. You are now Mr. Jerry Hoopsma, owner of several fast food franchises. Wherever you are, if anyone asks, you're in town scouting for new locations. You can pick and choose. Fast food is far and wide. You can probably get a Big Mac on Mars now, so possibilities for entrepreneurial Jerry Hoopsma are infinite. Nobody will blink an eye."

A man who appeared as if he took all his meals at junk-food outlets, Bob Chance gaped at Ted Snowe, trying to process the encounter.

"Snap out of it. Consider yourself in an improved variation of the United States Federal Witness Protection Program, Bob-Jerry, compliments of yours truly."

"My family and friends."

The meek reply sealed the deal, Ted thought, the flat tone confirmation that Chance was on his way, that he could not care less about his family and friends. Ted didn't know much about them except that Chance was married and he had a girlfriend. His clients wanted this job done *fast*. They were extremely pissed at Chance and Ted needed the money, so he zeroed in on the embezzling.

Tunnel vision and sloppy homework he'd later regret.

"Sorry about the loved ones, but, come on, you really are eager to be free as a yellowthroat, aren't you? You can bring your squeeze along. Brenda Smith will jump at a chance, bad pun intended, to leave the beauty salon where she works and help you spend your ill-gotten gains in earnest."

"How do you know all this?"

"Does it matter?"

"I guess not. What's in it for you?"

"Don't you know that it's rude to ask a person about his income?"

"Sorry."

"Just kidding. Twenty percent of what you've stolen so far."

"But that's almost one-hundred-and-fifty-thousand dollars."

Damn. Birdwatcher Bob had embezzled close to $750,000 so far, somewhat more than Snowe guessed. Chance hadn't been there all that long. If he had severe money woes or simply seized an opportunity, Ted didn't know and didn't care.

"You know, South Seattle Industries was only my second full-time job after graduating from college and passing my CPA."

"I didn't know. Is this relevant?"

"My first job was with a small firm, a family firm. They were in a small-town storefront and had long-standing relationships with clients. The owner had a little kid. I'd play with her when they'd bring her into the office. Bought her ice cream. For her fourth birthday, I got her her first tricycle. She eventually went off to college. Got her degree and passed her CPA. Then just like that, she was in. I was out. Over twenty years with them. I was out on the street. Not even a gold watch."

Some of Ted's disappeareds had broken down in tears. Chance was on the verge. He needed to move this along and seal the deal. Ted was nearing forty, the portal for a midlife crisis, so he could relate to Chance's angst.

"Nepotism sucks," Ted said.

"Tell me about it."

"Bob, life —"

"If you, whoever you are, if you tell me life isn't fair, I am going to scream," he stammered.

Ted was going to tell him that. So much for homilies. Time to get tough.

"Listen, Chance, enough self-pity. Man up. I have a large investment in you. Those documents didn't come cheap, nor did the series of investigators I used to learn your recent biography. Jerry Hoopsma is brand-spanking-new too. He wasn't taken from the gravestone of a died-at-birth Jerry Hoopsma I've resurrected. I recreated you from zilch. Be cool, exercise common sense, and they'll never find you. My overhead is sky-high and assembling the package was risky."

"You were paid to kill me and I'm paying you not to?"

"I am and you are. I'm double-dipping, an ethics violation, I realize. I'll try to sleep at night."

"You said Russians."

Ted Snowe was hired by intermediaries, associates of associates of associates, electronic barbed-wire fences he dearly hoped were impenetrable. *Russians* was a complete bluff. They made great bogeymen. Everybody knew they were blood thirstily crazy. There were tales that when they whacked somebody out, they took along entire families, down to second cousins. It was said that the Gambinos and their ilk held them in awe and kept out of their way.

It logically followed that his insistence that Russians weren't in the mix meant that they were. An interesting if unwelcome surprise.

"Don't sweat it. Use what's in those envelopes and they'll never find you."

"What if I say no?"

"Haven't we covered that ground, Jerry-Bob? I won't clip you now or tomorrow or the next day, but don't make any long-range plans," said Ted Snowe, who hadn't murdered a soul in his life and didn't intend to start with this sad sack.

Bob Chance looked at the envelopes in his hand, then cocked his head. "*Dee-dee-dee.* Black-capped chickadees. They're very common hereabouts."

"We're wasting time, Bob."

"I lead field trips as a volunteer, you know."

"Bob."

"I don't ask for a penny, even for gas money."

"Bob."

"I'm respected for my knowledge and willingness to work with all age groups and levels of experience."

Ted moved a step closer to him.

"Bob."

Chance moved a step backward. "When do I have to decide?"

"Now. We're an hour south of Seattle and the Eastside burb where you live. It's up to you, but I recommend that you drive close to the airport and take a room at one of the big hotels along the highway. You're ten minutes from the rest of the world."

Ted gave him a slip of paper. He had written two rows of numbers on it.

"First priority is to transfer my money to this account and don't get any cute ideas. No bargaining, no negotiating. One hundred and fifty grand. Next, if you choose, call your girlfriend. That's up to you. Have her stop halfway through a haircut if she has to. Like most hairdressers, I assume she changes jobs often."

"She does."

"Good. They won't miss her for a day or two. Tell Brenda to pack a bag and meet you at the hotel. Both of you use the time in your room to study the documents for as long as it takes to learn the new you. Alter your appearance slightly to adhere to the new photos I tweaked. Flat-lens glasses and hair dye should do the trick. Hairdresser Brenda can do it perfectly. Get on a plane and fade into the sunset of your choice."

Bob hesitated and said, "I don't know. I think I might go solo. Brenda's a sensitive gal, maybe not up to it. She has issues. I have to think this over."

Regardless how you dressed him, a true sociopath, Snowe thought. Mr. Robert Chance, CPA and family man, was no better or worse than the murderous folks who employed him. He simply lacked a violent streak or if he did, the gonads to act on it. Leaving his wife and kids and lover behind was a mere inconvenience, an entry in a ledger. He'd sow his wild oats at his destination.

"That's your call. What isn't your call is my fee. My money comes first and it comes very soon."

"Don't worry."

"You'll be worrying big-time if my money isn't there."

"Don't worry. Please don't worry."

"My employers may've written off their embezzlement loss, settling for you being six feet under. Blood's more important than money and you're off the payroll so you can't embezzle more. That's how they think."

Bob Chance said, "Listen. A song sparrow in the trees to my left. They're named song sparrows for a reason."

"This is my first birdwatching trip and maybe not my last," Snowe said. "I'm impressed by your insights and your skill. You picked a terrific venue too. Swamp, shrubs, salt water. All easy to get to because of the boardwalk. How you'd hear a bird sound, identify the species, and have your scope set and aimed before the rest of us knew anything. It's a nifty hobby. Hey, wow, that big bird standing on the stump not fifty feet from us."

"A great blue heron. They're common in our area."

Bob Chance–Jerry Hoopsma finished packing up his scope and tripod, and said, "I have six-hundred and ninety-eight birds on my life list. I'm looking forward to exceeding one thousand."

"You were fudging. You told us seven hundred."

"I was rounding off."

"Good luck."

"Have you ever heard of a resplendent quetzal?"

"I haven't. As you know, I'm not a regular birdwatcher."

"As I said, we prefer to be called birders."

"Pardon me. Birders."

"In my opinion, the resplendent quetzal is the world's most beautiful bird. Its tail feathers can reach two feet in length. The quetzal is extremely rare. It's found primarily in tropical cloud forests in Central America. The ancient Maya executed anyone who harmed a quetzal by tearing out their beating hearts."

Ted laughed. "That increased their life span. The birds, that is."

"The Guatemalan monetary unit is the quetzal. That's how much they're revered in that part of the world. Books have been written about resplendent quetzals and their history."

"You have the time and money to chase down that quetzal and spend it too, Mr. Hoopsma. Have a nice day."

As Ted walked to his car, Chance yelled, "You, sir, are a desperado."

Desperado. He'd been called an abundance of things, but never that.

1

A Rare Breed of Cat

Desperado, Ted Snowe thought a week-and-a-half later, smiling as he walked toward the beach late on a flawless day, savoring Bob Chance's complimentary insult.

When he'd first gone into European exile, Snowe knew he had a pair of choices. Stay in his burrow and risk dying of boredom. Stick his head out of it and risk having it shot off.

He chose the former *and* the latter, living incognito and fairly well on a budget that was not lavish. For the second time in his life, Theodore Spangler Snowe Junior, was attempting to make a dishonest living by fraudulently disappearing people, committing a lesser crime to avoid fulfilling the larger crime, a capital offense. He rationalized it now as he did then that he was saving lives. And stuffing filthy lucre from two sources into his pockets. A hypocritical Robin Hood, if one wished to be overly critical, not a dictionary-definition desperado.

Ted Snowe was playing it relatively safe during his encore, declining assignments on violent individuals, citing a cockamamie conflict of interest. Since he was an uncontrollably violent sociopathic psychopathic individual himself, an essential on his CV, he might be recognized by his prey, a past colleague or fellow inmate. He'd been in the business "since, like, fucking forever, man."

His clients were buying his crude justification.

But for how much longer?

Ted had presumed that white-collar criminals, supposedly cerebral, educated and analytical, would exercise common sense and caution, and remain disappeared.

The first time around, he had taken on tough guys and neutralized them with a blowgun and curare-tipped darts before giving his pitch. He likened the curare to a beekeeper's smoke.

Jimmy (Knuckles) Brutto, was his first and foremost lesson in Murphy's Law, the beginning of his troubles. Jimmy was a Mafioso goon and degenerate gambler, a subhuman wrecking ball nicknamed for his vast résumé of broken jaws and crushed eyeballs. He sported the lowest hairline Ted had ever seen outside of a zoo. Ted pictured Jimmy Knuckles moving his lips while reading a STOP sign.

Jimmy had gotten into the worst sort of trouble with his bosses, skimming from a variety of rackets to feed his gambling jones, doing so without an iota of finesse or restraint. Intellectually limited as Jimmy was, Ted had thought he grasped the importance of sticking to the background and the altered appearance he provided. Jimmy was to be a Midwesterner named Charles (Chuck) Abbott, who liked shooting pool and watching stock car races on TV. A quiet blue-collar life out of harm's way.

But no.

Charles (Chuck) Abbott did not disappear into amber waves of grain, pool-shooting taverns, and Sunday band concert country with the good ol' boy identity that cost Ted much time and money to construct. Jimmy (Knuckles) Brutto turned up mere months later in a Mobile, Alabama courtroom, dressed in tarp-sized orange, charged with manufacturing and trafficking methamphetamines worth millions on the street. Jimmy was also charged with contributing to the delinquency of a minor—his curvaceous fifteen-year-old girlfriend who was in juvenile custody.

Ted's employers were exceptionally annoyed by Ted's breach of business ethics. They sent a *real* hit man after him.

Further, Beth Palmer Brutto, Jimmy's "widow," had collected on a $100,000 life insurance policy she had taken out on Mr. Brutto, after forging his signature on a junk mail application from some gyppo company, Grim Reaper Life and Indemnity or the like. Her rationale was that by littering her mailbox with the offer, the insurance company was just asking for it. Despite no corpus delicti, few doubted that Jimmy wasn't wearing concrete galoshes, communing with the fish.

When Jimmy returned from the dead, the insurance company wanted their money back from Beth, and Beth wanted that money (she'd mostly spent, paying bills and fixing up her mother's trailer home) from Ted. Fair was fair. Beth Palmer Brutto tracked Ted down and stuck her hand out. No money was paid. A failed business transaction morphed into a rather unconventional first date.

Beth became the only woman Ted had ever truly loved. And probably ever will love.

Thanks to their high-flash-point romance and inseparability, Beth joined Ted as a target. After a bit of harum-scarum by all parties, Ted's prospective assassin met his end by one in his own profession. Ask Ted and Beth who hired that person and they'll take the Fifth.

Several years ago, Ted went on hiatus and the couple moved permanently to Vila Nova de Milfontes, Portugal in southwestern Europe, a charming beachfront town of white stucco and red tile roofs. They had the naïve notion of living happily ever after, Ted thought as he waded into the Atlantic on a typically balmy autumn evening.

A half dozen other people were out doing the same. The summer crowds had dwindled, though in high season, while the town's population inflated, the visitors were less than overwhelming. Milfontes primarily attracted summering Brits and weekender *lisboetas*.

Vila Nova de Milfontes was a fishing village where the Mira River emptied into the ocean, offering paragliding, ecotourism in the surrounding area, and little else for a visitor. If Ted craved utter solitude, he could with minimal effort hike to several adjacent beaches and have them to himself.

He slogged into the water and stopped when chilly swells lapped at his kneecaps. Vila Nova de Milfontes was the same latitude as the Bay Area, so temperatures were not in bathwater range, but its sunsets were hard to beat. Filtered as it was by haze, Ted watched the orange fireball plate the horizon copper and finally, as if losing its buoyancy, descend behind it.

Waterfowl skimmed the surface, wheeling out to sea. Ted made a mental note he'd probably forget to search for them in a field guide to birds of the Iberian Peninsula. He had picked it up in Lisbon immediately after his return flight from Seattle. Birdwatcher Bob Chance hadn't completely hooked him on the hobby, but Bob had whetted his interest. Ted stood in the water until his toes were numb and trudged out.

Vila Nova de Milfontes was a two-hour drive from Lisbon. You might go days without hearing American English spoken there. The English speakers were predominantly the visiting Brits.

Ted's neighbors were friendly, but kept their distance. His Portuguese was better than he let on. He confined it to greetings and basic needs, and he intended to keep it that way, a barrier to camaraderie.

Bom dia, senhor.

Bom dia, senhora.

He had taken an indefinite leave of absence from faux-assassination, and with Beth was having an extended and passionate honeymoon without benefit of clergy. After eighteen months of unwedded bliss, however, paradise was becoming bor-ing.

They were restless and there were limited ways of stretching one's legs when there was a price on one's head, an open-ended contract. The no-necks he had betrayed neither forgave nor forgot. Beth and Ted came to think of them euphemistically as "the Fellas." The exact price on Ted was surely sizable and as long as Beth was with him, she'd be two for the price of one.

Ted came out onto warm sand and headed home, thinking that exactly 214 days ago, he was doing the very same thing. He had walked into their small house and found a note on the kitchen table:

> *Dearest darling yummy Ted, it's not you, it's me. I need*
> *my space. I'll take my chances. Don't try to find me.*
> *Love you forever. Beth.*

Terse, unsentimental, no frills, twenty-six words, thirty if you eliminated the contractions.

It could have been done in verse.

Beth had carefully planned her escape, too, thoroughly blindsiding him. She was packed and gone in less than the forty-five minutes he was on the beach and in the water.

Ted Snowe was nearing the end of his thirty-ninth year. A tip-off on what was coming, which he hadn't seen, was her teasing him that as he zeroed in on the big four-oh, he'd changed. Gone was the rogue con man with an edge, a zest for the risk vs. reward game. He had changed into a businessman, anxious how full their piggy bank was, and in interest rates.

She had said it with a twinkle, but he'd missed her true meaning. He'd rebutted by kidding her that his career was as long as a professional athlete's. With the exception of football placekickers and soccer goalkeepers, you were flat-out done at forty. He *wasn't* kidding and she knew it.

Their love life was atrophying too, something that went unspoken. Spontaneity had given way to rote, no less than once and no more than twice a week, always after dark, always in their bed. It had been months since a secluded beach or a hammock on the patio, one time in a rainstorm, or half-looped in a Lisbon hotel room while on a shopping trip.

He guessed that Beth's first stop would be Butte, Montana and her mother, whom she fretted about constantly, and presumably vice versa. Gladys Marshak Palmer Wiley Johnstone Higgins Dickey lived in a trailer park. Ted had resisted the immediate urge to set out after Beth, a wild and reckless chase that would accomplish nothing but create a scene if he caught her and quite possibly expedite their death sentences.

Ted walked onto his verandah and the undersized basketball court he'd installed on uneven asphalt. His yard wasn't large, but it was long and narrow. Imaginary center court was a meter from the alley, demarcated by waist-high flowerpots, the contents of which had wilted after Beth's departure.

Illuminated by twilight, he picked up a ball and drained ten straight from the chalk-marked foul line, nothing but twine. He unsuccessfully persuaded himself that he had lost little since his playing days as a point guard at Purdue, second-team all Big Ten in his senior year. For a ballplayer, in dog and cat years, he was in his enfeebled nineties.

Ted went inside, feeling a twinge of queasiness, as he had for the past 214 evenings, irrationally expecting to see Beth and her suitcase, her flying into his arms. But there was nobody there for him, and nothing of the slightest interest except the things on his dining table, how he'd left them. Salt, pepper, a laptop, an ancient (c. 1950) Remington typewriter, and his excuse for a chapbook, a ringed notebook like kids took to school.

The day's *International New York Times* was on the table too. The *Times* was Europe's English language paper, and Ted walked to a store every morning for it and a cup of coffee. All the news he wanted was on the laptop, but the ritual was homey, even though the paper made him achingly homesick. The online English-language *Portugal News's* stories were predominantly in-country.

For a life so mundane, Ted Snowe's existed with a multitude of contradictions. Lonely as could be, he resisted every urge to mingle with others. After Beth's departure, he could not, in fact, bring himself to troll Lisbon tourist bars and pick up American women, giving them intensely lurid tales to take home. Something out of a Technicolor movie.

Ted put the newspaper on his bookshelf to get it out of the way. The shelves badly needed dusting, but he lacked the energy and motivation to take on the task. It had been Beth's responsibility.

The book titles were hand-me-downs from past occupants and eclectic. The history of the Messerschmitt Me-262, the world's first operational jet fighter; a mystery novel set in a mythical Southeast Asian nation; organic vegetable gardening; a coffee table pictorial on the postimpressionists; a biography of Benito Mussolini; a thin Kierkegaard tome; a true crime potboiler about a serial killer; a short story anthology; a soccer coaching text with a foreword by German great Franz Beckenbauer; a 14-year-old *World Almanac and Book of Facts*; a road atlas of Great Britain; a Portuguese phrasebook; a guide to ancient Roman archeological sites; Ted had read and reread them all, and added to the shelves until some were two deep.

Once, after he'd had more than a few beers, he decided to fill the hours usefully, in any way possible, even housecleaning, an unnatural act, drunk or sober. He tackled the most difficult chore first, cleaning out the attic.

From atop a rickety ladder, he'd crawled into it and found the Remington inside a leatherette case that had been gnawed by rodents. It was keeping company with bent curtain rods and brittle yellowed newspapers that dated to the Antonio Salazar regime, things that had been forgotten many tenants ago.

Oddly, around the time of the Remington find, Ted had decided to scratch a dormant itch when he came upon some English languages books of poetry in a tiny bookshop on a cobblestoned Lisbon street. He read and reread Jim Harrison, Ferlinghetti, Corso, Bukowski, edgy stuff like that.

In college, he had taken a course in poetry appreciation, which he hadn't in the least. They were made to study the work of poets dead before the invention of the steam engine. Nuances known to the professor and better students were lost on him.

This was different beyond different. Aided by loneliness and Super Bock beer, Ted saw in the typewriter discovery and poetry enjoyment as a synchronicity not to be ignored.

Filling those hours, he wrote on the Remington he had meticulously cleaned and lubricated. It was his belief that poetry should not be slickly word-processed. A fountain pen or manual typewriter were the only acceptable tools.

His best (so he thought) effort was an ode to the planet Mars.

At the time, the planet was visible low in the night sky, bright and tempting. Ted had been drinking, a beer in one hand and binoculars in the other. His alcohol consumption had not decreased after Beth's departure.

Properly inspired, typing with index fingers, herewith:

RED

The Red Planet is not
red. The Red Planet is reddish.
The Red Planet can appear golden,
ecru, brown, tan, grayish, bluish,
the hue of a butterscotch sundae.
Of late, an alien prowls the surface.
It is not the first.
This metallic beast sports
black rubber feet, a glass eyeball,
an insect's worth of shiny appendages.
It is a gleaming cyclops, hideous and menacing,
slow and clumsy as it negotiates the endless desert
and slaloms around boulders and slabs.
Martians play peekaboo with the invader, who lacks
peripheral vision and an elastic neck.

They are not scared shitless of it.
Martians have no digestive tracts.
They are not scared to death of it.
Martians are not born, nor do they die.
Millennia of solitude, and now this.
What does *this* extraterrestrial want,
probing and digging?
If it comes to a slab with inscriptions,
then what?
To the sacred scrolls,
then what?

Three months ago, recklessly, he read *RED* aloud at an English-language poetry slam in Alfama, Lisbon's oldest district. Alfama was hilly, unruly and labyrinthine. It was there when the Visigoths were. Some narrow streets hadn't seen direct sunlight in a millennium.

The open-mike slam was held at *Café de Canção* (Cafe of Song), a watering hole where *fado*, the mournful Portuguese folk music, was sung live. Wednesday nights were devoted to the English-language slam, which drew bohemian expats and a smattering of curious locals.

Astoundingly, Ted had won first prize, a certificate, and ten Euros. He framed the award with the 10 € note and mounted it on the living room wall.

Ted would love to earn a living as a poet, but knew that he could only do so in a fantasy world. The infinitesimal percentage of poets who were published at all could expect to pull down $400 over twenty-five years. It would take until the 30th Century to make what he made on one disappeared.

So he had resumed his former career as a "disappearer" on a parallel track, climbing back on that horse. The firewall worked both ways, so he never ever used a name, but he had valuable phone numbers. A little trial and error and Ted connected with someone who had not heard of his past deviousness or connected his voice to his deceptive business practices.

The assignments came infrequently—only four thus far, two before and two after Beth's departure—albeit enough to marginally maintain his lifestyle. Keeping oneself pseudo-disappeared was expensive, and the allure and isolation of Milfontes could be a trap of its own making. He'd have to force himself to move on soon.

The call-in procedure with the Fellas was more sophisticated than the last time around. Daily, he was instructed to go online and open the classifieds section of the top twenty-five American newspapers, in order of circulation, then check under *Pet City, Cats,* or the equivalent. If there was an advertisement for a Clarkson medium-hair cat, an animal as fictitious as if it had come from Mars, he was to call the number from a pay telephone or a throwaway cell. The search was usually busywork, but he didn't want to chance that it wasn't by skipping a single day. If the Fellas demanded obedience to uniformity, that's what they'd get.

Next morning, on his 215th Bethless day, Ted reached the twenty-first newspaper in line, the *Dallas Morning News.* And there it was, a Clarkson medium-hair cat, available for a bargain price of $599, as if a used car priced to sell. Every picture of these critters was different. This was a short-hair tabby. Ted was a cat person. He'd love to have a cat again, but the traveling his career demanded would be unfair to the animal.

He wrote the phone number down. It was always a different number and he always spoke to a different Fella. To weed out calls from the curious and from crazy cat people, a recorded message said that the Clarkson medium-hair had been sold and thank you for your interest. Ted was to punch #35 and wait for one of the Fellas to answer.

He got up, but went no farther than the fridge for a bottle of Super Bock. Southern Europe was wine country, not renowned for beer, but this Portuguese brand, a robust lager, wasn't too bad.

How many was that today?

He sat, drank, and thought. It had been only ten days since he disappeared Birdwatcher Bob Chance. Subsequent assignments never ever came that frequently.

Was it an emergency on their end, a colleague ratting them out to the law, agreeing to air filthy linen to one and all, a la Joseph Valachi? Or was it a trap, to bring him back to the States to get him out of their hair once and for all?

He finished the beer and thought it couldn't hurt to make the call and decide what to do from there. He had enough money left to live comfortably for another year, frugally for two. Ted wasn't deceiving Bob Chance when he said that he had high overhead.

Ted subcontracted investigative work on each assignment, making sure no one entity could dope out the big picture. After all expenses, his net on Birdwatcher Bob was only $84,533. It was tax free, but still.

Then what? He needed to squirrel away a bunch more for retirement. He couldn't do this until Social Security kicked in, a miniscule monthly amount as he'd paid little into it. Beth was right about him and retirement too. It was becoming a hang-up, him thinking that they could someday have actual friends, backyard barbecues, and double-dating to movies and ball games.

Beth hadn't taken much money with her. Less, he thought, than she was entitled to. Pocket change and airfare, really.

Previously, he made these calls from land lines. He'd drive to Lisbon and use a pay phone, with a pile of Euro coins on the shelf. No longer. Pay phones were getting harder to find than Clarkson medium-hairs, and even low-tech gunsels had caller ID.

In the States, Ted had bought a bundle of disposable cell phones with domestic and foreign area codes, enough of them to raise the sales clerk's eyebrows. Let the Fellas think that Ted (the Desperado) Snowe was in New Jersey or Vladivostok or Timbuktu.

2

Brenda Lee Smith

Bobby said there'd be a little bit of bleeding. Just some spotting, that's all. The doctor, he said so too. Well, I think he said so, but his English was bad and I could hardly understand him. Bobby said it'd get better and eventually go away and sure enough it has, along with the cramps they said would go away too, as they for the most part have.

Bobby helps me keep a close eye on my situation. He says there are all kinds of doctors where we're going if a problem crops up. Bobby treats me like porcelain and I love him for that too. You gals out there, you should be so lucky to have a guy as thoughtful and caring as my Bobby is with me. I'm number one!

They said I might get hot pants too and they're right. I surely do have 'em. I'm hornier than a three-peckered goat, yes I am, but that's the last time I'm gonna say it that way as Bobby doesn't like me talking dirty, so I'll leave it to your imagination. It (me not having horniness) and (me having it) infection, they were my biggest fears, but there's no infection either, not that we know of. Bobby was correct on that count too, saying to hang onto the antibiotics if there's a flare-up.

When Bobby says no worries from now on, I'll try not to. I'll leave the worrying to him as he does enough for the two of us, (he's a worrywart-and-a-half), although he pretends he doesn't and says we're as good as home free.

The first of last week, he called me up at the salon when I was halfway through a cut and a perm and said drop what you're doing, pack a bag, and let's go. I already knew something was up. He had me on what you'd call red alert, so he didn't have to twist my arm.

Ever smell that chemical you have to use for a perm? Yuck. I'd told my client (her name is Janice) I was going to the back room to get something and kept right on going out the door.

My client, I'm not losing any sleep over her. Janice is a real nasty old bitch. Nothing is ever right and if she ever gave me a tip I'd faint dead away. It's what they call poetic justice that I'd cut just one side of her hair, so if she has to walk out of the salon like that, she'll be a lopsided Little Orphan Annie with her mile-wide butt, wrinkles and sagging boobs. It's a sight I'm almost sorry I missed.

The other gals who didn't have clients were outside smoking and shooting the breeze and didn't think a thing about me going straight to my car, as there are no set hours for stylists. If your appointment calendar was blank you were free to go. Besides the bitch in my chair, I'm leaving behind my clippers and the rest of my tools, and three more clients on the day's calendar and I don't know how many scheduled for the rest of the month. Tough bananas. They can deal.

Bobby said he had a plan and said to go when he said go, so I went when he said go.

Bobby. The first time we met is when he came into the salon without an appointment. I could tell right off the bat that he was embarrassed. Guys his age who come in to get a haircut where they don't know anybody, nine times out of ten their hair's thinning bad. Like Bobby's was. *Ten* times out of ten, when they hop in your chair, they want you to do a comb-over, making it not look like one. I'll tell you, it isn't easy, but if it can be done, I'm the gal to get it done.

I think the first time I ran my hands through what was left of his hair, I knew he was the one for me, how he smiled at me through the mirror. He came in like a week later for a trim he didn't need and I knew he knew he was the one for me too.

Karma. That's what I think they call it. Bobby says it's fate, which is the same thing, isn't it?

So. We're in this big and swanky hotel, out close by the airport, Bobby has us changing rooms like mad. Playing musical rooms is what we're doing. Just a precaution, leaving no stone unturned, he tells me. Better safe than sorry.

He says it's okay to help myself to the rooms' minibars, but don't get tipsy. I don't know how you do that but I try. The bottles are so little, they're sneaky, you know, and before you know it you get a buzz on. In three separate rooms I got a little bit buzzed. But what the heck, if this isn't a celebration I don't know what is.

All Bobby will say on the room changing is there's a lot of money in the picture and he doesn't want to needlessly frighten me. He'll explain it all later when we're in paradise. Paradise is a big improvement to where I've been most of my life, it sure as shootin' is.

I've got some of my work equipment with me that I had at home and I'm dying to do my magic on Bobby as I'm a magician at my craft with scissors and clippers and gels and rinses. Bobby says not to get carried away. He has to look like his new ID and his new name he won't say much about. I can play around with his thinning mop later on in paradise.

He's happy with the result, though. When he looks in the mirror, he can't tell the difference between the face in the mirror and the picture on his passport.

My first and middle names, Brenda Lee, you know, she was that singer from a long time ago. My daddy used to love her and had her songs on photograph records, the old black vinyl kind you played on a turntable. Her picture was on the cardboard jackets and she was as cute as a button, like Bobby tells me I am. I can still hum some of her hits like *I'm Sorry* and *Rockin' Around the Christmas Tree*.

When Daddy passed away I don't remember who got the vinyl.

Him and me and Momma too, we were what you'd call estranged. We weren't on speaking terms either, and Momma and me still aren't. I'm not leaving any close-knit nuclear family behind. Bobby's my family.

It's pitch black outside and Bobby says it's time to go. He bought us tickets on his laptop and the plane will be leaving in under three hours. We're off to lay on the beach and drink mai tais and mojitos. Bobby, he'll be birding too, not "birdwatching" like every no-nothing idiot says, but birding. Bobby says where we're going is a birder's paradise. They have I don't know how many different species of birds.

I'll be honest with you. A bird to me is fried chicken with mashed potatoes and country gravy, but I'll try real hard to love looking for birds up in jungle trees, not just on menus.

Bobby's got himself into a panic attack now after he looked at his laptop in the middle of last night. He changed our flight, moving it up as far as he could. As we're flying first-class, they're jumping through hoops for us.

He said that some of his money is all of a sudden dribbling away to parts unknown. He uses technical talk about the Internet and stolen passwords and encryption and laundering (not clothes), stuff that flies fifty miles over my head. I don't ask for details on what this crisis is, I wouldn't understand it anyway. He says he's right now done a quick transfer of his money into new accounts or we'd be flat broke before you know it.

Bobby's as smart as a whip, 'specially about numbers as he is a certified accountant who got a raw deal. He's been taken advantage of long enough and I'm with him on that 100-percent.

When we get where we're going, Bobby has his heart set on this rare bird he calls a ketsal or katesol, I can never remember exactly. The pictures he has in his bird books, it's positively darling, with this long long tail. It makes me think of Rapunzel's hair, its tail's that freaking long.

But as somebody's been messing with him and his money, we gotta get on an airplane and the hell out of here, so we're tossing our stuff into our bags willy-nilly. Bobby says not to worry over wrinkling. We can pay somebody to press it later on. We can pay to have everything we want done for us.

We're in the elevator now and I stroke Bobby's hair. I cannot for the life of me keep my hands out of his hair. Bobby tells me to spit out my gum. It irks Bobby when I chew gum, which I do a lot and he hates it when I pop my gum. It's white-trashy, he says, hurting my feelings, which he can do when he's stressed out, but he always apologizes later.

He says I can chew gum on the airplane to keep my ears clear. That's the only exception. Into my purse the gum goes.

I have got the shivers, I'm so excited.

Just as the elevator door opens, Bobby hugs me and says it'll be over soon.

But he's trembling when he does.

3

Mr. Nameless' Exit Interview

"You're getting sloppy, pal."

Ted Snowe didn't reply.

"Yoo-hoo. You there, buddy?" said a second Fella.

"Yes. Yes I am."

"What you been doing for us, we liked it. They just up and go away, you know. No muss, no fuss."

Past tense?

"Thank you."

"See, this is how these things gotta work, how you did it for us. It can't work no other way or there's a shitload of problems down the road."

"Absolutely."

"You done good for us."

Compliments from the Fellas were as rare as Clarkson medium-hairs and they were alternating, two on one. Were they playing good goon, bad goon?

"Thanks again. I appreciate it."

"So why'd you go whack the motherfucker in broad daylight in the middle of a hundred fucking people like you're Al Capone or some A-rab terrorist, him and this broad of his? Why didn't you just call the TV news, have them be there when you did them, to catch it live, shitbird?"

"You don't have to yell. I'm not deaf."

"Don't tell me what I got to do and what I don't got to do."

Ted held the phone away from his ear. "Sorry. Please explain."

"You saying you didn't?"

"Hell no. I'm confused. Please explain further."

"I'll explain as farther as you want. We paid you for doing him like you do them, where they just go away. Now this."

In any circumstance, errors in usage grated on Ted Snowe, who had majored in English, and this was one. But it was not an ideal time to point out that "farther" was used for distance and "further" for all else. "I do what you pay me to do. I always have. What is *this*?"

"You said you made him go away? It's where this one you say you done and took money from us to do, you're saying he rose from the dead like he's fucking Jesus H. Fucking Christ so you had to go and do him again?"

"I disappeared him," Ted said, knowing that it was a pathetic rebuttal.

"Yeah? What you went and done, you made him and this broad into a Swiss cheese in front of this big hotel across the street from this airport in front of a million people. That ain't disappearing nobody."

According to what he was hearing, Mr. Bob Chance—slash—Jerry Hoopsma had reappeared even more spectacularly than Jimmy (Knuckles) Brutto. That is, unless this was a bluff, a tall tale, an attempt to test him and his dedication to customer service, to ascertain if he was giving value for money received. An employee review of sorts.

Ted tried to match their bluster, working a semi-snarl into his voice. "You're not making any sense. What the hell are you talking about?"

"The hell I ain't making no sense. It's you who ain't making no sense. This better not be no trend. They're supposed to go away. Vanish."

"They do. How I did it, see. I'll say this regarding the individual in question," Ted said, thinking and talking fast. "That individual went for a swim. What can I say? How did it go wrong? Maybe the guy played possum before we went out for a midnight boat ride. He did an underwater Harry Houdini, slipping out of all the ropes and concrete blocks. I'm not saying it can't be done. If it did happen, I certainly underestimated him, an error I won't repeat. I can't answer for the woman with him. This method, in deep water, I believe, is far superior to burying. In the ground, you run the risk of an animal—"

"Don't tell us, you and your methods, how to get rid of a stiff. We know how to get rid of a stiff."

"Sorry. All I'm trying say is that we inhabit an imperfect world."

"Don't be talking down to us on your imperfect worlds, shithook. You keep acting like you're some fucking gunslinger, you're dead fucking meat."

An atheist who had not been close to his mother, Ted said, "I swear on a stack of Bibles, on my mother's grave."

The Fellas hung up on him.

"Rude," Ted muttered as he twisted the phone, snapping it into pieces.

He had been his wiseass self, telling Bob Chance that he was conducting an "exit interview" with him. That's what the knuckle-draggers were doing with *him* and he had failed the interview miserably. Whether the fireworks were true or false, they had teetered him off-balance.

Ted dropped the phone parts on the floor, then stomped on them as if they were cockroaches. He went to the fridge for another Super Bock and began looking on the laptop for that story. If it had happened, it'd likely be in the Seattle and/or Tacoma newspapers not long ago. And there it was, page-one in *The Seattle Times* and *The Tacoma News Tribune*.

In summary, Robert N. Chance, forty-four, and Brenda Lee Smith, twenty-eight, were shot multiple times with a nine-millimeter automatic pistol at the entrance to a large hotel on Highway-99, near the Seattle-Tacoma International Airport. It was early in the morning, before dawn, and Chance and Smith had been standing with their luggage, waiting for an airporter shuttle to take them to the terminal. They were shot from a moving vehicle, an older small car with tinted windows that was driving fast through the parking lot. It was deemed either a "random drive-by shooting" or an "execution-style" slaying.

A handful of others were outside waiting for a ride and ducked down, so nobody had a good look at the car's occupants or its license number. Mr. Chance was an accountant and well-known volunteer in local birding circles. Not much was known yet of Ms. Smith other than that she was employed locally as a hair stylist.

Birdwatcher Bob must've gotten horny and changed his mind about leaving his hairdresser behind, Ted thought. Loaded with dough or not, the guy was no stud.

Ted searched *further*, finding a follow-up article the day before yesterday that was bad news for him too. Mrs. Robert N. (Mary Ann) Chance, was in equal parts angry, stunned, and grief-stricken, convinced that the double murder was not random. Mrs. Chance had pushed hard for a full investigation. A couple of days before the slaying, her late husband went away while she was at work, leaving a vague note that he had a last-minute invitation to attend an industrial-metals accountancy seminar when someone else dropped out.

She had "smelled a rat." It was so unlike her Bob, who was always so precise, so orderly. He had to think and rethink the smallest change in his life before "making the plunge." However, before his employment at South Seattle Industries, he had been laid off from a job he'd held for over twenty years. She had noticed behavioral changes, "moodiness" and "irritability." The existence of another woman, though, had been a "complete shock."

A police spokesperson said that Bob Chance's Jerry Hoopsma identification did not jibe with his actual ID, which the nitwit had hidden in the lining of a suitcase. He had taken Ted's advice and tinkered with his appearance, though, (per detective comments on the corpse) with flat-lens glasses and a blondish dye job (no doubt done in their hotel room by Hairdresser Brenda).

In the articles, Chance's supervisors at South Seattle Industries refused to comment on whether they were digging into things too, or if they had discovered any irregularities, a sure indicator that they had. They were saddened by the loss of a valued employee and friend, and their hearts and prayers went out to the widow and the remainder of the family.

"Broad daylight" and "a million people" were exaggerations that did not offer solace. Two people were dead and Ted Snowe was not entirely blameless.

Ted was perspiring in places he didn't know one could perspire. He was feeling sick, and it wasn't the Super Bock on an empty stomach. It was a feeling of responsibility to his three other second-generation disappeareds. They had to be advised that the odds were good that they were wearing bull's-eyes. They were who Ted had made them and they'd damn well remain remade.

Not to mention targets drawn on Ted's own ass and Beth's. It wasn't impossible that someone was closing in on him, eager to dig the true story out of his hide one chunk at a time.

His callers hadn't demanded their fee back on Birdwatcher Bob: the standard $15,000. You can return a defective washing machine to the store, so it was logical he'd be asked for the money. But he hadn't been.

Nor had embezzlement recovery been brought up when he received the assignment on Birdwatcher Bob Chance. Then or minutes earlier. It made no sense for the Fellas to write off what could add up to a million bucks. Ted should have been instructed to hold Bob's feet to the fire, literally if necessary, until he coughed up the money.

South Seattle Industries and their titanium? What had Bob Chance taken to bookkeeper's Valhalla he alone was privy to?

It seemed that professional assassins were playing in Ted's sandbox too.

Russians? Ted's fictional Russians perhaps weren't fictional.

A fine mess.

Some desperado he was. Beth had accused him of being a "businessman," an epithet whether she was winking or not. A businessman. If that's what he had degraded to, he was a piss-poor one.

Bob Chance had done exactly what Ted recommended and landed on a coroner's slab instead of in tropical nirvana.

Ted began packing, throwing things into a suitcase, throwing hard. His three remaining disappeareds: a sticky-fingered bond analyst, a Ponzi artist, a retirement planning scammer. Not solid citizens, but the jerks deserved a heads-up.

First priority, of course, was Beth. Admittedly, it was a great excuse to seek her out.

Ted sat on his suitcase so he could zip it shut.

Thinking that a conscience can be a terrible thing to have.

4

The Fellas

"What're you thinking? What's on your mind?"

"Same as on yours is what I'm thinking."

"You think?"

"Yeah. The guy, is he fucking us over?"

"Yeah he is."

"How he talks to us, sometimes normal, like we talk, then he switches over and talks like a college boy or something."

"Maybe he got that split personality thing. Schizo-nutso, I think they call it."

"Yeah, him and the stiff's magic swim in the water, his Houdini bullshit. Chance croaking and turning up to die again. He's like that other one who used to fuck us over before he fell off the planet a few years ago. Remember him?"

"Yeah. The one who said he done Jimmy Knuckles, but didn't do Jimmy for real. This one, he come well recommended too, but you never know about human nature, who's a rotten apple and who ain't."

"Hey, what's going on with Jimmy?"

"They busted him peddling speed with this young poon, you know."

"I know. I remember, the dumb ass."

"Well, they still got him locked up down in Alabama or one of them states down there. He ain't gonna be busting no heads when he

33

gets out. He'll be so old and decrepited, he'll have to hire somebody to wipe his ass for him."

"We gotta keep an eye on this guy who didn't do Chance."

"We gotta."

"The guy we sent to clip the one who screwed us before with Jimmy Knuckles, he ain't been seen since."

"I know."

"We gotta keep an eye on this motherfucker who said he done Chance, in case he does business just the same as that other guy."

"That's what you said."

"We gotta."

"You pay somebody to do something and they don't do it, it ain't right."

"It ain't."

"You can't trust nobody in this day and age."

"You can't."

"Society, morals, all that, it's in the toilet. Business ethics is all gone."

"You're right. There's no integrity no more. Know what I think it is?"

"Uh uh."

"That Internet shit and these little tablet things everybody carries around staring at. Nobody lifts a finger to work no more. All anybody does, they look at them little things day and night. We was raised with values and a work ethic. There's no values. They're walking across the street staring at one of the things, it oughta be legal to run over them. You're doing a public service."

"Ain't that the truth. Now, are we ever gonna see any of our money back we paid on Chance and what Chance took of ours?"

"I'm working on an angle. I put out feelers on sending this guy out to where Chance worked."

"I think I know who you're talking about. Tony."

"Yeah, Tony. Guy's batshit crazy."

"That's him. That's our boy. He can do it if anybody can. I said we gotta get things done last week, but he already flew out there last week. He's way ahead of us. I don't know who sent him and I ain't asking. The important thing is he got sent."

"Yeah, that's good."

"He's like a live grenade, you know. He's the best at what he does but, you know."

"Yeah, don't I know. He's an expert numbers guy and he can take care of what got to be taken care of too. He likes doing it. The man enjoys his work, the bloodier the better."

"It's his whole life. A man shouldn't be married to his work. It ain't healthy to take your work home with you."

"Him, you gotta be careful of. He's funny in the head. He's fucking creepy. Looks like a movie star and he's a fucking mad dog with rabies."

"Doing what he does to a stiff after he'd made him into a stiff, slicing and dicing it into cat food. That ain't normal."

"A normal person, you give him a hit, he does the hit and moves on. It's just a job. This guy, though."

"They say you give him a broad to do and he gets his rocks off. He ain't queer but he don't like broads neither."

"He'll find what's left of the money and have his fun too."

"Whoever the money belonged to, we don't need to know."

"We sure don't. A little knowledge is a dangerous fucking thing."

"They hired a hundred-percent legit bookkeeper at that titanium joint and look what it got us. A goddamn crook is what Chance was. No values, no morals."

"I'd like to fly out there myself and piss on his grave, the motherfucker."

"Anybody else there who cooked the fucking books, he's gonna get his ass fried too. There's a shitstorm waiting."

"Let's check our phone the fucker called us on. What's the area code? We gotta trace down his neighborhood so we can tip our guy to pay him a visit when he ain't doing his arithmetics at the titanium joint."

"It's good we work that angle. Keep talking nice as we can to the no-good motherfucker without blowing our stack. I know I did when he called. It ain't easy to be cool, but we gotta try."

"I'm looking. Yeah, here it is. Oh one one and a six one and a three. Hobart, Tasmania."

"Where the fuck is that?"

"Don't you know nothing? It's where they have that Tanzanian devil."

"That's a long way off."

"More than halfway around the world. Hell, my guess is two-thirds of the way around the world. That far."

"Motherfucker does get around, but the world ain't big enough for him to hide in."

5

Serial Matrimony

Call me paranoid, John Q. Paranoid, Ted Snowe thought. He disliked coincidences to the extreme. Disappearing someone his way and having him promptly disappear for real, for instance.

Jimmy Brutto, fine. A complication, a headache. In the long run, though, a smooth ending.

Bob Chance and his lady friend. Not so good.

Ted was thinking this on a red-eye from Amsterdam Schiphol to Chicago O'Hare. He had time to think because he couldn't sleep. He couldn't sleep because he was flying coach, back in steerage, Row 42, Seat E, upright with zero legroom, sandwiched between a pair of guys, Seats D and F, who had BMIs the same as their row number, wide bodies on a wide body.

Why this Row 42 parsimony? With the current development, Ted's untaxed income was plummeting from comfortable to precarious, so he was flying coach rather than business class, as he had on all four second-generation assignments. That was an extravagance he absolutely could not afford. He had a hunch that cleaning up this mess was going to be a long expensive haul.

A "rogue" con man with a violent streak flying business class transmuting to a "businessman" flying coach. Rhetorical irony. As ironic as a hit-man-who-isn't whose subject was nonetheless hit.

Ted almost smiled.

Truth be told, he wouldn't be comfortable flying even if he were in the cockpit, hands on the controls, knowing what was going on. The poem that he scribbled in his chapbook pretty much told that tale:

SILVER

> Observe the lustrous silver bird on the tarmac.
> Ground crews swarm it as if picking off ticks.
> Like feathered vertebrates,
> this silver bird is clumsy on the ground,
> its spindly legs and feet
> gratefully retracting when airborne.

At 38,000 feet, you ride in an aluminum eggshell,
nibbling on complimentary peanuts.
At 550 MPH you drive over an ethereal pothole.
You crank up the sound of your $3 headphones,
veering your mind from fragility.

An infantile piece of work, he thought, wondering how he had cluelessly scored a B- in that poetry appreciation class.

Strangely, shoulders numbingly tucked, he could now sleep and didn't wake up until the pilot announced that the Great Lakes were below. Not that he could lean over and verify it even if he cared to.

Ted wondered how high the highest-flying birds flew. Not as high as silver birds, any of the Boeing or Airbus species, but high.

Birdwatcher Bob Chance knew.

Bob knew how high a resplendent quetzal flew too.

Bob, what the hell did I do to you and your lady?

* * * * *

Priorities. Numero uno, find Beth ASAP and update her on current events. Last time around, the bad guys got to him through her. History repeating itself? If so, not wonderful. She had to be whisked out of jeopardy. He was her tarnished knight/desperado riding in on a soiled-gray, swayback charger.

Secondly, learn who clipped Birdwatcher Bob Chance and his lady love, Brenda Lee Smith, and why. Ted hoped that law enforcement would have this wrapped up by now, the killers in the slammer, saving him the trouble of sticking his neck out further, playing amateur dick and savior of a trio of shady disappeareds.

Ideally, it had nothing to do with his fictional (?) Russians and embezzlement.

Or fellow birders (not birdwatchers) enraged that Bob fudged on tabulating his life list? Ted had no idea what bird aficionados were capable of.

Or maybe an old boyfriend or ex-husband of Chance's girlfriend.

Please, anything to get me off the guilt-ridden hook.

Ted knew he was dreaming.

From Chicago, Ted shuttled to Kansas City to Salt Lake City to Butte, in smaller and smaller aircraft. He got into Butte late and picked up a rental car as Doug Miasma, his pseudonym de jour, and drove toward town, thinking he'd get a room at a hotel or motel, but not until he went into Beth's mom's trailer park.

The erratically-blinking sign in front of Eden Mobile Home Estates had not changed: V CACY. Also unchanged was the goodly percentage of homes that featured major appliances on front porches and vehicles up on blocks.

Gladys' was on the second row in, a single-wide dating from the 1970s in a park full of elongated shoe boxes of that vintage. Even in the dark, Ted made out a slight longitudinal twist. The original white and beige had faded in spots to earth tones.

Lights were on in every window and he could hear loud twangy music. Among the vehicles clustered around the trailer was an old SUV with JUST MARRIED sprayed on it with shaving cream.

Beth?

Ted's heart sank. To Beth and Ted, marriage was the dreaded m-word, a surefire passion snuffer. Had she been swept off her feet by a NASCAR-centric redneck who wore more advertising on his jumpsuit than the Yellow Pages? Or much worse, a lantern-jawed cattle rancher who owned a spread the size of Rhode Island?

His stomach roiled until he saw the GLADYS ♥ BILLY BOB banner that hung above the front door. Serial bride, Gladys Marshak Palmer Wiley Johnstone Higgins Dickey, had tied the knot with hubby number six. Hopefully, Beth was in attendance.

Ted went to the door and Gladys answered, accompanied by even-louder twangy music and a solid block of cigarette smoke. The new Mrs. Dickey was wiry and leathery, an old fifty-seven or fifty-eight. She wore bifocals and a gray perm, probably a permanent wave done today for the occasion. She held a cigarette in one hand, a sixteen-ounce can of beer in the other. Dressed in a white pants outfit, she had a flowery white wreath around her neck, confirming that she was indeed the blushing bride.

Unless an interior decorator had surveyed the scene, shrieked in horror, and gutted every room, the inside of her immobile mobile home was out of a Watergate-era time capsule. Shag carpeting, a popcorn ceiling, an avocado-colored refrigerator older than Beth, dark woodgrained paneling. A working lava lamp on an end table, for God's sake.

Gladys may not have been mother of the year material, but she'd been protective of her two daughters. If any of Beth's stepfathers had been inclined to teach them about the birds and the bees, Gladys would have gelded them on the spot with whatever was handy in the silverware drawer.

She squinted at Ted and said, "I know you. You're the soccer player."

He'd never participated in a soccer match, but once upon a time, Ted Snowe had played minor-league basketball, drifting at the fringes of the game with fantastical dreams of the NBA. Among other venues:

Sioux Falls, Grand Rapids, Topeka, Albany, Fargo and Yakima. He was a six-foot point guard (if you insist on being precise, 5'11⅝"), a midget in the sport, who, as he liked to say, compensated for being short by being slow.

He compared himself to the baseball player who languished in the minors because he couldn't hit a big league curve ball. Or fast ball.

One night, Ted was playing for the Rockford Lightning of the Continental Basketball Association, against the Grand Rapids Hoops. He'd had a crummy game. Twelve minutes, three points, two turnovers, and a last-second 20-footer that would've given them the lead and the game if it hadn't been an air ball. Rockford lost by one and the fans let him know badly he stunk. When you have 1,600 people scattered in the stands, critiques can be very personal.

Sitting in the locker room, slumped on a bench, towel around his neck, the last man there, he knew then and there that it was time to call it quits. But he didn't.

Beth's mom had it imprinted that Ted played professional soccer, and this was no time to correct her.

"Yes, ma'am."

"I don't understand soccer and I don't get how come you still don't sound British."

"I've worked bloody hard to eliminate the accent, mum."

This wasn't her first beer. It took her a moment to process his remark.

"You're a good-looking boy who's built for sports, but what did the good Lord give you hands for if you can't use them?"

"I didn't make the rules. So how are you, Gladys?"

She grinned, exposing the roof of her dentures, and held out her cigarette hand. There was a plain gold band on her ring finger.

"That's how I am as of six hours ago."

"Hey, good for you. Congratulations."

Just before Beth and Ted fled to Portugal, Beth's mom and a gentleman by the name of Floyd Dickey had tied the knot. He wore white socks with black slacks, and a slick pompadour with long sideburns, what Elvis's hair would have looked like. The couple seemed happy, but Gladys' marital bliss had a history of fizzling fast.

"I'd introduce you to Billy Bob Blamey, the happy groom, but Billy Bob's had a little too much to drink when everybody was toasting everybody else and is passed out in the bridal suite. The man has no endurance." She cackled and winked. "That's okay. We had our honeymoon in advance. If I can get his hung-over ass out of the sack at oh-dark-thirty one day this upcoming week, we'll be going to our official one, to Branson, Missouri. Once he can get a fill-in at work. That's all that's holding us back. Fall weather in Montana, you know, one day it's eighty degrees, the next a blizzard. We gotta hit the road while we can. Wanna come in for a drink, Fred?"

"It's Ted and no thanks." He took a deep breath. "Let me guess. Beth was your matron of honor."

Gladys exhaled smoke and looked upward at it. "Oh how I wish. Adele Johnson, two spaces down, filled in for her. Took the night off from the convenience store to do so."

"Beth hasn't been living here?"

"Nope."

"You don't know where she could be?"

"That child of mine dropped out of thin air months ago. She was here for less than a week, said hello and goodbye, and I haven't seen her since. I thought you and her were on the move again, living in sin in Poland or somewheres where you went with her before, doing whatever slippery business you and her do that she can't even talk to her own mother about."

"Any idea where she went, Gladys?"

"Didn't you just ask me that?"

"In a different way."

She squinted at Ted again. "I don't have the slightest hint. None."

"Oh."

Bottoms up. Gladys crinkled the dead soldier.

"If you and her do hook up some fine day, you finally gonna make an honest woman out of her, Fred?"

"Uh."

"And not slap her around like that Jimmy Brutto gangster?"

"Absolutely not. I'd never touch her. That way."

"Jimmy Brutto, who I told her not to marry. If she had to go and run off to New York City and marry a gangster, why couldn't she marry a presentable one, not some drunken ape? That's what I said to her more times than I can remember. Tony Soprano was cute as the dickens. Jimmy wasn't cute."

Moving on from Jimmy and the m-word, Ted said, "No idea at all where Beth went?"

"I wish I did. You tell me and we'll both know."

Ted congratulated her again and went to his car, wondering what next. He felt like he was on the edge of the earth, one step from falling off into oblivion. He opened the door, deciding to stop at the first bar he came to and get roaring drunk, oblivion out of the tap, glass after glass of it.

"Boo."

6

Beth ♥

Ted turned around and there she was. His Elizabeth Palmer Brutto was tall and slender, only two inches shorter than him, a honey blonde with big hair and a hardening baby face. She was a cross between a bombshell and the girl next door.

The dim, fly-specked trailer park lighting cast a glow on her gorgeous freckles and her alcohol and perfume fragrance was pleasant and then some.

Beth kicked a tire. "Is that little thing the car you came in?"

"Yeah, it's a rental. Why?"

She took his wrist firmly and said they were going to her car.

"Why?"

"Stupid question. You must have jet lag," she said, "It's darker there and my back seat is bigger than your entire car."

Ted could take a hint and she was correct on both counts. It was pitch black and she was still driving a 1990s land yacht, a Crown Vic put out to pasture by a taxicab company and auctioned off to Beth and her mom. It had enough miles on the odometer to reach the moon and partway back.

It was the vehicle she owned when they first met, when she tracked Ted down and demanded the $100,000 from him that Grim Reaper Life and Indemnity had demanded from her. No money changed

44

hands, though their hands soon found each other, and their lives dramatically changed.

Not many minutes later, they lay entwined in the back seat on a blanket that softened the duct tape and vinyl beneath. Ted's pants were on the floor with her panties. Her skirt was up, the hem neck-high, the windows fogged. They were bonded with bodily fluids after having behaved like a couple of sex-crazed teens at a drive-in movie.

"Memory lane," he said. "Like in the hammock."

"Without the rainstorm," she said.

"I've never seen you in a dress before, have I?" he said, kissing her moist, salty forehead.

"Still haven't. You yanked it up so fast, you didn't get a real look. I found it at the bridal department of a thrift shop. Considering Mom's track record, I bought it for durability. If you didn't tear in to pieces while you were ravaging me, it's good for two or three more of her weddings."

"While you were ravaging me too. I was using my imagination. I'm sure it's a very nice dress."

"It should be. It cost fifty bucks. Mom's wedding was sort of a special occasion," she said. "Sort of. I've always wanted to pop up when the preacher asks if anybody objects to this union."

"Did you?"

"No. I lost my nerve again."

"I'd like to have been there for that."

"We'll have other chances. Tell me the honest truth, why did you come for me, Mr. Theodore Spangler Snowe Junior?"

"Would you believe that I can't live without you?"

"Sounds good. Keep talking."

"You first. Why were you so easy to find?"

"I knew you'd come some day and I can't live without you. I almost wasn't. Easy to find. I saw you coming to the door, got cold feet, and told Mom to lie for me, and went out the back way."

"And?"

"I changed my mind, okay?"

"I'm glad as glad can be that you did. Were you your mom's matron of honor?"

"I was."

"Your mom said Adele Johnson was?"

"Adele made the tuna casserole with crushed potato chips on top, her signature dish. That was her contribution."

"Who caught the bouquet?"

"I made sure I was out of range. We have a low ceiling, you know. It bounced funny, then off Mom's hands. She fumbled it onto the Velveeta slices, crackers and ranch-dressing dip. The bouquet was too gooey, so we improvised. That's why she was wearing that wreath instead of carrying the bouquet."

"Sounds logical to me."

"Believe it or not, Mom catches the bouquet at every wedding she attends no matter how hard she tries not to."

"I was going to ask her about that, if the neck wreath was a local custom."

"You know what the wedding cake was?"

"Let's see. A cake?"

"Not even close. It was a keg of beer with shaving cream written all over it like used car dealers do on windshields. The 'JUST MARRIED' on Mom's rattletrap SUV too."

"Again, why were you so easy to find?"

"I've been hiding in plain sight. Besides, if anybody's still on the hunt, it's for you. I'm just the damsel you put in distress, deflowering me and everything, then abandoning me," Beth said. "I had a sob story all worked out."

"Deflowering you?"

"We were out of circulation so long, I took a shot at a normal life. I've been living with Mom the whole time and tending bar again."

"The same establishment?"

"Yeah. The same old rut. Greasy burgers, cold beer, drunks telling me they're gonna take me away from all this when they can't even take themselves away from all this. The owner sprang for a couple of humongous wide-screens. Being football season, the TVs keep the wildlife sedated."

Ted remembered The Pub and Casino, a generic sports bar, a squarish cinder-block affair that bristled with satellite dishes, the casino portion an alcove of video poker and keno machines.

"You're sticking your neck out a mile, girl."

"I left Milfontes with a little money, but I feel useless if I'm not working, sitting around with Mom while she chain-smokes and watches all that mindless crud on daytime TV. It'd be a set routine. You and I had a different set routine, but a set routine is a set routine. That's why we were boring each other to death."

She sat up and looked at him. "I haven't been with anybody since you."

Ted believed her.

"Likewise," he said truthfully.

"Not even hitting on tourist ladies when you went to Lisbon?"

"No. Why did you ask that?"

"When we went to the big city, I saw how they looked at you, the tour groups of librarians or schoolteachers."

"Not like the guys in those groups ogled you."

"I'm sorry I split on you like a coward," she said.

Ted didn't reply.

"To be honest, I wanted you to track me down without too much trouble. I didn't want you to mope around in Portugal and get a cat to keep you company. I didn't want you to turn into a crazy cat guy. A cat whisperer."

"I resisted the urge. The Clarkson medium hairs were my only pets."

"Lemme ask you a question. A question I don't think I ever asked you?"

"Whatever it is, you've asked it."

"When you played basketball, did you ever have groupies? Who waited for you outside the locker room and hopped in the sack with you at the bat of an eye?"

An old question. Get reacquainted time.

"What brought that up? Because you and I didn't waste any time?"

"Did you? Hot babes?"

"No," Ted Snowe lied.

Minor league groupies were not up to NBA standards. Hot babes were in short supply. But that was semantics, a technicality cancelling out a lie.

"Not once. I resisted."

"Are you sure? When I was in school, star jocks got more ass than a toilet seat."

"Including yours?"

"No," Beth Palmer Brutto lied. "We did move along pretty fast, didn't we? We'd known each other for, like, twenty-four hours when we jumped each other's bones."

"Almost that long." He kissed her shoulder. "Is that another question?"

"This one is. When it's that quick, how come the girl's a slut and the boy isn't?"

The renewal of an old debate.

"You're not a slut."

"That's not what I asked."

"You posed an age-old question," Ted said, nibbling her ear. "A trick question. A minefield of a question."

"Brat."

"I am a slut," he said. "I confess. I'll take the rap. I will be your faithful slut, doing any depraved thing you want."

She began playing with him, getting a response.

"I believe," she said. "Congratulations. You passed my polygraph."

They needed to talk about Birdwatcher Bob, Ted thought, but the subject wasn't that urgent. By the time they finished, the steamed windows were running.

"I'm dying for a cigarette," she said.

"You'd kicked the habit before we went to Milfontes and stayed clean."

She shrugged. "I'm back with Mom and the old environment. I'm really really trying to be good. I haven't had a smoke for I don't know how long."

"How long ago is I don't know how long?"

"Don't ask."

They snuggled for a few minutes.

She said, "You being here because you can't live without me, that isn't the only reason, is it? Not after all this time."

"Two hundred and sixteen or -seventeen long days."

"I'm reading your body language."

"From this close range?"

"I'm not liking your vibes, Snowe. Talk to me."

Ted told her about Birdwatcher Bob, Brenda Lee Smith, and the Fellas.

"Shit," she said. "That does not make any sense."

"It doesn't. In hindsight, I wish the Clarkson medium-hairs had gone extinct."

"We both know Jimmy Brutto's bosses don't do it like that. They're low-profile psychopathic killers. That's why they hire you. What you're saying, it's the Roaring Twenties and tommy guns. Unless, you know, it's actually Russians."

"We can't rule anybody out."

"So what should we do?"

"Beth, think. Has anybody been snooping around here?"

"You mean, to find you through me?"

"Yeah."

"Now that you mention it." Beth wiggled upright and slipped on her panties. "Two weeks ago, I suspected that my room had been searched. I don't know what it was. Things were a little bit different in my underwear drawer, but nothing was taken."

"The blushing bridegroom?" Ted said, putting on his skivvies and pants after getting both on backwards on the first try.

"I don't think so. Billy Bob's a likable drunk who's somehow able to hold a job driving a tow truck. He's around here a lot and will be permanently now, but no. I told Mom and she told Billy Bob and he swore that he never went in my room for any reason. Mom would've kicked him out if he had. I haven't the foggiest who."

"I used to play in your underwear drawer, picking out that part of your wardrobe for you."

"I know. It was adorable, kinky but adorable."

"We need to find out who did Bob Chance and his gal pal, and why. Who put me in a bind. Us in a bind. My three other disappeareds too."

"Well, three's a crowd. Billy Bob will be moving in permanently from his apartment."

"How long will it take you to pack?" he asked. "There's plenty of luggage room in my rental car. We can't play house in it, but we can travel."

She pulled him back down into a prone position. "You're gonna take me away from all this?"

"Yes ma'am."

"I've been keeping a bag halfway packed just in case my hero came. My desperado."

"That's me."

"Bob Chance really called you a desperado?"

"He did."

"I'll make excuses with Mom and phone in my notice to the bar. Mom will be okay with it. She thinks the world of Fred, my soccer player."

7

A Clear/Unclear Game Plan

They drove west on Interstate-90 but capitulated to fatigue two hours later and spent the night at Missoula. The motel was sprawling, multi-storied, and the parking lot was two-thirds full. Ted paid cash, showed no ID, and pulled the make, model and license number of the rental car off the top of his head, and signed in as Mr. and Mrs. Fred Tedrick. They didn't know if anyone was hot on the trail, Beth's room searcher, representatives of the Fellas, the gunslingers who rubbed out Birdwatcher Bob and Mary Ann, whomever, but anonymity as the Tedricks was comforting.

In the morning, Ted went out for sweet rolls and coffee, and brought their breakfast back to the room and to bed, careful with the hot coffee on bare skin.

"You know, if we were smart, we'd be hightailing it back to Milfontes before someone else does," Beth said.

"If we were smart," Ted said, nodding in agreement.

"And packing up the rest of your belongings in ten minutes or less and going someplace else in Europe or any continent but North America."

"Leaving no forwarding address. I agree," he said, thinking of his vintage Remington.

"The Riviera."

He looked at her. "Good. You're thinking of sunbathing topless? They do that there."

"Don't give me any ideas. Anywhere else but where we were and are."

"Also good."

"Search your memory, Ted. The dead birdwatcher was your fourth assignment after you rose from the dead. As did Bob Chance. For a few days. What the hell happened?"

"I've been thinking and thinking. You know I've been turning down hardcore bad guys. No Jimmy Knuckles, no labor racketeers, no shifty lawyers with bad-ass friends. No violent types, nobody I have to disable and disarm. I stuck strictly to white collar this time around. The first was a bond analyst, the second a Ponzi schemer, the third an investment counselor, then Bob. Yeah, they were scum, especially the sleazebag investment guy, who targeted seniors, but they were smart scum.

"None of them had put up their dukes since the fourth grade and the last weapon they used was a squirt gun. They had triple-digit IQs and knew what was good for them, guys who go through life thinking of nobody but themselves. They played ball with me without much persuasion. The closest to confrontational Bob got was correcting me for saying he was a birdwatcher not a birder. That and calling me a desperado."

"I remember the first two you did, you commuting from Portugal while I was there," Beth said. "Those douche bags. They were oil slicks, but physically harmless."

"In retrospect, I have learned my lesson. Give me an old-fashioned, brass-knuckles type, a master criminal who breaks heads but can't break into a parking meter."

"In your lesson plan, is there a chapter on going into retirement for good?" she said, looking hard at him.

That again. "And retrain as what? Wait, I could attend job fairs."

Beth sighed. "Good point. You told Chance *Russians* and he instantly said impossible."

"It was bat guano, right off the top of my head."

"He didn't know that, but he acted like he knew for sure it wasn't Russians."

"True," Ted said.

"Or lying through his teeth, knowing for sure it was Russians."

"True," Ted said.

"What bugs me is that the gorillas who had you do Birdwatcher Bob, they didn't ask you to scare or torture it out of him what he did with all that money he embezzled before you whacked him, which, of course, you didn't do. If they bought you telling them that you took Bob for a moonlight swim, they'd maybe think Bob confessed all, down to the last penny to save his ass. Wouldn't they?"

"That crossed my mind. The embezzlement has to be nudging the million-dollar range. The street gang who put an end to Bob's life and his life list may've been motivated by money to do the job but maybe not the South Seattle Industries money. They were likely hired hands paid a flat fee."

"I'm unclear what your game plan is," she said. "Our game plan."

"Not as unclear as I am."

"I'm unclearer that you are."

"No, you're not."

"Yes, I am."

"Not."

"Am."

They made a grab-ass game out of it until Beth said, "Hey, I have a brainstorm. Volunteer your services to the police to help solve the dead birdwatcher case. As a good citizen, handkerchief over your mouth on one of your phones or a pay phone. Drop the Fellas names, say 'Russians' and hang up."

He shook his head. "I don't know the Fellas' names and don't want to know their names."

"Make some up."

"The law would not be grateful and the tip would lead nowhere. I'd be written off as a nut."

"Yeah, you're right."

Ted said, "Besides scooping you up to save you from whatever the hell I'm saving us from, and saving my three other disappeareds, who are unworthy but objects of my guilt just the same, The Fellas think I cheated them and made a gangbanger-style commotion. They are brutally pissed. Them and/or Russians. As a good citizen, I have to straighten things out."

"That is a mouthful and it is a problem, my dearest."

"A large problem. But, you know, the Fellas ask a helluva lot out of me for their lousy fifteen grand per hit, so they shouldn't complain every time there's a small glitch."

"You're joking."

"Kind of. They are unlikely to file a complaint with a consumer protection agency, though."

"They would have a solid case against you for the Better Business Bureau."

"Look at it from my side, Beth. The fifteen K is gross, not net. All my expenses come out of it. The remainder's slim, less than half. The marketplace is overcrowded with underemployed hit men, so I have to take it or leave it."

"But you don't do the job they hired you to, bozo. Your major expense is researching and creating new identities. You're cheating them."

"I'm saving lives."

"That's beside the point. They aren't paying you to *save* a life. Look, I'm not criticizing. You should be up for the Nobel Peace Prize, but I'm just seeing it from where they do, as a devil's advocate, okay?"

"Okay."

"So you need to know why the Fellas hired you to disappear Mr. Chance and who really disappeared him from amongst the living."

"Well put."

Beth brushed crumbs from Ted's chest and lap, brushing them a little farther south than necessary. "Where to?"

"The best of all worlds is me starting off by stashing you with a maiden aunt or in a nunnery."

She kept her hand where it was. "Nah, that's no fun. My only aunt is on her fourth husband, trying to keep up with Mom, and nuns would interfere with my social life. You're taking me with you to the scene of the crime."

"Why?"

"Why not. We have to start somewhere."

"I rescued you when you probably didn't need rescuing, and stuck your neck out as far I've stuck mine out."

"Stop with the gibberish and finish your breakfast, Snowe."

He knew when to give up and shut up. When Beth dug her heels in, nothing would change but the decibel level of their discussion.

"Yes ma'am."

Beth studied Ted's profile as he sipped his coffee. Something about him had changed. For certain, something was drastically different. When he'd described his encounter with Bob Chance, he'd spoken enthusiastically of the different birds he'd seen on the field trip, naming some. Great blue this and little yellow that.

Her man seemed kinder and gentler, and he already had been kind and gentle to her from day one, bless his heart. If he had changed, she'd take it.

Mutual boredom split them up in Portugal. It wasn't apt to happen here. They might get killed, but they wouldn't be ho-hum yawning at the time.

8

Roses Are Red, Violets Are—

According to Ted's off-the-top-of-his-head calculation, the drive from Missoula to Seattle was 476 miles, plus or minus a mailbox or three. The adjoining town of Sea-Tac was a bit farther to the south.

"How do you know how far," Beth Palmer Brutto said as they left the motel in their mirrors. "There's no GPS on the dashboard of this deathtrap."

"My GPS is folded in the glove box. It's an easy ride, mostly freeway."

"You do your homework, big guy. The sign of a professional. I've always liked it."

"On the Bob Chance assignment, the dog may have eaten my homework."

Around eleven, as they crossed into Washington State, opening time for The Pub and Casino, Beth called in.

"No, Madge, I don't know when I'll be back. My aunt lives in Pittsburgh all by herself."

"She's got what?"

"Uh, whooping cough I think she said it is. She was coughing after every other word."

Ted had met Madge, a large woman who had no need for bouncers.

"No, wrong. It wasn't eradicated years ago, not before she was born. That's smallpox."

"I'm positive, Madge. Not in Pittsburgh."

"A cigarette cough that turned into pneumonia. That's a possibility. I think she'd had a few toddies when she whipped her diagnosis on me too. She is my aunt, though. Somebody has to look in on the old bat."

"You're right, she may be as fit as a fiddle, but she's gone a little funny in the head and that's a worry in itself. Sorry, Madge. Bye."

"Think she bought it?" Ted asked.

"Probably not, but I don't steal out of the till, so I have job security."

If they were of a mind to enjoy the scenery, they had their choice, passing snow-capped peaks, dense evergreen forests, and flat farmland, irrigated and not. In the eastern part of the state, something knee-high was being harvested on both sides of the highway.

They were trying to guess what it was when Ted said, "I have a confession to make."

"Oh God."

He dropped the typewriter find and poetry bombshell on her, capping it with the slam victory in Lisbon and his 10 € prize.

A bombshell that turned out to be a dud.

"Wow," Beth said, stifling a yawn. "You said confession and I was thinking, hell, I don't know what I was thinking."

"A half-baked *wow*? That's it?"

Beth looked at him, realizing what was different: artistic sensitivity. Hell, he already was Mr. Cuddles.

She said, "I'm sorry, but nothing surprises me about you anymore."

"Is that good or bad?"

Beth evaded by saying, "We had to study poetry in high school in an English class. The teacher was hung up on that mushy Browning shit. You know, 'let me count the ways'. You're not doing that kind of stuff, are you?"

"No."

"Or roses are red, violets are blue."

"No. No way."

"And you say you have to write your poems on a Middle Ages typewriter that was in the attic, or you can't write them?"

"While in Portugal I thought I did, but I wrote one on the plane."

She took her time answering, observing the same cute guy she adored.

"Does this have anything to do with you turning forty real soon? They say those milestones have side effects."

"Jesus."

"A midlife crisis thing?"

"Forty isn't midlife. It's the attainment of maturity. Wisdom."

Beth hesitated before asking, "Have you written a poem for me?"

"Not yet. Would you like me to? I can find an old typewriter at a thrift shop if I come down with poetry block."

She'd been told that poems were sometimes part of the pitch guys made when popping the question, a springboard to the m-word. She'd heard that from a drunk at The Pub and Casino. But the guy had also seen a UFO and a werewolf.

"Let me think on that one. When I was taking the class, Mom was on her third hubby, who was our fifth live-in. Romance of any kind then, barf."

"I see where you're coming from. I'll resist the urge."

"Love poems, I think, barfy or not, the bottom line should be getting into a girl's britches, you know, like sending her flowers and candy. No offense, but the guy poets in the textbook we had pictures of, they were taken a million years ago, where everybody had funny eyes, but they did look a little light in the loafers, which you're obviously not."

"I haven't tried writing an erotic poem, but you're inspiring me."

She rested her head on his shoulder. "No hurry, but if you do, let me help you with it. There has to be a bunch of dirty words in it or it's not worth the paper it's written on."

"Paper it's typed on. I promise there will be."

"Wheat," Beth said, snapping her fingers. "That's what they're harvesting."

Ted drove fast and they stopped only when they had to. At one rest stop in the Cascades, overlooking rolling hills, he saw a Clark's Nutcracker, a gray and white bird Bob Chance had spotted in the tide flats, saying that they're almost never seen at sea level.

"It's cute," Beth said after he told her in the car. "Poetry and bird watching too, I'm back in your life in the nick of time."

"Afraid I'll take up flower arranging next? Fashion design?"

She honked him. "If you do, I'll have to check this stud-o-meter on a regular basis."

* * * * *

The fateful (and fatal) hotel was a full-service high-rise in Sea-Tac, across Highway 99 from the airport of the same name. Bob Chance and Brenda Smith had been a five-minute shuttle ride from the airport terminal and their flight to utopia.

Beth and Ted took a room late, but before going to it they went into the cocktail lounge for drinks and food. It was half-occupied by dazed, wrinkled folks and their suitcases on wheels. They had their luggage with them too, weary, butts sore from the drive, so they blended right in.

Seated at the bar, they ordered sandwiches and beer. The suds went down easily, so they were ready for a second when their food came. After their meal was gone and they were well into their third, the place emptied out and the bartender had some free time.

Attempting to be casual, after trading stale complaints about Seattle's drizzly weather and their admiration for the powerful Seahawks, Ted said, "Didn't we read that something crazy went down here recently? A double murder?"

The barkeep was in his forties, lean and balding, and was halfway successful at hiding his annoyance about being asked this for the thousandth time.

"Something you never expect to happen here. This is no flophouse, you realize. This is serious expense-account land. We've had coronaries upstairs. That's it for deaths on the premises."

"We can see it's no dump," Beth said, looking around admiringly, playing the rube. "Cool. Class all the way."

"It was right out front here. Walk straight out of the lounge and you could see it happen if we'd been open then. Lucky we weren't. Two guests staying here shot down in cold blood while waiting for a ride to the airport. I'm still not believing."

"A lot of shots, wasn't it?"

The bartender spread his hands and said, "I wasn't here, but that's what they say. There were shells all over the turnaround. It was like one of those drive-bys those gang members do, hopped up on drugs, blasting away with their stolen pistols. Don't get me wrong. I've got nothing against those minority boys who live in those neighborhoods and run in packs like wild animals. That's all they have to do. One in a hundred has a father in the household. Those kids get pissed off if you make the wrong hand signs and have the wrong tattoos or spray-paint the wrong crap on the wrong wall. You'd think we were in downtown Seattle where those troublemakers hang out. I'll tell you, law and order is a thing of the past, and kids aren't raised with any values, not some of them."

Meaning non-whites, Ted thought. He kept his mouth shut. Beth, a bartender who had heard it all, knew better than he how to organize this parade.

"Weird," she said. "Those people who were killed, they certainly weren't gang members, were they? Certainly not people their age, staying here."

That she made a show of hanging on the bartender's words seemed to energize him. Holding court was part of his gig and he was up for the task.

"No way. I never saw or met them, but they were an average couple, so you'd think at first glance. The people at the desk who remembered them thought so because they didn't remember them. Know what I mean?"

They nodded in unison, rapt.

"Well, the cops and the media, they've been uncovering some interesting things. The guy, it turned out he was maybe a serious embezzler from a small aerospace company right here in town close to a Boeing plant. This South Seattle something. They're making no comment, so you can draw your own conclusions. The guy, he'd disguised himself and had fake ID on him. He'd skipped out on his family and was running off with that gal. A younger gal."

Beth tapped Ted's knee with hers and said, "When guys get to be a certain age, it's always a younger gal, never an older one."

The bartender smiled. "You said it. Not me."

"Where were they headed?"

"Someone let it slip that they had first-class tickets, but the cops, they're keeping the destination hush-hush. I'd bet wherever it is, it's got palm trees and sandy beaches. If it was me, that's where I'd be going."

Resplendent quetzals, Ted thought.

"You say you weren't here when it happened," Beth said.

"Nope. Whoever it was, they were up with the chickens. Like five-thirty. It was still dark out. Last time I was up that early, I was in the Army."

"Witnesses?" Beth asked.

"There were three or four others out there waiting for that shuttle. Everybody was half asleep. When the shooting started, they woke up fast, hitting the deck or running for it and dodging behind something. I'd do the same thing like any sane person would. Nobody got a look at the shooter or shooters, or a good description of the car or its license plate. All anyone knew was that it was gray or silver and old."

"Not much to go on," Beth said.

"Yeah. If you ask me, it's a dead end. Must've had something to do with the guy's phony-baloney situation. His embezzling nobody's officially admitting to. The law's not telling the exact amount he made off with, but it had to be a bundle. They might not know. You don't get yourself killed over peanuts."

Two couples walked in and sat at the bar, so that was the end of the conversation.

Ted and Beth finished their beers and found their room, disappointed that they'd learned nothing other than the bartender was a racist. Exhausted, they set the alarm so they'd be downstairs before five-thirty tomorrow morning.

In bed, she said, "Quit fidgeting and get to sleep."

He said, "Can't."

"Count sheep."

"I've run out. It's the end of the flock."

"Impossible. You can't."

"I have. First-class airline tickets are gamboling over the fence. That's the problem. They flap. They're a bitch to count."

"And that may be a vital mystery clue," Beth said.

"What? How?" Ted said, but she was snoring.

9

Scene of the Crime

Without benefit of caffeine, they arrived in a near-empty lobby at 5:15, standing with their suitcases, waiting for a ride, pretending to be eager to fly. Carpeting was being vacuumed, faux marble swept, bric-a-brac dusted. Banquet and meeting rooms were dark, and the business office was unused. Four bored rent-a-cops moved out of the way when they had to, wasting as little motion as possible.

Seated at his desk, the concierge had nothing going on either. He was young, chipper, smiley and vigorous-looking, clinical characteristics of a morning person, Ted thought.

"That's sickening behavior," Beth whispered as they walked toward him. "He needs help. Professional therapy."

"Our shuttle bus is on its way, but it's running late," Ted said to her loudly, per the script they polished in the elevator. "A slew of flights must've just got in."

"Can we wait here with you. Inside. Until it's time to go?" Beth said in her best little-girl voice. "I'm kind of, well, you know, after what, you know."

Also per their plan, Ted rolled his eyes at the concierge who winked, a heavy mist of testosterone discharging, one virile man to another, sensitive to the little gal's fears and anxieties.

"The shooting? Oh heck, folks, I wouldn't worry about it," the concierge told Beth. "It'll never happen again. It was a one in a million thing and management's beefed up security. There's a good half-dozen security people out in the lot from sunset to sunrise, plus the ones you see in here."

"Do they have guns and know how to use them?" Beth asked.

"They've been trained," the concierge said. "I think you have to be."

"They say those poor people, they were just an average-looking couple," Beth said, shaking her head. "Not hardened criminals or anything."

The concierge said, "The criminal issue is up in the air. I vividly remember the guy because when they checked out I tried to take his suitcase for him, he jerked away like I was trying to steal it. I hate to speak ill of the dead, but he wasn't her type. He was chubby and sweaty. She was taller than him and could have been an athlete in her younger days. After hearing about them later and what they had in the suitcase, well, I can't blame him for hanging on to it."

Ted wondered why the concierge was opening up so readily to strangers. Then he answered his own question by watching his eyes, which were darting between Beth's shoulders and knees, her strike zone.

"An average couple except for that?"

The concierge rocked a hand. "They never left their rooms. Everything was room service. That's not totally unusual. Same with the 'do not disturb' sign always hung on the doors, them picking up their trays after they were left in the hall."

"You said *rooms?*"Beth said. "*Doors?*"

"Yeah. Odd, isn't it? Everybody here thought so. I don't know if it was reported in the media. The time they were here, they changed rooms once or twice a day, packing up and moving lickety-split."

Ted and Beth looked at each other. Their vital mystery clue? Was Bob merely paranoid, buying Ted's warnings, or was somebody really nipping at his heels?

The concierge tapped an ear. "You hear things. Desk clerks talking, Hispanic maids who know more English than they're given credit for. They were heard talking about passports. There may've been trouble with them."

"Why?"

"They'd clam up if an employee got too close."

"Did they explain why they switched rooms?"

"No reason given. No complaints about the ones they vacated. We're half empty, so it wasn't a problem. They paid cash and tipped real nice." He laughed. "In that case, the customer's always right."

"The gal, did she have anything to say to you?" Beth asked.

"Only one thing stuck in my mind. She asked if the shuttle takes them right to a first-class check-in. I had to explain that you went to the first-class line after you went inside and found your airline counter. I guess she hadn't traveled much. She acted like she was afraid of flying too."

"So you were here then?" Beth asked.

"I was on duty, but at the front desk, going over the morning's checkouts. I heard pops, like firecrackers being shot off."

"How many?"

"Four or five or six. It didn't register at the time. Then a guy came running in and said to call nine-one-one. There'd been a shooting. They did at the desk. The others ran in too. One guy said there was nothing we could do for the victims, so nobody did. Maybe we were cowardly, but we had our own skins to think of, you know, in case the shooters came back."

A taxi pulled up. The concierge excused himself and went out to meet its passengers. Beth and Ted scooted back to an elevator and went to their room, where they crashed, aware now that Chance and Smith had fussed with his disguise, matching it to his passport, as Ted had recommended. Birdwatcher Bob had been fearful of uninvited company far more ominous than South Seattle Industries auditors.

The big question: how had the assassins' timing been so spot-on?

"There went my vital mystery clue, swirling down the drain," Beth said.

"It's a semi-vital clue. First-class means Bob had some bucks left hidden under the mattress. The couple was suffering justifiable paranoia," Ted said.

"That's no answer. Please turn off the light."

They fell right asleep, spread-eagled on the supersized bed. Instead of first-class tickets, Ted dreamt of resplendent quetzals and yellowthroats and great blue herons gamboling over shrubs in triple-canopy jungle.

10

A Soccer Mom Scorned

They barely slept, two hours max.

Ted came out of the shower, towel around him, saying, "We can't sleep because powerfully perplexed puzzlement—pardon the alliteration—is counterbalancing exhaustion."

Beth was putting on lipstick. "I'm glad you cleared that up, Mr. English Major. I'm starving."

They ordered room service breakfast: eggs, toast and coffee.

Forgetting who Ted had registered them as, Beth signed for the meal with an illegible physician's scrawl and told him, "This costs more than the twenty-four ounce Death by Cholesterol T-bone at the Pub and Casino."

Before checking out, they sat on the bed, looking at Ted's laptop, reviewing what they knew about the late Bob Chance and Brenda Lee Smith.

He said, "By all appearances, there's nothing we don't already know. We do know my prep for the job was sloppy. The Fellas had a rush order, probably to stop the bleeding at South Seattle Industries. They wanted Bob whacked posthaste.

"Other than parking tickets, my boy was squeaky clean. Eagle Scout. Honor student. Sang in his church choir, volunteered at a food bank, the whole deal."

"Really?"

"Nope. Just kidding, I think, but he was clean, no police record, or it'd be in the news. I can't stop obsessing about when I said it was Russians and Chance was emphatic that it was not Russians."

"Therefore he knew or thought he knew who hired you," Beth said. "We can't rule out anybody on the planet who is or isn't Russian."

"Yeah. Take a number."

"Bob was bitter about being laid off from his first job he'd held for twenty years, replaced by a family member. A girl even."

"He was collecting retroactive back wages on his next job, the dummy."

Beth said, "You didn't do the job you were assigned to do on him. For shame."

"You can't get good help these days. Even mediocre help."

"Well, somebody was on the ball."

"Who was hired by whom?" Ted said.

"The little woman was proactive?" Beth said. "Mary Ann Chance, driving with one hand, spitting lead with the other."

"Spitting lead?" Ted said, thinking that she may've heard that one from Jimmy Knuckles.

"She raised holy hell for a full investigation, saying that he'd left a note that he was off to a seminar."

"She who smelled a rat," Beth said. "A rat named Bob."

Ted said, "Maybe she'd learned what was going on and made a call. Only one thing is wrong with that theory."

"Yeah," Beth said. "Who'd she contact to buy the hit? The PTA president who moonlights? A substitute teacher without enough work to make ends meet? From what we know of her without knowing her, Mary Ann Chance strikes me your basic soccer mom."

Ted said, "Bob being riddled with bullets, after she learned the truth about him, I have to believe that was her favorite nonsexual fantasy. That's about the size of it."

Beth said, "Yeah, sexual fantasy or not. After she found out her hubby was diddling a beautician. And maybe even found out he was diddling his company's books to spend on the diddled beautician. You know what they say about a soccer mom scorned."

"But how would she have found out first, ahead of the Fellas?"

"Bob talked in his sleep? Beats me. We're yakety-yaking in circles."

"Ninety-nine-plus percent of the populace don't act on fantasies that would land them in the slammer with the choice of the chair or the needle," Ted said.

"I know, I know. I'll bet she's putting on a brave front for the kiddies, but she's not crying herself to sleep."

"Too many variables," Ted said.

"Where do we go from here? The next disappeared on your list? If some maniac is planning to gun them down too and you're gonna warn them, we have to get moving."

"If that is what's happening," Ted said before he picked up the phone to call downstairs and extend their stay. "We go from here to nowhere yet."

"Mary Ann Chance?"

"If we can get to her, maybe Mary Ann can clear up some of those variables for us," he said.

Beth said, "That's my department. Since you've swept me up and along for the ride, I may as well earn my keep."

11

Dirty Pool

Cleaned up and ready to go wherever they were going, Ted and Beth talked it over. They didn't want to rudely barge in unannounced on the perhaps-grieving Widow Chance, so they decided to play dirty pool.

"Dictionary definition of?" Beth said.

"Underhanded or unsportsmanlike conduct."

"Is dirty pool dirtier than rude?"

Ted said, "Not if you play polite dirty pool."

"I'm in."

On the laptop, they found the Robert L. Chances in the White Pages and Beth called Mary Ann, surprised that her number was unchanged and that she picked up on the third ring.

Hoping she wasn't laying it on too thick, Beth asked forgiveness for intruding, saying that she and her partner had been on a field trip with her husband and had some property of his he'd loaned them they had forgotten to give back.

"I feel so so sick about all this," Beth said, crossing her fingers. "I feel like a thief, keeping that book after, well, you know, everything."

Then Mary Ann did most of the talking, Beth nodding.

"We are so so sorry for your loss," she finished as she squeezed her neck to make her voice crack.

When she hung up, Ted said, "You should've been an actress, girl."

"You're an actress every single night tending bar, making the drunks and Romeos think they're as smart and sexy and cool as they think they are so the assholes will tip."

"It didn't take long for you to learn this part," he said, putting his shoes on.

"If only you were a Hollywood agent," Beth said. "Mary Ann Chance said to come on out any old time before three. She'd taken some vacation days off from the bank, and was cleaning things out. School's probably out at three for her kids."

"Nice work. What was her tone like?"

"Neutral. Flat," Beth said. "We could've been talking about a bake sale."

They stopped at a strip mall not far from the hotel. At a bookstore, Ted bought a field guide to birds of the Pacific Northwest. On an impulse, hurrying to the shelves and back, Ted grabbed one on birds of North America; it was the size and heft of a brick. He bought another on tropical birds. The resplendent quetzal was one of its stars. Red and green and white, with iridescent-green tail feathers twice as long as its body. He tucked the page over.

"For you?"

"So?"

"My man, a birding, birdwatching poet. Wonders never do cease."

"Check this little guy out."

"It is a cutie," Beth said, looking at the plate. "Bob expected to find a splendid quetzal at his destination?"

"It was his dream, so I know he was going to Central America or southern Mexico."

"That's why you bought it."

"You look skeptical."

"Is that flying sweetie-pie our next vital mystery clue or are you really and truly turning into a birdwatcher?" Beth asked, paging through it as they walked back to the car.

"A birder," he said. "Not me, not seriously. I don't think I am."

She laughed. "You and that Clark's Nutcase we saw at the rest stop, you liked to've peed your pants."

"No comment."

"A birdwatcher's life list, you said that was a big deal."

"It is."

"What's yours?"

"If I tell you, will you lay off?"

"I will."

"I don't know."

"That doesn't count as an answer."

* * * * *

Ted drove onto Interstate-405 northbound while Beth roughed up the Northwest field guide to make it appear well-used.

It took them 45 minutes to reach the Chance home. Thanks to single-occupant cheaters, the HOV lane wasn't much help. Mary Ann Chance lived in Bellevue, a city sprawl of 125,000 on the east side of Lake Washington, which divided Seattle from the eastside towns and burbs. Downtown Bellevue was newish, high-rise and sterile, with horrendous traffic and lights that took forever to change.

"The construction crane looks like the city bird," Beth said, looking upward.

The Chance home was on a cul-de-sac north of downtown Bellevue. Her neighborhood was typical, a cookie-cutter ring of split levels with manicured lawns, SUVs and Black Forest yupmobiles in the driveways. Deciduous and evergreen trees were puny. Ted figured that if you counted their rings, you'd have fifteen tops.

"No dandelions, no poverty, no trigger-happy gangbangers," Beth said.

"American dream," Ted said.

The Chance garage doors were open and cardboard boxes were in the driveway. A minivan was parked on the street.

"Soccer-mom-esque," Beth said, looking at the van.

A woman in her forties, in jeans and sweatshirt, presumably Mary Ann, was carrying men's clothing from the garage and dumping it into boxes. She was plain and nondescript, with short hair and blue eyes. She was pale and not made up, thickening around the middle. The ten extra pounds she carried rendered her on the verge of shapeless.

Ted thought that if Grant Wood had been around lately, searching for *American Gothic* models, the Chances would have been strong candidates.

Beth gauged Mary Ann as neither attractive nor unattractive, and not getting any younger. She admired the woman for not fighting Mother Time with chemicals and trips to the gym, but saw how Bob could be easy pickings for a hot chick after him and his stolen money.

She looked at them with no discernible interest. "You phoned?"

Beth handed her the field guide and said, "Yes, I did. I'm so so sorry for your loss."

Ted said, "That goes for me too. Though I didn't know him very well."

"Sure. Thank you," Mary Ann Chance said, either for the book and/or the obligatory statements of sympathy.

She tossed the field guide into a box half-full with other books, many with birds on the covers. Other boxes had male clothing including a Boy Scout uniform and framed certificates, most upside down, some with the glass broken.

Bob Chance in the CPA Hall of Fame? Ted wondered.

Mary Ann held up the Boy-Scout merit badge sash and said, "Do you know what these things represent? I think this one is for voyeurism, that one for masturbation."

Ted and Beth nodded, each thinking that they'd heard everything. Before this.

As the grieving widow slam-dunked it into a box, Ted smelled alcohol on her breath.

"Sunday, there was a memorial service for Robert. He was a lapsed Catholic who dragged me there twice a year when he went on Christmas and Easter. It was at Our Lady of Exquisite Agony, one of those. They have this picture of an Aryan Jesus in the lobby. He looks like a Swedish homo."

Beth and Ted nodded.

"Before we were married I refused to take instruction at the church. His parents insisted. An outsider like me had to in order to be married there. We eloped to Coeur d'Alene. A couple of wild and crazy kids. The excitement went downhill fast."

Bronzed baby shoes: an NBA-hard slam-dunk.

Ted and Beth nodded.

Mary Ann said, "This is probably a wasted trip for you. A charity is coming by later for anything usable. I'm keeping nothing of his. Zip, zilch, zero."

Mary Ann Chance was obliterating any sign of her late husband, Ted thought.

From the womb to a hole in the ground, Beth thought.

Ted said, "It was a terrible thing. I hope they catch them. Do you know if the police have any leads?"

Beth said, "However you feel, you know, murder is murder."

She looked at them blandly. "Well, I think they finally eliminated me as a suspect, which frankly is what I care most about. The spouse is always the leading suspect, you know. I had an alibi. I was getting myself ready for gridlock traffic and work. Neighbors saw me and my car. I work in Seattle and rush hour taking either bridge into town is a living hell. They ruled out me hiring anyone to do the job too.

"I've made no big withdrawals lately and I had no knowledge of his dirty money. I work in a bank too, in IT, but as a college-degree-less flunky under a glass ceiling. I taught myself how to write code and can write rings around the pimply nerds who make twice as much as I do, but I can't transfer money. The only things I can steal are leftover doughnuts in the cafeteria."

Beth asked, "What exactly do you do?"

"Much of the day, I fine-tune the bank's website's mortgage refinance page, sending out endless emails, pestering our customer's to refi. Do it today or the low low low rate's gone forever. If the suckers bite, I maintain those pages too."

"Sounds complex."

"It is. When I'm off, I get four or five calls a day from the managers and whoever's handling my desk. How do you do this, how do you do that?"

Beth said, "It's nice that you've been cleared."

"The manager and his managers went over me with a fine-tooth comb. The cops too. I don't know how many times they asked me where Bob's Jerry Hoopsma identity came from. His phony fast-food magnate background. How the hell should I know? When it comes right down to it, I didn't know Robert any better than this Jerry Hoopsma."

"Jerry Hoopsma. That is odd," Ted said. "Any distant relatives with that name?"

Beth pushed against him.

"Who knows? He's an only child and his parents are dead."

"Hoopsma. It sounds Karjackastanian, one of those countries," Ted said. "One of those you see in the news that're always fighting with the Russians."

Beth and Ted noted that she didn't react to "Russians."

"It is odd. No one in his family down to distant cousins are named Jerry-anything, no colleagues of his past or present. He didn't have real friends that I knew of. Just the bird people in his groups. Whoever fixed him up with that ID was probably a stranger and a real pro."

Ted thought it might not be a good idea to thank her for the compliment. He said nothing.

"They put the fake ID on a par with expert counterfeiting. Whoever did it for him needs to be in a federal lockup."

Now wait a minute, Ted thought.

"Well, I hope they catch them real soon," Beth said. "You can't have people running around shooting people."

Mary Ann Chance dropped a set of binoculars in with the birding books. "These ought to fetch a pretty penny for the charities. They're German, top-of-the-line. Nothing but the best for him and the birds he chased out in the boondocks." She held up the tripod. "Look at this. Light as a feather. They don't come cheap. It's some exotic metal like titanium. Thousands of dollars he spent on this gear without ever asking me. Could I use the money and take you to Cabo for a romantic week instead, my dear?"

It's aluminum, Ted thought.

Clunk thwack went the tripod.

"I don't want anything that he's had his hands and face on. I can write all this off on my taxes."

"Are there any leads?" Beth asked, repeating Ted's question, wondering why she hadn't answered it.

"Are they hot on the trail? If they are, they're not keeping me up to speed. His supervisors at South Seattle Industries, maybe they're also satisfied that I never saw a penny of it. Or not. I haven't heard word one. They could've sent me flowers, couldn't they? I didn't take their money.

"He had a good job there too, but he couldn't get over being dumped at the prior job. Get over it, I said. Grow up. There's no corporate loyalty these days. It happens all the time, I'd tell him. We weren't starving, for Christ's sake. Stupid blind me, I hadn't seen the bimbo factor."

"Speaking of titanium, was titanium important? In anything?" Beth said.

"Only that South Seattle Industries did something with it. Bob didn't say and I gave up asking when he stopped talking about work. We weren't communicating as it was. About anything."

She shook her head. "Bean counters. Why did it take until—this—for them to catch on? Did he have somebody there in on it? I told the cops that they should dig into it there, but their body language said that they wouldn't or didn't know how. They weren't taking advice from little old me."

Beth and Ted thanked Mary Ann Chance for her time and she thanked them for the book, saying, "It'll find a home. You'd be surprised how many bird watchers there are who think their life lists are more important than anything else in life. Their families, kids, anything. I guess that's why Robert and his whore were going to Panama, the fucking asshole. They say they have rain forests down there and oodles of birds."

"Panama?"

"That where I think his first-class tickets were for. One of the detectives grilling me let it slip. Panama City with a plane change in Houston."

Fucking asshole. She was bitter and didn't care who knew, but that was over the top, Beth thought.

"Panama?"

"An educated guess on my part. The cops told me in so many words when they asked if he knew anyone in Panama."

In the car, Beth said, "Mary Ann's handling her grief well, isn't she?"

"She is brave," Ted said. "Chin up. Stiff upper lip. But why the dog and pony show, right out in the driveway for us and all the neighbors we didn't see who were peeking between curtains?"

Beth asked the windshield, "What was the whore gonna be doing in Panama while the fucking asshole was watching birds?"

"I have over seven hundred birds on my life list. I'm looking forward to exceeding a thousand," Ted said. "Among Bob's last words to me."

"Before or after he said you were a desperado?"

12

Memories

The prediction of dry, unusually warm weather was correct, so Beth and Ted decided to take the rest of the day off and sightsee. Ted remembered the NBA Seattle Supersonics semi-fondly. Seven or eight years ago, some carpetbagger bought them from the local coffee magnate, then moved the team to Oklahoma City.

While they were still the Sonics and Ted was at Purdue, a Seattle scout came to check him out when they were playing Illinois. He had an okay night, twenty points and eight assists, but he never saw the scout again. Ted missed a wide-open ten-footer as time ran out and Purdue lost by one. The scout was long gone before the team walked off the floor to a gloomy locker room.

Ted Snowe, Choke Artist Extraordinaire, a malaise that he carried with him to the CBA and other minor leagues. That was his rep. Not conducive to being a go-to guy.

Referring to a tourist guide and map they picked up in the hotel lobby, they took light rail downtown, walked the hilly streets, rode the Great Wheel, and toured the Pike Place Market. They walked to the Smith Tower, a thirty-eight-story jewel of neoclassical architecture. When built in 1914, it was the tallest building west of the Mississippi. Today it was lost in a forest of steel and glass.

They came back to the hotel and drove to the Woodland Park Zoo, especially fascinated by the animals that looked at them.

"Who's caged? Is that what they're thinking?" Beth asked.

"Good point. They're fed every day and they're not paying the mortgage and utilities. No car payments, no alimony."

As they were leaving, Beth said, "Would you believe I've never been to a zoo before?"

"Why not?"

"Butte has no zoo and I never got around to going to one in New York before Jimmy and I had our whirlwind disaster. Him and his pals were a two-legged menagerie anyway."

Ted said, "If the cage doors were left open, how many of the inmates here do you think would leave?"

"That's an odd question."

"A metaphor."

"Metaphor for what, English major. No, wait, I get it. Your three remaining disappeareds. Are they staying put?"

"Give that girl an A."

* * * * *

In bed that night, after they came up for air, calling him a desperado more than once, Beth said, "Tell me again how you got into your, ahem, line of work."

"Memories," Ted said, "This is ancient territory, you know."

"I know, but we've been apart for eons and I love to hear it. We have to recycle those memories. Have to. The sound of your voice, period. After I ran off, that's one of many things I missed about you, Snowe. Your zoo metaphor got me thinking. Humor me. I'm the only one now in the whole side world who knows and that it so cool. We would not have met unless you were a crook, you know."

He held up twin V-signs. "I am not a crook."

She tickled him in a place you would not tickle one in public.

"C'mon. Whip it on me."

He complied, beginning when he'd graduated from Purdue, a free-agent tryout with the Detroit Pistons upcoming. Wedded to a knockout of a yell queen, he had the world by the ass. The marriage didn't last much longer than the honeymoon and his tenure in NBA training camp was even shorter than that, as he was out-quicked by established point guards who towered over his six-feet (precisely 5'11⅝"). He stubbornly refused to give up on a pro ball career, so he bounced around in the minor leagues, a walking-talking-dribbling travelogue of medium-sized cities.

"You were a frat rat at Purdue, weren't you? I forget."

Spoken like an accusation. "I doubt that you've forgotten, but, yeah, a Phi Delt."

His comeback was right on, Beth thought. She was insecure at times about having only a middle-of-her-class high school diploma. Her teachers told her repeatedly that she was an underperformer and college material, a scholarship in her reach if she buckled down.

The Underachievement Nazis would not leave her alone. Beth had tested a 121 IQ and they wouldn't stop throwing that in her face. If you didn't want to go to college, you didn't. If you wanted to smoke between classes behind the wood shop, you did. If you didn't want to be like your older sister, the reincarnation of Betty Fucking Crocker, you weren't.

That 121 score was one of the few secrets she kept from Ted.

"You had keggers, wild drunken parties?"

"We did."

"Montana colleges do too. After a couple of beers, the frat rats think they're God's gift."

"You've been to some of those?"

"A couple. May were turn to basketball?"

"You're the one who veered us off that road."

"How were you at the foul line? Small guys are good free-throw shooters, aren't they?"

"Eighty percent."

"When the game was on the line, were you eighty-percent good?"

"Now and then."

"You choked?"

"Everyone does, but do it more than once or twice and you get a rep that's hard to shake. They don't remember the forty-footers you made at the buzzer."

"That sucks."

"It does."

"Did you ever make a winning forty-footer at the buzzer?"

"No."

Ted continued: Non-hit man. That's how he thought of himself. Ted had blundered into the profession following that life-changing Continental Basketball Association game in La Crosse, Wisconsin. After a few brews with his teammates, he went to his room.

In the fourth quarter, his assigned roommate had had his legs cut out from under him when he drove to the hoop, and was in the hospital for X-rays. Ted opened what he thought was a closet, but instead an adjoining room.

A short, balding, sweaty guy with a cane nearly jumped out of his shoes. He begged Ted not to kill him, promised that he'd give every penny back, and wouldn't utter a peep. Ted was feeling no pain and thought the guy had half a bag on too.

Out of curiosity, Ted invited him into his room for a drink, a share of the six-pack he'd bought across the street. His guest brought along an attaché case he white-knuckled on his lap, as if it contained the President's code to launch nukes.

He claimed to be one Shorty Hammerhill, bookkeeper for a Mob family who had gotten too old and knew too much, now on the lam. He'd thought Ted was who they'd sent to whack him out. His retirement gift was not to be a gold watch, but a .45 slug.

Shorty pleaded to stay the night in Ted's room. Ted said not a chance. Just then, they heard a commotion next door, things being kicked and tossed and slammed. When it was quiet, they peeked in on a tornado aftermath. The visitors had even torn the Gideon in half.

Shorty told Ted that if he'd get him to an out-of-state airport he'd make it worth his while. Shorty's own car was possibly being wired with a bomb as they spoke. Ted asked what worth his while meant. Shorty opened the attaché case and tossed a banded slab of hundreds that exceeded a season's pay for the entire rosters of Rockford and La Crosse.

Without further urging, Ted rented a car, took Shorty Hammerhill to Milwaukee, and put him on a plane to Cancun. Shorty talked shop during the drive. Ted listened to Mob gossip. He listened to who provided flawless false identification, for how much. Unemployed and marginally employable, Ted Snowe listened to an opportunity.

En route, at a truck stop, Shorty had him pull over. He got into his luggage and gave Ted an artificial leg. The one he'd been born with had been a casualty of diabetes. Shorty said it was why he was gimpy and that it was a spare. He told Ted to send it to the Mob as if a proof of purchase sticker for a rebate.

"So they believe you're as dead as a doornail?"

"You got it, Ted. Play your cards right and it's a cinch."

Ted was fined for missing the bus back to Rockford. He was cut three games later when a better player came off the injured list.

Scared witless and half-looped, he had phoned the number Shorty gave him, told them not to "send boys to do a man's job" and received another nice slab of money at a PO box he'd rented per Shorty's instructions. After collecting for the Shorty Hammerhill hit, Ted embarked on a career even more tenuous than minor league basketball.

At this point in time, on his encore in the hustle, Ted thought he was being more selective about assignments, certain he had convinced them to keep their heads down and relish their new lives.

Until Birdwatcher Bob Chance.

"I'm not complaining, doll, but you took a step off the deep end."

"Beth, the alternative was to teach high school English and coach basketball and marry the girl next door," he said. "I bounced around as a kid. I played at three different high schools, so there's no hometown to go home to. And what do I put on my résumé for the last dozen years? Minor-league basketball bum and fraudulent hit man?"

"The part I didn't get and never will get is, you have a college degree. You had options."

"But I was an *English* major. I don't think I told you this one. Science grads ask why. Engineering grads ask how. English grads ask if you'll be having fries with that. Nothing has changed and I am not getting any younger."

She laughed. "Point made. And food service sucks. I know firsthand. And you're not getting any younger. The big four-oh, you know."

Something prominent in the back of Ted's mind floated to the surface.

Up on an elbow, he asked, "Beth, did I inadvertently kill those people, Chance and his woman? Is it misplaced guilt or did I? Be honest."

She pinched his gut. "Stop beating yourself up, Snowe. Chance brought it on himself. If they didn't hire you to, you know, they would've hired the real thing."

"His girlfriend was an innocent victim."

"You didn't know if she would've been with him. You could've known. He said he might go solo. We're off to warn the others too, so saving three out of four ain't bad. Ted, sweetie, goddamnit it, stop, okay?"

He stopped.

He stretched out and stared at the ceiling he couldn't see.

"Hush, my sweet."

"I have. Hushed."

"Your brain hasn't. Switch it off, okay."

"Click," he lied.

"We never talked about her," Beth said.

"I'm asleep."

"We didn't."

"Okay. Who?"

"You know who. I never brought it up. I was too insecure about her. Was she blond too? If you ask who again, your next word will be *ow*."

"My long-gone wife was not a natural blonde like you, baby. She was a peroxide blonde. To be a cheerleader then, you had to be blond. It was in the rules. Those blond jokes, they don't apply to you. No way. It's fashionable in the same vein to make fun of SUVs and TV anchors, but you're no dingbat."

"Flattery will get you on top of me, but not off the subject. You said the marriage to Peroxide Blondie was over super fast."

"It was."

"Why? Didn't you love each other?"

"Tough question. We thought we did, but we didn't. There was the expectation that we did."

"Like Cinderella and the Handsome Prince."

"You got it. I was a BMOC jock and she was a head cheerleader. We were ornamentation. We left campus and I was an underemployed English major and she was a C-student dropout whose looks qualified her to be a receptionist."

"You turned into pumpkins."

"The guy who served me the divorce papers made an analogy kind of like that. I decked him. May I switch off the gray matter now?"

"You may."

"Click," he said, meaning it.

13

Mary Ann Chance Redux

They were packed, checked out, having breakfast at the hotel, ready to contact the closest disappeared, who Ted had dispatched to Portland, Oregon, less than 200 miles south on Interstate-5.

But for the fantastic motel room sex and the city tour, they had achieved little. They had learned virtually nothing about the double murder, the who or the why. Bob Chance and Brenda Smith were skedaddling to Panama to hunt resplendent quetzals, spend an undetermined amount of embezzled money on an presumably-opulent lifestyle, and live happily ever after, but didn't.

"Wait a minute," Ted said as they studied Portland hotels on his laptop. "Birdwatcher Bob was going as Jerry Hoopsma and Hairdresser Brenda Lee Smith was going as Brenda Lee Smith."

"You remade him, not her too."

"That's my standard policy."

"Do you give group discounts?"

"That's something to think about, but most of my disappeareds *have* preferred to go solo. If they had a significant other they wanted in their new lives, they made contact later."

"Yeah," Beth said. "He was Mr. Alias and she was still Brenda. Easy to track."

"Bob changed rooms to avoid the footsteps, which he didn't hear."

"If he had, she was gonna be thrown under the bus, don't you think? He'd tell her he was going out to buy a paper and keep on going, the prick."

"Agreed. That's my Bob. Too bad for both of them that he was tone deaf," Ted said. "Could be the shooters traced him through her."

Beth said, "Maybe Brenda couldn't keep her trap shut to one of her gal pals at the beauty parlor, and the gal spilled the beans accidently or on purpose."

"If I hadn't rushed."

"Goddamnit it, Snowe. Will you please stop beating yourself up?"

Beth's cell chirped like a bird, species unknown to Ted.

"What did you do?" Ted said. "Before, it was a classic Alexander Graham Bell ringtone."

"Thinking about the situation, I changed the ring-a-ding while you were in the shower. It's robin redbreast, one of the choices. Cute, huh? Hello."

She listened and said, "We'll be there as soon as we can."

"Mary Ann Chance," she told Ted. "She asked if we can come right out."

"Did she say why?"

"No. But there was some life in her voice. She was rattled and wasted no words."

They left their remaining breakfast and did the best they could, but this was rush hour and the traffic was brutal, a twenty-mile trough of automotive sludge.

Beth kept track of middle digit extensions when vehicles cut off other vehicles changing lanes or speeding up so vehicles couldn't change lanes in front of them.

At their exit, she said, "Fifty-seven."

"How does that compare to a commute in Butte?"

"You're rhyming. Is there a poem coming on?"

"My poems don't rhyme."

"Traffic-related, we have that many middle fingers per year. In the bar, that many on a lively Saturday night."

When they got to Mary Ann Chance's, her garage door was closed. Nothing was parked in the driveway and her blinds were pulled.

Mary Ann opened the front door before they could ring the bell and ushered them in to the entryway and slammed it behind them.

Without preamble, she said, "When I got home from running errands, a black SUV the size of a dump truck was parked across the way, one I think I saw last night cruising through, stopping, looking my way and I know what you're thinking, that my mind is playing tricks, but it did it at least twice, and while we have our share of nosey parkers in the neighborhood, none of them has that model or guests who do, thank goodness.

"Both times the driver was looking straight at me, window down so I'd have a good look at him, I think, so I'd wet my pants, which I damn near did, and for a second I thought he might be one of Robert's birdwatcher friends, except this one, he'd be the type to go along on an outing with a bazooka to check out a species, so I thought I'd run it by you, whether you ever saw him on a field trip, and, please, I'm not accusing you guys of anything, it's the timing, you then him, and I apologize for calling you, but I didn't know who else to call, the timing, you know."

Mary Ann had spit it out in a single shaky alcohol-tinged breath.

No expert on spirits, Ted thought she could be drinking anything from wine to bathtub gin.

Beth didn't recognize the scent either. She'd never served it at The Pub and Casino, a beer and whiskey establishment.

Beth gave Mary Ann a hug. "We're glad you did call us, dear. We're on your side. We're here for you."

"Can you describe him?" Ted asked.

"I can do better than that. A little better," she said, taking a cell phone out of her slacks pocket. "I kind of panicked and was set to call nine-one-one, but what would I tell them? The police think I've been a nuisance anyway, a royal pain. They're pissed that I'm totally innocent and I didn't fall apart and do a Perry Mason number when they gave me the third degree so they could close their case and get promotions, the bastards, so I snapped a picture with the phone camera. They aren't good shots, not studio quality, you know, but, well, here."

Ted looked at a man with dark shades, dark hair, and a jutting jaw. Sans sunglasses and with a vacuous smile, he could be an anchorman or a real estate salesman. He was driving a Hummer, in Ted's opinion, a member of the SUV species at its vulgar worst.

He shook his head and gave the phone to Beth.

Ted looked at her as she looked at the phone, and saw every bit of color drain from her face. Her freckles stood out like measles.

She said, talking as fast as Mary Ann had, "I don't know him either, but I don't like the looks of this, Mary Ann. I really don't. He doesn't belong in a nice neighborhood in this. He could be a child molester for all anybody knows. So, *please*, if you see him again, keep your kids inside and call the cops. Don't risk it. You could be in danger."

"Hey, calm down. You're as rattled as I am," Mary Ann said.

"I just don't want you taking risks, okay? In light of what's been happening."

"Don't you worry. I sure won't. He doesn't look dangerous, but you're right. With what's been happening."

"That old saying," Beth said. "You can't judge a book by its cover."

Mary Ann thanked them, said it was good advice, promised she would call the police immediately if she saw him again, and that she was sorry to trouble them.

In the car, Ted asked, "What's the matter, kiddo?"

Beth looked at him. "Ted, I know who that guy is."

14

The Guy Beth Knows

Everybody needs a hero, do they not?' A role model, an idol even?

Mine happens to be the late Theodore Robert Bundy, Mr. Misogyny himself. Sir Necrophile.

Are you shocked?

People who know me would not be the least bit surprised if they knew.

Be thankful you don't know me.

Nobody knows me. My employers. Nobody.

Do not misunderstand. Ted and I are not cut from the same cloth. We are and we aren't.

True, Ted disassembled lifeless human bodies, as do I. But he did it for fun, confining himself to females. I do for fun and profit, and I do not gender-discriminate. The clients make that call.

Ted could have been an earner, as I am, and I am not referring to my other profession, accounting. He was a college graduate, though, a learned man.

If he had happened upon clients unhappy with their ladies, who knows? He may have gone down that path. The man could be living a life of luxury while fulfilling his dream.

We will never know, will we?

Mr. Bundy's life (1946-1989) was tragically short, abbreviated by a seat in Florida's Old Sparky.

Such a waste of talent, of potential.

As I sit at my South Seattle Industries cubicle and toil at my other profession, attempting to unravel accountancy legerdemain, I think often of Ted as I sort through the numbers Robert Chance cleverly juxtaposed and outright disintegrated, in search of the lingering funds and the whole truth, of others who may be party to this heinous crime, coconspirators of the deceased embezzler.

Among my other duties, I have been asked to answer questions regarding Mr. Chance's spectacular demise.

Retribution. Let me count the ways. My preferred method is the ice pick, through the ear canal to the brain or the rib cage to the aorta. Scant muss, scant fuss; an unobtrusive prelude to the fun.

Ted worked with blunter, cruder tools.

Those are small quibbles.

If my ice pick plunge misses the aorta and punctures smaller vessels, and the subject isn't dead yet, I allow them final words, which annoyingly are pleadings and prayers. I inform them that begging is futile and that prayer is also a waste of their last words, their deity as apocryphal as the tooth fairy. There is a finality to death; when it's over it's over, I say. Accept it and call it a day.

Regardless, in the aftermath, as I dispose of the evidence, I always ask myself what would Ted do.

15

No Pinky Ring

Beth said, "You know my story, my pre-Ted Snowe life, but I need to tell it again, to focus and explain and elaborate, to lead into why I was on the ragged edge of coming unglued. I can't answer multiple-choice questions. It has to be this way."

"You're going to keep me in suspense, aren't you?"

"Hush up. Mary Ann Chance's mystery man is the end of the story I have to tell, even if you heard a lot of the beginning and middle before, okay?"

"You're saying I should yield the floor?"

"Do you know the definition of 'hush', Mr. English Major?"

He was driving from Mary Ann Chance's to—Ted hadn't the foggiest where the hell he was driving to, aside from staying on surface streets, doing curlicues in cul-de-sacs, and making slow passes through strip malls. "I'm listening."

"I am a divorcée and a bartender and for all intents and purposes, an only child and like you get off on saying about yourself, an only adult.

"My family is really only my mother. I have an older sister. Kimberley's the second coming of June Cleaver. Kimberley is perfect perfect perfect. She set an example in school, The Girl Most Likely to Succeed, that I rebelled against. I kicked her off her branch on my family tree long ago. Deleted, obliterated, erased.

"Gerald, her hubby, is a bank veep. They have his and hers SUVs. Their two-point-four kids have braces and are in advanced placement classes. Kimberley lives in Arizona and has washed her hands of Mom and me, and vice versa. We're on the phone like five minutes during the Holidays and the conversation turns into a lecture. On me not reaching my potential and how it's not too late, uplifting shit like that.

"When we were younger, she'd criticize everything about me. For one, she'd go, why don't you do something with your hair style?"

"I like your hair," Ted said.

"Keep your paws off it and drive. She said I had big hair and big hair was so low class, *so* white trash."

"She actually said 'white trash'?"

"She did. I liked to've slapped her face."

"You don't have big hair. Marge Simpson has big hair."

"Last time we talked, I was totally fed up with her lecturing, and told her that she oughta play hide the salami with Gerald more often. That'd calm her down and get her off her high horse too. I don't think we chatted last Christmas."

"I'd wager she wasn't at the Gladys-Billy Bob nuptials."

"Since her and Mom are on the outs too, she wouldn't be caught dead in a trailer park. You make smarter wagers than my ex did."

"Moving right along."

"Okay, when I was younger and dumber, I wanted in the worst way to be out of Butte. I'd had a hang-up on the Big Apple for I don't remember how long. Not to be a star or a big shot or anything. New York just seemed like the farthest thing in the universe from Butte, Montana.

"I'd cocktail waitressed and tended bar at home, so I had experience. I got a bartending job at a pretty classy place in Queens. One night, in walked this gorilla in four thousand bucks worth of pinstripes, and, wow, everyone's practically falling down to kiss Jimmy Knuckles' pinky ring, the managers and customers alike. I went gaga too because everybody else was.

"One thing led to another, to the world's tackiest Vegas wedding, perfumed plastic flowers, a preacher lady out of Grand Old Opry, an Elvis hired as his best man, you name it. My honeymoon was in the room watching TV. His was downstairs losing his ass at the sports book. As you well know, Jimmy would bet on anything, spring training baseball, women's college volleyball. *Anything.*

"In hotter and hotter water with the Fellas over various issues, gambling debts at the top of their shit list, Jimmy Brutto had taken it out on me toward the end, drinking all the time and batting me around. He'd gotten constant grief from them that he'd married an out-of-town cocktail waitress, a blonde no less, rather than a respectable girl from the neighborhood, who'd go on to have eight kids and a mustache.

"I'll leave Jimmy there. That's where you came into his and my life, my hero."

"For which I'll always be grateful to the big galoot," Ted said.

"Back in Queens, this other guy came into the bar once in a while. When he did, the regulars liked to've pooped their panties. Jimmy gave him a wide berth too. His name was Antonio Spazento. He was known as Tony Whack Job."

"Whack Job. A double meaning?" Ted said.

Beth twirled a finger at the side of her face. "Oh yeah. Jimmy was Mahatma Gandhi in comparison to Tony. Everybody in the room, he made their sphincters tighten. And he was gorgeous too, a living doll. All the gals, he made their hearts flutter. He looked like a game show host. He could work as a catalog model for men's wear."

"He made your heart do backflips too?"

"He isn't as pretty as you, Mister Green Eyes, okay?"

"So long as that's cleared up."

"There were whispers that he's a private kind of guy, how he takes care of business, you know. Tell him what you want and stand clear," Beth said. "Tony Whack Job works alone with tools that make no noise. He likes ice picks, through the ear or rib cage, whichever's the handiest.

"Then he'll cart off the corpus delicti. He'd yank teeth, chop off fingers and head, and bury the separate parts here and there in the sticks. If anything's found by a coyote or backpacker, it might as well be a piece of the Unknown Soldier. He's never spent a day in jail either.

"And get this. No pinky ring."

"The Jack the Ripper of mad-dog killer mobsters, and he has *no pinky ring?*"

"Correct, no pinky ring. He wears a college class ring on his ring finger."

"No way."

"Honest to God."

"In gangster movies, a pinky ring's part of their uniform."

"In real life too. You know what's even scarier? Tony Whack Job's a CPA and has advanced business degrees."

Ted shivered as his right foot slipped to the floor and he ran a STOP sign. "Jesus H. Christ. And you're sure it was him at Mary Ann's?"

"Ninety-five percent. Even with shades on, those eyes burn through the lenses like lasers."

"The Chance-Smith murders don't strike me as his style. Or did he want to be Al Capone or Albert Anastasia when he grew up, and acted on impulse?"

"No. He has to be here to find the Fellas' money and maybe find the killers too. The money's the priority, don't you think?"

"I agree."

"Tony and Bob, dueling CPAs. Wow."

"Gives a new meaning to number crunching. Dueling. Didn't there used to be a song?"

"Yeah, with banjos," Ted said, "I wonder if Tony Whack Job partners up with Russians. On loan from the Fellas."

Beth said, "I doubt it, but he may've buried a few Russians."

"Chicken or egg?" he said.

She said, "Am I reading your mind?"

"I'm reading your mind reading my mind. Mr. Whack Job showed up at Mary Ann Chance's later in the day after we paid her a call. He's watching us too, not just her."

"Afraid so."

Ted said, "Let's lead him astray."

"How so?"

"Let's try this. We'll pay a visit to Birdwatcher Bob's former employer. See for sure if we can if they're being audited by Tony."

"Makes sense that they are and makes no sense that we do if we care about our health."

* * * * *

South Seattle Industries, an aerospace subcontractor, allegedly manufactured parts made of titanium. It was a low, sprawling building located near the now-demolished Boeing Plant Two, which had turned out a kazillion B-17s and B-29s during World War Two. A sign tacked above the door not much larger than the street number identified it. Beth and Ted supposed there wasn't a lot of walk-in trade for a cast titanium doorstop or paperweight. At the side of the building, an American flag hung limp on top of a pole. It was not flying at half-mast in homage to their fallen CPA and embezzler.

The waiting room was small and bland, like that of a hard-up dentist's. The woman at the front desk was young and businesslike in a tan pantsuit. Blond hair couldn't hide a wide-faced, dark-complected East European look. A nametag on her blouse identified her as Tami.

Per verbal script-writing done in the car, they told Tami that their teenage daughter was interested in majoring in engineering with a special interest in metals and if we brought her by, could a tour be arranged? Ted had wanted to say "son," but Beth insisted on "daughter," telling him not to be such a sexist oink-oink. Just because she stunk at math didn't mean the daughter they'd never have would too.

"What's that class you brains take after algebra?" she'd asked, remembering how hard the Underachievement Nazis had nagged her to take algebra, not business math.

Ted had said, "It's calculus, the one that steered me from a rocket science major to English."

"She's in advanced placement math," Beth proudly told Tami. "Calculus."

"We do not have guided tours," she said with no accent whatsoever. "Some of the processes can be hazarding. Give me a second and I will find some material that may be useful for your daughter."

Tami went through a door and they took seats, Beth a bit perturbed that she hadn't batted an eyelash at them having a teenage daughter.

At thirty-nine point-nine-plus years of age, Ted was more than old enough. In her early thirties, Beth would've been a child mom. She made a mental note to remind Ted of that later.

They paged through esoteric magazines on metallurgy and the aviation business, periodicals not found on newsstands. They had jazzy ads for flanges, fasteners, and high-strength drill bits. Many of the products were made in China, big surprise.

Tami came back with folded pamphlets.

She sat down with them and said, "You are welcome to take this for your daughter. The majority is on the properties of titanium itself. Did you know that titanium is as strong as some steel alloys, but forty-five percent lighter and that it is twice as strong as aluminum, but only sixty-percent denser?"

"I didn't know," Ted said.

"Wow. I had no idea," Beth said.

"And did you know that titanium is the world's ninth most abundant element, but very difficult to process from the ore and to work with after it is smelted? Titanium has many uses, from aircraft to ultra-hard machine tools to even jewelry."

"Jewelry?" Ted said.

"Yes. It is hard and durable and very attractive and it does not corrode." She held up her ring finger, displaying a lustrous silvery band that held a small diamond. "My fiancé is in there. He is a machinist. As I said, titanium is difficult to work. Bending and fashioning requires advanced skills, as it does when welded. He made this ring for me."

They congratulated Tami on her engagement and thanked her for her time.

Outside, Ted said, "I can understand why she's a titanium evangelist. It's neat stuff."

"If you're thinking ahead to Christmas or my birthday, titanium won't replace gold," Beth said. "I don't give a damn what you can do with it when you build an airplane."

"What do you think of Titanium Tami's English?"

"It's close to perfect," Beth said. "Right out of a textbook, worthy of straight As."

"No slang, no contractions, no accent," Ted said. "It's her second or third language. Tami isn't from anywhere."

"If Mister Whack Job is watching from the back room, while he's doing an audit and sharpening his ice pick, he's thinking we're carrying out a volunteer audit or trying to dip into the till or doing wherever his imagination takes him. In reality, South Seattle Industries would never let us get near the books."

"That's the general idea, but I can't say I like being bait, although it's our fault that we are."

In the car, he said, "See any massive black SUVs parked here?"

"*Nada.*"

They drove out of the lot, southbound for the next exit to I-5 and Portland.

Two or three buildings along, a small white sedan pulled onto the highway from South Seattle Industries.

Beth saw it through her mirror. "Am I paranoid or is it following us?"

"If Tony Whack Job was last seen in a big black gross vehicle, it's logical to switch to a small, environmentally-friendly white vehicle."

"Game plan?"

Ted got into the next center lane and U-turned northbound. "Eyes ahead. See no evil."

They went by the little white car. Before it was out of sight, it also U-turned northbound.

Beth said, "He bought our visit to Bob's employer, us trying to con the hired help and walk out with balance sheets and such. He really was in there doing his CPA thing for the Fellas."

"I'm a believer," Ted said.

"Where to?"

"I have a sudden inspiration."

Beth looked at him.

Ted took a left. The next right was I-5 northbound.

"I'm inspired to go where we'll have plenty of company if Mr. Whack Job drops by to say hi."

16

Tony's Field Trip

There are so many misconceptions about everything and everybody in this old world of ours, Tony thought, pulling onto northbound Interstate-5. Some people are born to what they become, some do so through childhood influence, some both.

For example, Ted Bundy, and me, myself and I, he had reflected moments earlier, as he closed his eyes to rest them from number upon number dancing on the computer screen.

Integers pirouetted and frolicked, concealing the key. Truth be told, Tony didn't even have the lock in which to insert the key he couldn't trace. His computer screen had become a hideous, tormenting video game, counterfeit spreadsheets from hell.

Robert Chance was good, gosh-darned good, Tony conceded. The digits were flipping Tony the middle digit. Chance's embezzlement was proving to be a remarkably tough nut to disembowel.

Angry and frustrated, within his clenched eyelids, he saw a bloody haze. He wanted badly to hurt someone now, anybody.

Antonio Spazento's late father hurt people too when things didn't go his way, at home and on the job. He was a numbers runner, his aptitude for figures passed along via genetics to his only legitimate child. Although the old man had little ambition and accomplished even less, his memory for numerals was prodigious, legendary. Never was a bet recorded on paper; it was logged in above his neck. This kept him out of jail and out of hot water with his homicidally-inclined bosses.

One of young Antonio's earliest memories was among his most traumatic. At the age of five, he announced to his mother while she was doing the dishes that he wanted to be an accountant when he grew up. She did not take it well.

She slung her dish towel against a wall and screamed in his face so loudly that his ears rang, giving him a month's worth of tinnitus.

"Next thing, you'll be playing with dolls!"

Traumatized by a mother who wouldn't speak, let alone look at him, in that same time frame, Tony had been relentlessly bullied by a nine-year-old who lived across the alley. It wasn't the best of times.

One warm evening, when the back door to the bully's house was opened for a breeze, young Tony lured their family cat with treats, set it afire with lighter fluid, and chased it back inside.

Three-alarm fire, serious burns to the bully, no sign ever again of the cat. It proved to be a seminal episode in the lad's life.

His father had witnessed the whole thing and gave him a hearty attaboy, even tousling his hair, rare father-son contact that didn't involve a whipping with the elder Spazento's belt.

Tony later overheard him tell his mother, "Don't worry about the kid. He'll turn out okay. He inherited my gift for higher mathematics is all it is."

Mr. Spazento did, however, put his foot down on Tony's ninth birthday, when he asked for an abacus, which the old man referred to as "Chinaman shit." A garrote one of his friends had fashioned in prison was an adequate substitute. A collector's item, his father said. A personal touch too.

"He used it once and nobody fucked with him after that, not even the coloreds."

A collector's item and then some, young Tony thought. Constructed of intricately-woven dental floss with pencil ends for handles, it was a masterpiece. The gift was an endearing rite of manhood.

With it, Tony had a load of fun with neighborhood cats and dogs, evisceration experimentation that prepared him for his future profession. However, the garrote gradually eroded and snapped while he was removing the *yip yip yip* from a Chihuahua. He dug through his mother's kitchen utensil drawer and came upon an ice pick, a revelation of a find. Woe be it to poodles and spaniels in a five-block radius.

Tony's mind leapfrogged from similar teen and young-adult antics to the present, professional polish having elevated him from amateur to consummate professional: From cats and dogs to Homo sapiens. What was the difference? A mammal was a mammal.

Take for instance, hypothetically, a hired assassin who fulfills his duty, services rendered for payment received (nothing gained, nothing ventured), and disposes of the evidence (i.e. the subject of the transaction) in a satisfactory manner, utterly professionally, leaving not a trace of remains.

To accomplish this properly, one transports the subject to a deserted Old McDonald's Farm, preferably twenty acres or more, then distributes the subject throughout. It is a given that one is a sociopathic psychopath with other undiagnosed disorders, but why embellish with labels? It is simply business and self-preservation, so why, boys and girls, do you regard such an individual as a nutcase on that alone?

How is that different than a janitor who upon sweeping his assigned floor, gathers the dirt into a dustpan and disposes of it? The job isn't done until the job is done. It's a no-brainer, folks.

Accordingly, if you utter the Tony Whack Job sobriquet in his presence, you are being irrational, nonsensical and unfair. Likewise, once, a man said that "You're so beautiful, you gotta to be a queer." He was rewarded with an ice pick in the auditory canal, shoved until the hilt struck the ear lobe. Everyone has feelings.

Unquestionably, for one in Tony's primary profession, his curriculum vitae is dichotomous and unique: He holds a CPA. The exam was no breeze, but he passed on the first try. This after a degree in accounting with a 3.73 GPA, a minor in European history, and an MBA.

His father attended no ceremonies, having been shanked and bled out by a cell mate for some unknown slight. Mother neither; the woman was stubbornly old school.

Like him or not, Antonio Benito Spazento was a Renaissance man, a polymath.

However, like professional athletes, those of his ilk have a limited window of satisfactory performance. It is a physically-demanding profession. If you're overwhelmed, weakened by fatigue, and careless, you will become a victim.

At age thirty-nine-plus, Tony estimated that he had two more years before being forced by common sense to retire. He would continue to audit for long-time employers. If he found discrepancies, a younger man could complete the job, with Tony serving an advisory role.

Tony took care of his money too, investing it well. He lived conservatively in a one-bedroom flat. His decor was concomitantly conservative. Photos of Ted Bundy adorned the walls. Mug shots, courtroom pictures when he served as his own counsel, his high school graduation photo.

There were palm trees and golden sunsets in Tony's future.

Tami had interrupted his reverie, to tell of a couple visiting with a nonsensical story of a technically-motivated daughter.

"In my opinion, they are snooping into our operation."

"About what we do or about Robert Chance?"

"How should I know? I am stalling them, with a story that I am getting them pamphlets on titanium."

Tony did not like this woman. She was an East European of some derivation, pushy and mildly unattractive. She made no effort to conceal her dislike of him either, a mocking quality in her Slavic eyes and in her tone.

Ted would know what to do with her.

The working conditions in South Seattle Industries' back room were also less than ideal. He did his forensic accountancy in an office within an office, flanked by cubicles, some manned by Tami's ethnic counterparts, who rarely spoke to each other and never to Tony. The place was soundproofed and who-knows-what-else-proofed. The walls had the acoustical shielding of a symphony hall.

"Let's see where they're going from here," he said, getting up and going out the back door.

Hateful and demeaning as the woman was, it was refreshing to be out of the office on a field trip.

Tony accelerated from the back lot as they were getting underway. He saw short hair in the driver's seat and ample blond hair in the passenger side, nothing familiar from the rear.

When they U-turned, they thought he would set out after them, Tony believed.

When he U-turned too, they surely knew he was on them.

Good.

Tami phoned when he was five miles along on the freeway, the subject in sight. "It is a rental car taken out in a Butte, Montana agency by a Doug Miasma."

"We'll just see what lies at the end of the trail," Tony said.

Tami hung up. She didn't tell Tony to be careful.

It was Mr. Doug Miasma and his companion who best be careful.

17

A Sweet Spot

Beth and Ted drove toward an eclectic skyline they would never tire of seeing if they were of a mind to settle here. That is, if settling anywhere was a practical option.

Their destination was a grand old hotel in downtown Seattle. It was constructed of stone, polished brass, marble (the real quarried deal) and money. They pulled up out front for valet parking. Though they'd lost sight of the little white car, neither Beth nor Ted were inclined to park in the hotel's basement, a concrete dungeon.

It was past lunchtime and they were famished. As soon as they took a room, registering as Mr. and Mrs. B. Hightower, they ate at a cocktail bar off the lobby, where they could observe comings and goings.

Beth wrote three numbers on a napkin and said, "I'm doing it before I forget. The first three of the license plate on the little white car."

Ted looked at the napkin, at "994," and at her.

"I kind of didn't look straight ahead when we passed him."

"As in kind of pregnant?"

"I had a finger in my eye like I had something in it."

"Like the little white car?"

"I was just glancing and he was looking straight ahead. He wasn't wearing shades. It definitely was him. Tony Whack Job. His posture, the whole bit, like he was gonna read the nightly news or ask which door the prize is behind. After he's sharpened his ice pick."

"Good peripheral vision." he told her.

"Thanks a load. I love it when a guy compliments me on my pretty eyes."

They had seen nobody suspicious in the lobby or the bar, so they went to their room and laid down for a nap, a genuine dedicated, worry-free nap, not the post-coital variety. Ted had faked a yawn and waited until Beth was breathing deeply. He tip-toed out of the room and into the elevator. The hotel parking lot was small, on three basement levels, dedicated to hotel guests. It was also quite dark.

It didn't take long to find a little white car wearing Washington plates beginning with "994." It was two slots from their car. The doors were locked and Ted saw no personal items inside it. The best he could do was let the air out of the tires. They could then move along to Portland without an escort.

Ted was about to kneel and remove a valve cover when he sensed someone behind him. Not felt, not heard. *Sensed.*

Although it took many years for him to accept it, he was never NBA material. But he was a professional jock, as talented and athletic as the basketball equivalent of a Triple-A baseball player. At six-feet (perhaps still 5'11⅝") and at his playing weight of 180, he was stronger, quicker and better coordinated than the average not-quite-forty-year-old.

Since the fifth grade, Ted Snowe had been accustomed to dribbling around screens, passing off to teammates who were in a position to score, and using his elbows if need be in the paint to snag the occasional rebound against taller foes. Much of his game was knowing where people were without seeing where they were. Sensing them.

With this instinct imprinted, he spun around and his left elbow connected solidly with a rib cage. The collision should have dropped the man to his knees, but Tony Whack Job Spazento bounced against the car to their left, stooped but maintaining a grip on the ice pick in his right hand.

"We took no papers from the titanium bullshitery you're auditing, Whack Job. Scout's honor."

"Don't call me that, Mr. Miasma. Don't you ever call me that," Tony said, connecting with a hard punch to a shoulder.

"Okay, sorry, How do you know my name, Mr. Whack Job?" Ted replied, driving his right knee into his jaw, clipping it, causing a sound like broken chinaware in an adjoining room, deflecting the thrust of the ice pick.

Tony wondered how Doug Miasma knew *his* name. Howling, spitting blood and tooth particles, he lunged.

Tony Whack Job was slightly taller than Ted and wiry, all sinew and mean streak, with zero-percent body fat, like Ted in aging-athlete shape.

Ted slipped his thrust, grabbed his wrist, and kicked his shin. With all his might, he slammed that wrist against the neighboring car. The door glass shattered and Tony released the ice pick. It fell against a tire. Unfortunately for Ted, no alarm sounded.

Tony Whack Job spat saliva and blood in Ted's face and butted his forehead with his own. It felt to Ted like a sledgehammer. The Marquess of Queensbury was gonna be a spectator today.

Ted was becoming winded, gym-estranged winded, sucking-wind winded, barely able to rotate behind Tony before his legs gave out. He wrapped an arm around the killer's neck and locked a hand to his wrist. He hung on as much to keep his balance as to strangle him.

Tony Whack swung backwards with both fists, landing kidney punches, but without the oomph to do any damage.

They were doing a goofy dance, Ted feeling as if he were a vertical bull rider. If this beast threw him, he'd be slaughtered.

"Who sent you, Tony?"

He growled in reply.

"I didn't do Bob Chance, Tony. I read about it like everybody else. Work with me on this. We have an out-of-control third party."

Tony Whack Job's herky-jerky intensified. Ted's arm was numbing from squeezing his tree-trunk neck.

Tony bent over sharply, to throw Ted over the top.

Ted let loose, catching him by surprise figuring to give him a stiff boot or knee. But Tony's foot came up first, slamming Ted into the car parked on the other side.

Ted clung to the mirror, seeing double.

As Tony retrieved his ice pick and aimed it like a lance, Beth clobbered the side of his head with a beer bottle.

Tony spun around, ankles tangled, and fell. His eyes closed, he flattened against the floor, as if completing a sit-up.

Two women with shopping bags walked by and paused, their mouths the configuration of Edvard Munch's *The Scream*.

Ted presented his best, painful grin, as if in a post-game interview after he'd been battered by heftier guards and power forwards.

Beth blew them a kiss. "Sorry, ladies. They're rehearsing for the big martial arts convention starting tomorrow at the hotel and it got a tiny little bit out of control."

At the elevator, out-of-breath Ted said, "What the, what the?"

"I was faking sleep, like you were before sneaking out. I knew you were up to something dumb. Somebody had left the beer bottle by the basement elevator."

"Babe, what you did, that was incredible."

She tapped a temple.

"Madge calls it a sweet spot. It doesn't take much force for a lights-out. I've seen it a zillion times at the bar when one of our boozehounds goes off his rocker."

18

The Final Three

"**Y**ou look like you've been in a turkeyshit shovel fight without a turkeyshit shovel," Beth said, dabbing Ted's forehead with a damp washcloth.

"Turkeyshit shovel combat? That's what you do for fun where you're from, that and stock car racing and tractor pulls and—ouch, dammit."

"How'd you hang on alive until I came to the rescue? Tony Whack Job isn't known for leniency or finishing second."

"I took his ice pick out of the equation early and fought dirtier than he did. Don't forget, I am a failed professional athlete, not your basic ninety-seven-pound weakling."

"Shush. You're heart rate is like six hundred."

"Christ, am I in sorry shape. In Milfontes, I should've been running and pumping iron, not drinking Super Bock and writing poetry. If you hadn't rode in to the rescue, it was curtains for me."

"Don't mention it. What you are is so swollen above the eyeballs, you could be out of a sci-fi movie, one of those characters with a bolt through his head."

They were in the bathroom of their hotel room, at the sink, Ted leaning against the counter, arms folded, pretending to be steadier than he was. He felt even worse than he looked.

"The man's a human battering ram." Ted hesitated. "Beth, do you think he recognized you? You were face to face for a second, before he went down for the count."

"Nah. I was just a bartender in Queens, just another little girl, who I got the impression he doesn't much care for, girls, I mean, any female in one piece."

"Okay."

"I hope okay. I don't think he did. Whenever he was in the room, he was holding court whether he said a word or not. The gang kowtowed but didn't get too close. Wanting to kiss his ring he didn't have, scared shitless too if he had a pinky ring or not. Does that make sense?"

"It does now," Ted said, beginning to shake his head, a painful gesture.

"Let's cut out the war stories. Why?"

"Why what?"

She sighed. "Why did you do what you did, dummy, sneaking out while I was faking a nap, knowing you were up to something dumb?"

"I'm your knight-errant, except you were the one on the white horse."

"You should've galloped into the garage carrying a spear. No, forget the spear. A flame thrower."

"It's better that we found him than he found us up close and personal, like when we were having the siesta we didn't take, if we were really taking it."

He stopped talking gibberish, thinking that he was nearing forty, a bad poet and fledgling birdwatcher. Correction, birder. Him in distress, rescued by a damsel. Ted Snowe was feeling a bit insecure.

"You know why he was hanging out in the garage?"

Ted said, "Tell me."

"He knew that you were gonna do what you did, check if he was there too. He set us up by making sure we were aware he was following us from titaniumville."

"I didn't want to disappoint him. Ow! Was that necessary? I'm not in critical condition, I don't think."

"Guys can be so grossly stupid," Beth said, kissing lightly, close to where she'd been dabbing. "They must have a shop in the lobby where I can get some ointment, bandages, and needle and thread to sew you up if the bleeding starts again. The sewing kit will be for mending clothes, but it'll work."

"Sew me up? You're not a nurse. No time either. We have to be underway to Portland."

"I'm good with a needle. Mom taught me to sew."

"My forehead isn't a buttonhole."

"Hold still."

"Gross stupidity is not our fault," Ted argued. "Not. It's how nature made us guys. It's testosterone pumping into our systems. We can't help ourselves."

"And what did you learn from this lesson?"

"I learned that Tony Whack Job did not communicate willingly before we did the tango and now he probably won't communicate willingly with a lisp," Ted said, giving her a line-by-line of their short conversation. "I hope for his sake that the Fellas provide dental coverage."

"So the goombahs who hire you really don't know who did Birdwatcher Bob and hairdresser Brenda, but they know whatever it is they know about you. What the hell did I just say?"

"You said what you said, whatever it was you said. Yeah, it does seem that they don't know. I'm at fault for everything because of neglect or malice or hanky-panky. Mr. Whack Job confirmed such."

Beth said, "Not a lot of useful info."

"We do have a homicidal third party out there, above and beyond Tony Whack."

"Not a bulletin."

"I had a thought."

Beth said, "Uh oh."

"I'm more convinced than ever that Birdwatcher Bob absolutely and positively may not be the only one in my merry band earmarked by our mysterious shooters. We have to act faster than I'd thought, to be certain that three pinheads have their heads down before they're blown off."

"Okay, let's focus. At the risk of sounding like a broken record, you did only four disappeareds after your return to the profession, right?" Beth said.

"Right. Two before and two after you deserted me. Owwwch!"

"You big baby. The Fellas paid for services you didn't render, so they're brutally pissed and are gonna take care of business, you included."

Ted nodded, another painful gesture. "If party or parties unknown sent Tony after me, don't send a boy to do a man's job. And a woman's job."

Beth waved a hand in front of her face. "Testosterone vapor's getting so heavy in here and some of it's mine, I can't breathe it or I'll grow hair on my chest. Refresh my memory on the final three. I think we were gonna on I-5, but let's do it now. Something to do while waiting for the bleeding to stop."

"I'm still bleeding?"

"Speak."

"Okay, the first, who we'll attempt to visit in Portland, was in his past life a Chicago bond analyst, Roger Higgins. No relation to one of your mother's ex-husbands."

"Toby. Toby Higgins. I barely remember him. Toby Higgins made a career out of mooching and drawing unemployment. You had to dynamite his ass to get it off the couch and a crowbar to get the TV remote out of his hand. Mom put up with him for like six months."

"The Fellas never tell me their exact problem with the assignments, and I don't want to know, though it's pretty easy to read between the lines. My guess was that they were laundering money through Higgins. Bond analysts, as far as I know, write reports filled with graphs and pie charts."

"Emptying truckloads of colorful bullshit on their clients?"

"That's about it. He started as a good boy, filtering their money into legit investments, but the returns were nil. He blamed the market, a slow recovery from the Great Recession, et cetera. Already suspicious, they were tipped off by brokers they knew that Higgins had gotten greedy and skimmed on them, the dumb ass. They had to be paying him well, too."

"Kind of like Bugsy Siegel's cost overruns while building the Flamingo."

"A good comparison, same retribution planned. Roger Higgins's name now is John Shannon. He was flighty, so I checked on him a month after I disappeared him, to see if he'd gone to Portland, Oregon, city of residence on his new ID. He had. He'd gone to work at a Portland-area nursery. Baxter Greenhouse and Nursery."

"Not a nursery for kiddies?"

"Nope. You wouldn't want any of my disappeareds around children. Plants and flowers. It'd been Roger's hobby. His thirty-eighth floor penthouse condo was a hothouse. I rode up the elevator with him and made introductions as I shoved him through the door."

"That's right. He had a nice piece of change left in his kitty to pay you."

"He did. I never leave my disappeareds starving. They'd do desperate things and I don't mean cardboard signs at freeway exits."

"The second had a Ponzi going, didn't he? It's hard to believe people still fall for those, but they do."

Ted said, "They do, every single day. You guarantee somebody ten percent per month and pay that ten percent initially. They're giddy, unwilling to believe that there's no magic portfolio, that they're being paid by money from future suckers. Happy as happy can be until the wheels come off."

"Dirty money laundered into it and he played games," Beth said. "For shame."

"Jack the Ponzi Bavard also got too greedy, a common denominator among Ponzi-ites. After I disappeared him, the law seized a waterfront mansion, twenty-seven luxury vehicles, including a Maserati, a Ferrari and a Lamborghini, a Cessna and a small yacht. If there is such a thing as a small yacht. It's all tied up in litigation and nobody's gotten a dime back yet. The Ferrari and a few other goodies have been auctioned off so far. The most optimistic guesstimate is eventually six cents on the dollar. The older victims won't live long enough to see 'eventually.'"

"Your clients had to've invested a large chunk into what wound up as Jack's toys."

"They did. One of the victims is suing to get the proceeds for the Ferrari sale back. Others are suing too. Good luck. No way can the Fellas risk that kind of exposure. They're screwed."

"I morphed Jack Bavard into Henry Green. I have him living in suburban Atlanta, tending bar, one of his former professions. That's where he perfected his gift of gab. He is a lady's man too."

"A pussy hound, huh?"

"An ass bandit extraordinaire. He broke hearts for fun and profit."

"I'd like to have Higgins-Shannon's pruning shears when we meet up with him," Beth said. "Make believe Mr. Green's privates are overgrown azaleas."

"That leaves my sleaziest of them all, him and his investment seminars. Al Selkirk was even slimier than the infomercial get-rich-quick-in-real-estate hucksters.

"He'd scare the hell out of seniors and recent retirees, saying they'd run out of dough and wind up homeless unless he was allowed to invest it for them. 'You don't want your money to succumb before you, do you?' Most of the investment went straight into his wallet."

"Yeah, Those seminars. Mom gets junk mail from them. Your choice of chicken or fish, then they bolt the door," Beth said. "They take old-timers for all they have. Some wind up in low-income shelters and even on the street. Mom had a neighbor who was skinned by one of them. She lives with one of her kids who doesn't want her any more than she wants to be there. It's either that or the street."

"I tried to refuse that assignment, saying I had the flu. I wanted a bona fide hit man on the job, to do it the conventional way," Ted said. "But the Fella I talked to was really insistent. Al Selkirk must've skinned somebody's relatives. I caught up to Al at a motel near the Miami airport and had a heart-to-heart with him before he gave his pitch. No chicken or fish for anybody that day. He was all done romping in Geezerland."

Beth smiled. "Selkirk didn't argue when you changed him and his career to John Doe, master janitor?"

"I'm almost disappointed that he didn't. I was hoping I could let off some steam in the form of a knuckle sandwich. He's John D. Dole, with a membership card in a janitorial union. I wrote his résumé, giving him a tenth-grade education and a generous sprinkling of misspellings and dangled participles, painful as it was for me to do it. He didn't like the new him, but he didn't argue. I had him cleaning up what he was dispensing it at his seminars. If there's any justice, he's mopping it up in bathrooms all over Seattle. First stop for him was a downtown hotel."

"Why didn't we check him out before going to Portland?"

"No way did he stick around town. I know my disappeareds. He was an arrogant ass, the least likely to behave. I'd wager that he was gone while I was in the air going back to Milfontes."

Beth resisted reminding Ted that he didn't know Birdwatcher Bob. No: salt in a wound.

"Okay, we have a psycho-slash auditor, gangsters and maybe Russians in the mix," she said, leaving it at that.

"The drive-by, this better not be no trend, said my caller verbatim before he rudely hung up on me."

"We may have a trend developing, big boy."

"I hate trends."

"After I wash your blood off, change your shirt. You look like an extra in a horror movie. It'll take me five minutes to pack."

Ted said, "At the front desk, we'll splurge on valet service again and have the car brought up from the garage."

"Please," Beth said.

The valet went for it, came back on foot, bug-eyed, and said, "Mister and Missus Hightower, it's like a porcupine on crack got in your car and went nuts. Dude, there's holes poked and slashes. Seats, headliner, dash, door trim, the works."

"Sounds like a dope addict went berserk," Ted said. "A random thing. I'm sure glad I don't have enemies like that."

"Society's gone all to hell," Beth said. "I'll tell you, law and order is a thing of the past, and kids aren't raised with any values, not some of them."

Waiting for a new car, Beth said, "Should we be getting a gun?"

"No way. I'm scared of the damn things. They can go off."

Beth said, "That's what they're made to do. I learned that from Jimmy when he was talking shop. If you change your mind, we can buy a Glock. They hold up to like twenty bullets. They say they're the shooting iron of choice for good guys and bad guys alike."

"Twenty ways to accidentally blow off a vital body part."

19

Just The Facts, Ma'am

A rental agency employee came with a replacement car for Mister Douglas J. Miasma. After inspecting the ice pick damage, he commented on how everything was going to hell in a handbasket on account of drugs and gangs and parents who didn't parent.

Beth and Ted agreed with him one-hundred percent, in a rush to get through the dialogue and paperwork so they could be on their way. Ted's own private handbasket hell was probably lurking in the vicinity.

Unable to resist having a little fun, Beth didn't help expediting matters by making the young clerk blush by suggesting that if the vandals had been breast-fed, they may have turned out differently.

Southbound on I-5, halfway to Portland, by the Centralia and Chehalis exits, Beth said, "I'm bored. Whip a poem on me."

"You say you're bored."

"C'mon. About a subject near and dear to your heart, but not too dear."

Meaning the to-be-avoided-at-all-costs m-word. But for an early misstep with the yell queen, Ted was a confirmed bachelor and Beth knew it. Closing in on forty, it was too late to think of starting a family, even if Beth was amenable. Besides, his idea of starting a family was going to the pound and picking out a cat, any breed but a Clarkson medium-hair.

"Yoo-hoo. Wake up, Sleeping Beauty."

"I know," he said, still locked on the shunned m-word. "How about money? It's called *Green*."

"I like."

"My chapbook's in the bag on the back seat. You read," Ted said. "Doing a poetry slam while driving is illegal in this state."

Beth found it and read aloud:

GREEN

Green is the color of money.
Money is the root of all.
Money can and cannot buy happiness.
Gobs of the green can buy
his and hers Benzes,
first-class to Heathrow to be fitted at Savile Row,
bottles of Chateau Froufrou 1924,
diamonds the size of legumes.
Gobs of the green can buy
hatred, envy, unfocused greed,
and an IRS bull's-eye.
Scarcity of the green can buy
late rent payments, mac and cheese,
cars that won't start.
Scarcity of the green can inspire
ambition, thrift, ingenuity,
circling of family wagons.

"I like it though I don't completely agree. There isn't much inspiring about an empty purse. I've been there."

"That's the thing about poetry. You don't have to agree."

She put a hand on his thigh. "Well, you do know how to tackle a subject without rhyming it. Any time you want to give me a reading on an erotic one, I'm game."

* * * * *

Baxter Greenhouse and Nursery was along a mixed-use stretch of highway east of Portland, with housing tracts galore, the Columbia River to their left, a terrific view of Mt. Hood to their right. The nursery was across the highway from a strip mall. It was small, with a plastic-roofed hothouse out back and no cars in the front lot. It was flanked by a sports bar with FOR SALE and AVAILABLE signs in its windows and a vacated pet shop on the other, likely victims of big box stores and megamalls.

Baxter's sole occupant was a sturdy, gray-haired woman in her fifties whose nametag identified her as JEN BAXTER. When Ted inquired about John Shannon, she said, "He's no longer here. I fired him."

Fired him. Just like that to total strangers. No inquiry who they were and why they wanted to know about Mr. Shannon, Beth thought, looking at Ted. Jen's expression bespoke the obvious, that she had not been pleased with Mr. Shannon's job performance.

Beth said, "May I ask why you fired him?"

"He knew more than I did about plants and everything else. I couldn't tell him a damn thing about anything."

That was the Roger Higgins Ted remembered, a know-it-all veneer that collapsed under pressure. "Do you know where he went?"

"It's been, hmm, how long?" Jen said, forefinger to temple. "Give me a minute."

She opened a filing cabinet and took out a folder. She opened it and wrote an address on a slip of paper. "That's where he lived when we parted company a few weeks ago."

"I guess he didn't use you as a reference," Beth said.

Jen Baxter laughed.

They thanked her and were on their way out the door when she said, "I think he was stealing out of the till too, but I couldn't prove it. He was taking small amounts I wouldn't miss, even with business as sorry as it's been. He was good with numbers, with money. I don't understand why he why he was here at all, other than he loved plants."

"It was a job," Ted said.

"A job on what little I paid him and what he stole from me, I don't think I'd call it a job suitable for him. I don't think he needed the money. He drove a brand-new BMW and his apartment's in a ritzy neighborhood, his and his wife's. And another thing. He always seemed to be looking over his shoulder."

"How so?"

"When we were both in back and heard the door ringer, he'd peek before going out to help a customer. If you can call it help. He had an attitude that turned people off."

"An attitude?"

"Like he was too good for this. As I said, he thought he knew more about plants too, more than me or anyone else. It was different with attractive young women, though. He'd hit a switch and on came the charm. He tried it on me. Once. I picked up the framed picture on my desk and stuck it in his face. Who's that, he asked? It's Lynn, my wife. That was the end of that."

Next stop was Casa Shannon, a half-hour drive from the nursery, a long commute from a job that paid pin money for the ex-bond wizard. The neighborhood and the apartment complex were posh. Any unit above the ground level had a view of a nearby lake. In the entrance directory, John Shannon and Marilu Shannon occupied a corner unit on the fourth and top floor, prime of the prime.

Out on the water, Ted saw what he believed was a flock of grebes. He did not share that observation with Beth.

He didn't have to. She watched him birdwatching/birding and

almost asked him what his life list was now that he'd seen those ducks with the sharp bills.

Beth said, "Did Higgins bring the little woman with him when he became Shannon?"

"No. His wife's name was Judy and they were either separated or on the brink."

"Not divorced?'

"For Roger-John, bigamy is a trivial offense."

"Like with Birdwatcher Bob, you home wrecker, you broke up an unhappy marriage."

They rode the elevator up and knocked on the door. A woman in her thirties answered. She held a cigarette, and had a store-bought tan and blond hair out of a bottle.

"You changed your mind?"

"We did," Beth said.

"Oh good. Come in and have a seat. I'm Marilu. The agency said they wouldn't take the case unless I provided more information about John and me," Marilu Shannon said. "I didn't want to over the phone. I have my reasons."

"A wise policy," Beth said professionally.

But for an inversion layer of cigarette smoke, the apartment was elegant, decorated with a pricey selection of leather, glass and chrome. It was right out of the Sunday supplement, circa 1990. There were house plants, all plastic, requiring as a green thumb only a dust rag. Ted's assignment, Mr. Higgins, was a non-smoker fifteen years her senior, so this must be true love/love of money and/or lust.

They sat on a couch as she continued, "You're the third detective agency I phoned. They all tell me to report it to the police. I go, I have my own reasons why I can't. They think something's fishy. So do I, by now definitely thinking fishy."

Marilu kept her eyes on Ted. He didn't think he'd been roughed up as badly as Beth's turkeyshit shovel comment, but he was in no shape to model for a magazine cover.

Getting into Beth's game, Ted shrugged manfully, touched an eyebrow, and said, "We do what we have to for our clients."

"And we mean *anything*. If there's rough stuff on the horizon, my boy here is just what the doctor ordered," Beth said, stopping herself before she overdosed on noir.

Marilu Shannon's eyes widened. Ted Snowe was officially the real Dashiell Hammett/Raymond Chandler deal and Beth Palmer Brutto was his dame.

Wondering if they were impersonating investigators of an agency Ted had used to research Roger Higgins initially, he took a notebook out of a pocket.

"Can you give me just the facts, ma'am?" Ted asked, blatantly plagiarizing *Dragnet* and Joe Friday. Last year, he'd sat through a *Dragnet*-a-thon.

Marilu Shannon put out her cigarette in an ashtray mounded with butts. "Well, three days ago John went out in the Mercedes to get the oil changed. He never came back. I called the dealer later that day and they hadn't seen him. We haven't been married long and he's never, you know, strayed. I started calling private detectives yesterday and that's about all there is to tell."

Beth asked, "Is there any reason you can think of that he would stray? Not that he would, but you know how men can be."

"Tomcat tendencies?" Marilu said.

"We have to ask, ma'am," Beth said.

"None whatsoever. Tomcatting around, that's how my ex lived."

"Could your ex be—"

"No way, even if Davey wanted to. The jerk works at a muffler shop. Him and his drinking buddies, they couldn't pick their own noses without a training manual. He's carrying a torch for me the size of the Statue of Liberty, the fool, but he's smart enough to keep his distance. John has the money to make his life miserable if Davey plays games with us."

Ted asked, "Would John Shannon's employer have any idea?"

"No. John worked a little while at a nursery east of here just because he liked plants. He'd retired superrich. John was self-employed before he retired. He had a high-tech start-up down in Silicon Valley. He sold it to Microsoft or Facebook or Apple or somebody for a big, big bunch of money. That was before I knew him."

Ted doodled in his notebook, tempted to step away and let the bad guys have at Mr. Shannon.

Beth said, "I really have to ask, Marilu. Why can't you call the police?"

"Well, I can say this much and that's all. A guy who worked for John in Silicon Valley said he invented this software, not John. The guy, he also said some icky things about him and this gal there he was in cahoots with filed a bogus attempted rape charge against him. They hired some muscle to go to his home to talk to him too. The situation was a nightmare for John. That's when discretion became the better part of valor."

"That's awful," Beth said. "I'm sure glad he started a new life."

"Oh, me too."

Roger the Weasel Higgins. Once a creative liar, always a creative liar. Ted closed his notebook.

Beth said, "There really isn't enough for us to go on, Marilu. I'm sorry. There'll be no charge for this consultation. I do have a suggestion, though."

Marilu lit a cigarette. Ted watched Beth's eyes as Marilu inhaled the smoke. Hungry eyes.

"Are you on the registration for the Mercedes?"

"John and me both. On the title too. We own it free and clear, it and the Beemer."

Laundered Mob money he skimmed and spent ostentatiously, rubbing their flat noses in it. Not smart, Ted thought.

Beth patted Marilu's hand. "Report the car stolen, but not John missing. They'll find the Mercedes, they'll hopefully find John too.

Even if it isn't good news, you need to know, dear. If it's the worst and John's hurt, somebody needs to be brought to justice."

Marilu Shannon blew a smoke ring. "Yeah. Cool idea. I'll do it. You know, our marriage isn't perfect. He's nuts about plants, but I'm allergic to half of them. I tolerate all these plastic plants and he puts up with my smoking. A compromise."

"Yes, ma'am," Ted said in closing.

In the car, Ted kissed Beth's cheek. "Quick thinking, lady, getting us in the door. Are you okay?"

"Meaning?"

"The smoke."

"Sure. Her place has nothing on Mom's trailer," Beth said. "John Boy is the mother of all bullshit artists. Is he on the run or is he at the bottom of that river we have a wonderful view of?"

"Neither," Ted said, looking through the mirrors. "Buckle up and hang on, sweet thing."

20

A Case Study

Antonio Benito Spazento didn't know how long he was out cold in the parking garage. A minute. Two at the most. He was prone on filthy cold concrete, how he remembered landing after the blow to the side of his head.

Mortified and in some pain, satisfied that he was alone, living up to his nickname, Tony Whack Job had retrieved his ice pick and taken out his frustration inside his antagonists' vehicle.

He drove to his motel, which was four or five miles from South Seattle Industries. He awarded himself the rest of the day off; he'd concoct a story for his absence later. He had taken a modest room in the bland three-story affair along a busy highway. Its sole claim to luxury was an indoor pool that he'd never seen used. Tony parked in the slot where the black Hummer had been. Having served its purpose of menace, it had been retrieved by the rental agency.

Home or on the road, life's pleasures did not come to this man from a cornucopia of houses and cars and women. Certainly not jewelry, clunky gold necklaces or, distasteful horror of horrors, cliché of clichés, the pinky ring.

Joy came from his work, his commitment to professionalism. He considered himself an ascetic, a rarity in any culture, any profession, in this day and age of free-floating gluttony and indolence. Asceticism was a satisfying contrariety to the curse of natural beauty, the Greek god syndrome.

Naked now, Tony went into the unlighted bathroom, avoiding the image in the mirror, and swallowed three of the aspirin he carried. He sat on the edge of the bed and felt his upper teeth with his tongue. Not good. Until he could find time for extensive dental care, he'd be going through life with his jaw clenched, like that hapless, thuggish, Italian dictator, his middle-name namesake.

Tony tried to remember the last events in the garage. Him struck on a temple. Losing his feet and consciousness. The woman, a blonde. Coming from a side, a sudden appearance. Swinging the bottle. Her face tense from the effort, yet smug. So familiar. That woman, like all others, a manipulator of the male with the malodorous thing between her legs.

Sighing, Tony gathered his courage. He flicked on the bathroom light and winced at the sight of a beautiful physique marred with bruises. He had underestimated his adversary, a man roughly his size and age.

He presented himself a sickening grin: Good Lord, Count Dracula in the flesh!

A puffy upper lip was the only collateral damage visible, a modicum of consolation. A shirt concealed the bruising.

Tony returned to the bed, stretched out, and fondled the ice pick, humming:

Through the rib cage and into the aorta.

Through the ear, penetrating the cerebral cortex.

Let me count the ways.

He tongue-touched his upper teeth. The incisors were broken at the gums, but the canines were sharp, ready for action.

He looked on the bright side. His injury was potentially utilitarian. Now he had an alternate weapon.

Ted Bundy was a biter too.

Wouldn't Ted have a ball with that blond bitch? Goodness.

Tony dug his telephone out of a pocket. He called home and see if his Neanderthal employers knew who the blond woman and her companion might be, giving them information on hotel registration and rental car only. To tell the full woeful tale of the parking garage fracas would be to confess weakness and failure at his *raison d'être*. He'd be an injured animal trailing the herd, fresh meat for predators. That was how their underdeveloped brains functioned.

The return call came less than an hour later. The Troglodytes were remarkably efficient when there was an expectation of mayhem.

The man and his blonde had registered at the hotel as Mr. and Mrs. B. Hightower.

Mr. B. Hightower had rented the car in Butte, Montana as Douglas J. Miasma.

Good grief, how much false identification did the pseudonymous Mr. Hightower and his blond harlot carry?

And who were they? His worthy opponent had addressed with the hated Whack Job neologism, indicating that he knew a world more about Tony than he knew about him and his woman. The man had him at a definite disadvantage.

Tony's headache was returning.

The blonde. If she were a natural blonde, the pubic hair told the tale. Lighter-skinned females were the easiest of all Homo sapiens to break down too and the most satisfying. They yielded so nicely to boning shears, he thought, hand on his erection.

Tony was a forensic accountant, as good as they came, but finding himself lost in the late Robert Chance's arcane detail. Algorithms plunging off double-entry (or triple?) cliffs into fog, dollar signs like lemmings. He conceded that Chance was brilliant, making critical moves in *quadruple*-entry bookkeeping.

Tony Spazento went into the bathroom for more aspirin, thinking of the interminable, mindless case studies he had to write in his MBA program.

Perhaps the drill with "real business issues" wasn't so useless after all. Perhaps he'd approach what was ahead with a case study. He'd develop a research strategy, a step-by-step empirical inquiry. Concrete data and human frailties; fine starting points, done with discipline, and a clear path to the goal.

Tony turned on the bedside lamp and picked up a notepad provided by the motel. He began to lay out the problem.

21

A Car Chase?

Ted backed with a mechanically-abusive lurch, as if in a carnival bumper car. Indifferent to the health and welfare of the rental unit, he jammed the shifter into DRIVE and squealed rubber, which he thought an impossibility in this tin can, semi-accelerating out of the lot onto a two-lane road, lucky that there was no oncoming traffic after failing to look both ways.

An oxidized-maroon 1990s Honda parked across the highway from the apartments pulled away fast too.

Beth said, "Jesus, you weren't kidding about buckling up and hanging on. I dated a guy who was a stock car racer."

"Do I need to know? Not."

"Okay. Watch out for that parked car."

"Missed it by a mile."

"That's Shannon?"

"It's him, our boy," he said. "Roger Higgins—hyphen/slash—John Shannon."

"Are you abso-posi-tiv-ilutely sure?"

"No mistake. He's my creature. I remade him, Beth, and I dream about my assignments. It's like going to a high school reunion and recognizing a long-ago classmate. They've changed, but not completely. Less hair, longer belt. But the jaw and nose, the profile.

The eyes. The eyes never change."

"Jesus Christ, another parked car almost jumped out in front of us."

"That's illegal. We have the right of way."

Hot on the Honda's tail, hesitating at four-way stops and lunching through, a spastic, half-assed car chase, a sum total of 175 horsepower between them, Ted blinked the lights, laid on the horn, as Beth waved out the window for him to pull over.

"I've never seen a car chase like this in a movie," Beth yelled. "Not with cars like this."

"The Keystone Kops."

"They had faster cars."

Belching a rooster tail of blue smoke, Shannon took them through several yellow lights and one red, numerous horns bleating from the last. Ted stayed right on him. Shannon gave up at a supermarket, drove into the lot, angled into a space, and stopped.

Ted and Beth went to his opened window. Shannon stared out the passenger side at sale prices on pork loin and green grapes in the store windows, drumming his fingers on the steering wheel, thinking that out of the corner of his eye, he'd seen Mister Cool standing there outside the apartments, him and some hot blonde.

He was in this fix because the bastard had waylayed him in his penthouse and robbed him blind, giving him choices, which amounted to just one choice. Now the son of a bitch was back for another pound of flesh.

Yeah, he'd been nabbed taking more than his cut when he was doing a wash-and-wear with Mob money, but why shouldn't he? It was *him* risking jail and they were paying him diddly with money that had blood on it.

There was something off-center about Mister Cool. Maybe he'd watched too many movies, but the guy looked like an FBI agent, not an enforcer for the bad asses. It didn't compute.

There was an edge to him too. If he didn't play ball, the guy could go Mr. Hyde at the blink of an eye, and the trunk of a stolen Cadillac in the airport garage scenario he gave him would come to pass, no doubt about it. Providing he didn't lose it and throw him out the thirty-eighth story window. It was too damn frightening to call his bluff. Maybe he should have.

Ted looked at Roger Higgins with both eyes, closer than the social distance. He had been a fashionable string bean when Ted disappeared him, a dozen pounds in excess of a Tinkertoy, but the new and debatably improved John Shannon verged on fleshy, with an impressive start on a gut.

Beth kept beyond the social distance, as close as she wanted to be to the creep. She couldn't picture Marilu in the kitchen, apron on, fattening him up with pot roast, fried chicken, gravy made from scratch, and apple pie. By the looks of this bozo, he did the cooking.

Higgins had had a full beard, which Ted made him shave to match the ID he had meticulously and expensively prepared. Flat-lens glasses and gray streaks combed into shortened hair completed the transformation.

Aside from packing on forty pounds, John Shannon hadn't changed much except for losing the fake specs and gaining the gray streaks, vanity overriding caution, that and the highly annoying arrogance he'd never abandon.

Ted smiled. "Johnny, it's been far too long."

"We had a deal, man. Get lost. I have enough problems without you."

"Why did you steal from Jen Baxter at the nursery, numbnuts?" Beth said, leaning over Ted's shoulder. "She can't afford it and you're loaded."

No answer.

"Your Marilu is fretting big-time, you putrid bucket of slime. She's going to report the Mercedes stolen. She doesn't give a damn about the car, but hopes that finding the car will find you," Beth said, her voice rising. "That's no way to treat the woman you love. If you do love her or anybody you're not looking at in a mirror."

Eyes unmoving from the grocery bargains, Shannon said, "What're you doing here?"

"Going to a helluva lot of trouble to preserve your sorry ass," Ted said. "Somebody else I gave a new identity to came to a bad end. You may be next in line."

"How bad an end?"

"The worst."

Beth said, "In your case, not necessarily so."

"That explains a lot of things. You may be too late. That's how come I lit out on Marilu, trying to draw them away from her."

"That's why we caught you lurking across the road from her?"

"Lurking?"

"Who's them?" Beth said.

"I don't know and don't want to know. Cars have been cruising through the lot in the last week or so. Different cars, three or four or five of them, but they had privacy glass, so I couldn't see who. It wasn't my imagination."

"What kind of cars?"

"Just cars, pickups too. None of them worth shit, all combined less than my Benz."

"Why did you think the mysterious cruisers were interested in you?" Ted said. "I'm open to ideas."

"Paranoia plus lack of other possibles in the building that I know of. There are a lot of long-term oldsters here who don't do anything."

"Did the oil in the Mercedes get changed?"

"No, but it was my intention. I was leaving as one of the cars came in. It followed me out and stayed with me for like ten miles. A freeway entrance was coming up, so I goosed it. They were in one of their beater cars. They got on it at the exit too, but no way could they stay with an SL500. I lost them, no sweat, and took the next exit, making sure they were out of sight.

"There's a used car lot not far from it full of junkers like this one, the last thing they'd expect me to be driving. I bought this from them, paying twice what they asked if they'd do the paperwork fast and stash the SL. They have a carport up in an alley to the rear of the lot.

"When you saw me, I was checking if they were hanging around home. I do it like eight times a day. This was to be the last time. I was pretty certain they've moved on by now, so I'll pick up the SL and bring it home, you know, but not all the way home. These apartments on the street behind us have unused garage space they'll rent me. Satisfied? Can I go?"

Ted shook his head and said, "Not a good move. You should go home long enough to pack and get you and your wife the hell out of town. You can explain later. Your glass is definitely half empty. You not knowing where they are doesn't mean they've given up. Haven't you learned that lesson by now?"

Beth said, "Your boss at the nursery said you were always looking over your shoulder."

"Like I said, I'm paranoid. Doing what I did, you have to be. I didn't see anyone then."

"Your nose is growing," Ted said.

He said nothing.

"You better ride out of town, pardner," Ted said.

"Marilu likes it here."

"You're not listening. You and her, go to another state. Get some land where you can grow plants to your heart's content. You have money to do what you want to do."

"Marilu likes it here."

"You're pussywhipped," Beth said. "That's adorable, but not too swift under the circumstances."

"Can I go now?"

Ted said, "Be my guest."

Shannon turned the key. The only sound was *click-click-click*.

"This happened yesterday too. The dealer claimed it was a new battery too. Would you mind?"

Ted said, "Hop in. It'll give us more time to talk some sense into you."

"Don't waste your breath. I get the picture."

They went as Shannon directed to the car lot, on a street that was atop a shallow hill. Hoods were open on the merchandise and balloons were attached. A trailer and a rickety-looking porch served as an office. Salesmen stood on the porch, smoking cigarettes. A slow day despite signs on many of the vehicles proclaiming SALE and BARGAIN and ZERO DOWN and WE FINANCE ANYONE!!

"Cream puffs," Ted said.

Beth said, "They ought to be hauled off to a wrecking yard and put to sleep."

They drove up the alley and stopped at the carport. Roger Higgins/John Shannon's Mercedes was backed in as far as it could go, covered by a blue tarp. Ted helped remove the tarp. The car was silver and gorgeous, an almost-new convertible with a retractable hardtop. It had to go for well into triple figures.

Beth whistled. "Nice ride."

As Shannon was getting in, Ted said, "If you're stopped driving a stolen car that's not stolen, you'll have some explaining to do."

"I'm not going far. I'll take my chances."

"Have a nice day," Beth said.

Shannon gunned it and started down the hill. Ted noticed small puddles by where the front tires had been. The transparent orangish liquid was too thick to be water and it was seasoned with metal filings.

Ted Snowe had earned a C in high school auto shop, the equivalent to an F in an academic course, but he knew what he was seeing on the ground.

He ran after the Mercedes, yelling, "No brake fluid! Try to stop. Pump the brakes."

Too late.

The Mercedes was accelerating. It hurtled onto a busy street. A taxi, a yellow Ford Crown Vic, coming from the right clipped his right-front fender and an SUV from his left nailed his quarter panel. Mr. Higgins/Shannon was spun 270 degrees, whereupon his right door and a utility pole made contact.

Dazed from being pummeled by the impact and multiple airbag deployment, he stumbled onto the street. Ted hadn't run this fast and hard since his last fast break. He lifted Shannon from his knees to his feet.

Gasping, he said, "I have to get back in shape, but not this way."

Beth wasted no time bringing their car, the floorboards hitting the pavement at the end of the hill. Ted dumped Shannon in the back and off they went, slaloming around the cab as it geysered steam.

The taxi driver was waving his turban at them to stop.

The SUV driver was squinting at crunched sheet metal, phone in hand, apparently in mid-text when it happened.

"A clean getaway," Beth said.

"Your stolen car validation on your mashed Mercedes," Ted said.

"Jesus," Shannon said.

"He can't help you," Beth advised.

"Does your warranty cover hacksawed brake lines?" Ted asked.

22

Tony on the Fabric of Time

Taking a well-deserved break from my case study regimen, I lay flat on my back. Sunlight enters from a razor-thin opening between the draperies. Refracted against a brass table lamp, the uninvited light has focused as a jaggedly-circular point the diameter of a pencil, playing an optical trick on the ceiling directly above me.

It is a harmless point of light, but it steers my mind far away from the cheap chain-motel fabric of the drapes to the fabric of time.

Albert Einstein posited that the past, present and future exist simultaneously.

So.

Let us say we have an orbiting telescope a billion billion billion times more powerful than the Hubble. Let us say that we zero it in on a planet similar to ours twenty to twenty-five light years away. Let us depict the surface of the planet as one big mirror.

If we observe the mirror image of the Earth twenty to twenty-five light years from that planet, are we not seeing ourselves forty to fifty years in the past? Could I not then fine-focus on Ted Bundy in his formative years? Good Lord, wouldn't that be a gas? Sitting at the knee of a master. A learning experience for sure.

Analogously, if conditions and technology permit, can I do the same beaming in on Uranus and Neptune, observing Mr. Miasma/ Hightower several hours ago, heading him and his blonde off at the pass?

Fantasy concluded, I sit up, tongue rubbing my nouveau weaponry, recalling that the area in my MBA studies where I fell down was "team building" and "networking." I work alone in my profession, of course. I begged off of team-building and networking class exercises because I was "bashful," a "problem" I promised to combat through therapy.

Team building could be the answer here, I think. An interlocking of it and networking.

Team building and networking. I write the hackneyed words in the margins of my case study.

Let us light that candle, shall we?

23

Canary in a Coal Mine

B eth and Ted drove John Shannon to the nearest car rental agency. With Ted's strong urging, hand on an upper arm so tightly that it left marks, he steered him away from the sporty models in the lot. In pain, Shannon selected a minivan with privacy glass.

They ordered him to hurry home to collect Marilu and pack a few things, and head straight to Portland International Airport. Once there, they encouraged him to throw a mental dart at the departure board, destination unknown. If he didn't know his destination in advance, neither would they or anybody else.

"The scenery in Greenland is fantastic," Beth said.

"Can't we pass on the van and have Marilu bring my Beemer?"

"Why the BMW for a trip to the airport?" Ted asked.

"You can't gender-bend for a minute and be a soccer dad?" Beth said.

Ignoring her verbal kick to his groin, Shannon said, "How about this? I'll leave it in long-term parking at the airport and try to sell it later, after we're settled. I took a big hit on the Benz today no matter if insurance covers it or not."

"You won't be around to collect on the insurance," Beth said. "Not to worry."

"This isn't the good old days," Ted said. "Think downsize, think small, think frugal."

"Come on. I don't want to lose two boss rides. The BMW, it's the M5 with less than a thousand miles. You can still smell the leather. It's aromatic, man. Five-hundred-and-seventy-five horses, zero to sixty in three-point-six. It goes for over a hundred grand and —"

"Whoa Nellie," Ted said. "If I were a cynic, I'd think you're not behaving like an ideal husband."

"What?" Shannon asked.

Ted said, "Aren't you afraid that there may be a surprise for you in that wonderful motor vehicle?"

"No, no, there won't."

"Is it garaged?"

"No, but it's been sitting in the side lot in front of God and everybody."

Ted said, "At nighttime too, while God's snoozing."

Beth said, "Yeah, then you drive it, not the little woman."

"Marilu loves that car and she's never driven a van."

Unable to summon sufficient obscenities, Beth's cheeks puffed and pinked.

"What a guy," Ted said. "Your lady love's your canary in the coal mine, huh?"

Shannon actually pouted.

"Okay, here's the deal. You start it after we call whoever we have to call to clear the neighborhood and hang yellow tape around it, or you do what we say."

"Which is?"

"Forget your precious car. Go home and pack. You and Marilu, be taillights down the road in fifteen minutes, in the van," Beth said.

"But that's not long enough to explain and pack."

"Do what the lady says, bunky. Or we'll duct-tape you to the hood of that precious ride of yours."

"Get out of the car before I do something worse to you. Right.

Fucking. Now," Beth said in a frighteningly soft voice.

Without further argument, Shannon quickstepped out of the car, to his apartment.

"Am I reading your mind again?" Ted said.

"Be a dear and park somewhere between here and the next freeway entrance leading to the airport."

Ted did, in a weedy vacant lot next to a convenience store, and waited. Sure enough, forty-five minutes later the van raced by, Mr. and Mrs. Shannon in it.

Beth called nine-one-one on one of Ted's phones. In a disguised voice that made her sound like Bugs Bunny on crack, she reported seeing a mean-looking man tampering underneath a BMW, license number such-and-such and such-and-such address, and could somebody please send out the bomb squad just in case.

She gave Ted the cell to twist apart. Out of the car, he stomped on the pieces and discarded them in blackberry bushes.

By the time they got back on the road, they heard sirens.

24

Amateur Hour

As Ted drove to Portland, Beth said, "Wanna hear a Tony Whack Job story? One that was floating around that Queens bar when he wasn't?"

"Sure."

"Before his final trip to the state pen, his dad was in a rehab facility for booze. Right across the road from it was a bar, Dry Out Bar and Grill, something like that. Big neon sign everybody at the rehab could see. Which even blinked at night. Getting the picture?"

"AWOLs?" Ted asked.

"By the droves, Tony's old man included. The customers from rehab weren't glass of chardonnay with dinner types. They were seriously thirsty. So Tony went to the bar owner and asked nicely if he'd turn the sign off or, better, shut down and move. The owner basically told Tony Whack that he was running a gold mine and to go fuck himself."

"Uh oh."

"Yeah. Next day, he was found dead in his storage room of an apparent heart attack. The family didn't believe it. He was in his forties, in okay health. They raised hell for an autopsy. They found the cause of death to be a punctured aorta. The mosquito bite by his ribs it wasn't. The case is still open."

"A heartwarming story."

Beth looked out at the Columbia and the land parallel to it, and said, "Most of those birds sure have dreary colors."

Ted said, "Yeah. Crows, sparrows, starlings. Colorful birds are a treat at this latitude. We saw a red-shafted flicker too, you know. Did you know that the closer to the equator, the more colorful the birds are?"

She said, "You're beginning to worry me."

"Me too. Bob Chance shared that with me after the field trip. While he was in disappearing denial."

"Think happier thoughts, man of mine."

"I'm trying, I'm trying."

"You did what you could for Birdwatcher Bob. You did what you could for our bond analyst. The dipshit knows the bad guys are in hot pursuit and he's smart enough to hear their hoof prints, so give it a rest. Tell me again. What's a bond analyst?"

"They look at numbers and trends and prices and yields and take your money and give you spreadsheets and bar graphs and pie charts in return, all in living color. If you swallowed the bait hard enough, our boy would connect you with a bullshit startup one of the Fellas concocted in cyberspace by nerds they owned and they'd split the profits."

"Shannon's problem was taking a second helping of the pie," Beth said. "That's all I have to know about bond analysis."

* * * * *

Portland, Oregon was a fun town to visit. This was Beth's first time, so Ted played tour guide. They got a room at an elegant old hotel in the Pearl District, near downtown. They did art galleries, nibbled lunch and dinner at food trucks, and had a few drinks at bars high in office buildings.

They watched the local evening news that night. Ordinarily to Ted, televised news and its giggly, preening anchors was akin to having a root canal. He said so.

"Stop with the same old lecture," Beth said. "They're honorary blondes, okay?"

The lead story was the anonymous phone call claiming a bomb had been planted in a BMW in a suburban apartment house parking lot.

The talking haircut on the scene interviewed a smiling detective who held the remnants of two potatoes and said, "Someone was having a little fun is all. These were stuffed in the exhaust pipes. The gas filler lid was pried open. A foreign material was added to the tank, we're pretty sure. Either sugar or, well, urine. The situation, if they wanted to make a political statement or any statement, it's amateur hour."

"The person who phoned nine-one-one, do you suspect they were involved?" asked the haircut.

Duh.

"The area code was Kuala Lumpur, Malaysia and the caller was hard to understand," the detective told the haircut. "He was definitely a foreigner and didn't take credit for any organization. We're continuing to investigate and the FBI may be called in too."

"You saved some serious engine damage to a luxury car today," Ted told Beth.

"Aw shucks," she said.

They looked at each other and chorused, "The muffler shop ex?"

"A muffler man scorned," Beth added. "Nah. Potatoes up the car's rectum. That's what you do when you're in the ninth grade."

"Yeah. Brake lines, though. That might be another story," Ted said.

* * * * *

"The good news is that your swelling's gone way down. In a month or two, you won't look like a monster from outer space," Beth told him in the morning.

They had decided to spend an extra half-day in Portland. It didn't seem to make any difference where they were. There was no conspiracy that included their wherever-bound German car aficionado, but they *knew* they always had company.

But for Antonio(Tony Whack Job) Spazento, their secretive companions had been unseen and unheard. With his CPA and MBA and smarts and track record, Ted had to believe that for unknown reasons Tony was intentionally careless.

"If you want a solid argument to back that up, sorry."

A must-do destination in Portland was Powell's Books on the edge of downtown. The main store was close to their hotel. It and its satellite stores were home to over 4,000,000 books, new, used, out-of-print, and collectible.

At the checkout counter, Ted bought four birding guides that covered half the planet. Beth cradled an armload of romance novels, many with lurid covers of damsels being ravaged by a variety of shirtless rogues. She was going to ask him if he thought he was being haunted by Birdwatcher Bob, but caught the wisecrack before it flew out of her mouth.

"You're an English major and that's it?" she said, making a face at his purchase.

"In college, they made us read beaucoup books. I took a class in modern literature where every author was dead before I was born. Bird guides are mostly pictures. Those things of yours, they're called bodice rippers, you know."

"Bodices or no bodices, those pirates use the direct approach. No luncheon dates and wine bar visits and moonlight walks on the beach and 'what's your sign?' before making a move," she said. "It's a turn-on."

"And I don't? Turn you on? I made the direct approach."

"I didn't say you didn't. And don't forget, I made the direct approach on you too."

"Yeah. We were a head-on collision. After what, the second date?"

"They weren't even dates. I'd glommed onto you trying to get that hundred grand."

"If I dress up with a hook and a peg leg, will that be even better?"

"It's something to think about," she said. "In the movies, the guys who play peg leg pirates, they have to bend a leg and strap the calf to a thigh."

"It'd be too uncomfortable to perform."

"I wouldn't care for a hook around me either."

After lunch, walking hand in hand along the riverfront, she said, "We've been going over the situation till we're blue in the face."

Ted said, "The searching of your room two weeks before your mother's wedding? That continues to bug me."

"A hunch that's gone past women's intuition. I'd kind of blamed it on my period, where things go off-kilter."

"You're positively sure it wasn't Billy Bob Blamey, her future husband?"

"Make that future ex-husband. It's only a matter of time," she said. "But no. We've been all over this. His elevator doesn't go all the way to the top, he's a drunk, and he may be closet kinky, but he knows better than to pull a stunt like that. If Mom caught him sniffing around in my underwear drawer, she'd make him a noose out of my bikini panties and hang him from that chain-lift thingy a neighbor down the street uses to pull engines out of his beaters to work on."

"You were living in plain sight tending bar too. Nobody hassled you?"

"Not until you took me away from all that."

"Beth, do you know the term 'Judas goat'?"

She laughed and said, "My mom gave up trying to get me to go to Sunday school. I do remember the guy and his thirty pieces of silver. I remember asking myself what that's worth in dollars. My allowance was fifty cents a week."

"A Judas goat is a goat trained to mingle with sheep or cattle, leading them to the slaughterhouse, while its own life is spared after it does its duty. They're used to track feral goats too, so they can be eradicated."

"How can a Judas goat sleep at night?" She stopped, stopping him too. "That's us, huh? Watching me, waiting on you. Now us."

"It's as good a theory as any. We lead whoever to whomever."

She said, "We don't get squashed like bugs till they have what they want, so we can rule out Tony Whack Job. He's a separate player."

Ted said, "Or is he? The Fellas are pissed that I, allegedly, did Birdwatcher Bob Chance Depression-era gangster-style rather than subtly. So they sent Tony Whack Job to handle business his style."

"There's enough maybes that I'm not following you."

"I'm not following me either. I'm just saying there's an X factor."

"A rival mob, then. I'm semi-convinced of that now. Russians or other foreigners. It's an equal opportunity profession these days," Beth said. "They've been known to have little spats."

"Why does a second gang care about my other assignments?" Ted said.

"How about this? It's personal. It's you, not any of them," she said. "Look. Seattle and Portland are two hundred miles apart. Us and Bob and the clown here we sent on his merry way, we're easy pickings."

"We'd better get a move on and check my last two fast. Just in case, we'll take a zigzag route."

Beth looked at the man she was hopelessly head-over-heels over, wondering if she'd hopped aboard an adventure or a disaster.

"Oh goody. I adore airline food."

25

Marilu Shannon

I don't know who my man is, but I know who he isn't, and that's who he says he is. Whoever my imaginary, fake, phony, fictitious John Shannon is, so long as the money's there and it stays ripe to be plucked off the tree, I'm staying along for the ride.

Him and his high-tech start-up down there in Silicon Valley he sold for more than God's worth? Hah! Daylight savings time ended and he couldn't even set the clocks ahead. He did a goofed-up job of trying to set them back, not spring ahead. I had to do it for him.

That's my genius techie. He won't touch my laptop or tablet. I can't make up my mind if it's computerphobia or he's afraid of what he might find or that somebody on the other end will find him. Your guess is as good as mine.

I'm not giving out a hint where we are now, so please don't ask. John swore me to secrecy like twenty times. It's where they never have winter, which narrows it down as far as I'm going to narrow it down. John says he's going to raise orchids. Out of doors. Him and his attention span, we'll see where that goes.

Those people who came to the door pretending to be private detectives, they could be the ones that have my John Boy jumping out of his shoes whenever he hears a noise, don't you think? The guy who looks like he ran into a door, but is still cute, that could've happened to him anywhere, not just like in a detective movie, you know, where he's jumped by a villain in the first act, but gets even at the end. They did get me and John back together long enough to split the scene and that's good. I don't know if he was running out on me or not. I don't think so or he'd've been long gone with his phony oil change. Or would he unless the fake detectives had intervened? So many unknowns.

But as they say, nobody's perfect. For sure not me. John caught me on the latest rebound from Davey. Love of my life, Davey, who I've busted up with and made up with so many times I can't count them, before and after we divorced for the second time.

Davey's been acting like a dippy teenager since John and I hooked up, which is par for the course for him every time I have a new squeeze. Dumb little pranks, hot-rodding out front at night, yelling and laying rubber, like kids working through a six-pack. Davey and his high school drinking buddies will never grow up. Call me a ditzy blonde, but I love Davey for it, the dopey kid in him.

Davey was playing it cooler this time, playing head games, trailing John around, making him paranoid as all get out. Fooling with his cars too. Right before he gathered me up and we lit out of town, I asked John about the Mercedes and he got white as a ghost and mumbled some lie I couldn't even understand. And the Beemer, let's not even go there.

Davey'd love to kick John's ass six ways to Sunday, but he's not mean unless he's been drinking. He wouldn't do anything to hurt John bad. He just wants John out of my life and himself back in it. It's the same old cycle, us horny and hot-to-trot for each other as all get out, promising eternal love, then fighting like cats and dogs, then me kicking him out or him leaving on his own.

God almighty, right after we met in high school. Me a sophomore, him a senior, Davey and me in the back seat of his cherried-out '66 Impala SS convertible, where he got my cherry. Ha ha. Us afterward, pants and undies all over the back seat floor, us stickied together with blood and sweat and you-know-what, looking up at stars and a full moon. There'll never ever be a time like that again *ever*.

Davey, bless his heart, hasn't got an ounce of ambition. He works at this chain muffler shop and that's as far as he wants to go in life and then some. But I'm at the age (not getting any younger) where I have to start thinking of the future, how if I'm going to grab the brass ring, have a chance at the finer things. The clock's ticking.

I'm not trying to fool you into believing I'm the best person in the whole wide world because I'm not. I'm doing what any girl who's not getting any younger would do. When I find out where Johnny's money's coming from and how to dip into the honeypot too, I'll send Davey a picture postcard and say come on down for a vacation. John has a roving eye too. I can tell whenever we're around these young native gals. He might leave me high and dry in an instant, so a girl's gotta do what she's gotta do.

We'll see what happens.

Davey, he can lose control of himself really easy where I'm concerned. Like I said, when he's drinking, he's another person altogether. It's sexy and it's scary too.

His tomcatting, I can do without. If he comes on down, it'd damn well better! I'm not jumping from the frying pan to the fire.

Davey's a smoker too, so we'll quit when we feel like it, quit together. The blond detective who dropped in, she was a smoker or ex-smoker. I could tell by that yearning look in her eyes when I lit up.

Anyway, whatever happens, it'll happen.

That's my plan: me and Davey and John's money.

That's what I'll do whether you or anybody else likes it.

26

A Hermaphroditic Hairdresser

At Portland International, while waiting for the first leg of their diversionary flight to Kansas City, Beth received a bird-call phone call, her robin redbreast. She looked at the tiny screen, then at Ted.

"What the hell. It's Mary Ann Chance."

"Were you girls sorority sisters in a past lifetime?" Ted said. "In a parallel universe?"

She shrugged and answered.

Beth's responses were mostly giggles and "You have *got* to be kidding!"

When she thanked Mary Ann, hung up, and regained her composure, Ted said, "No more anchorman-esque goons in the neighborhood?"

"Unless you count the ghost of Brent Lee Smith."

"Excuse me?"

"The Brenda Lee Smith autopsy results are in. Brent Lee Smith had had a sex change operation not too long ago and became Brenda Lee Smith."

"A hermaphroditic hairdresser," Ted said.

"Yuck. I wouldn't want her/his hands in my hair. Does this have anything to do with anything? Like, you know, a vital mystery clue."

"Other than the secret passion of a dead birdwatcher, no,"Ted said.

"Dead birder," she said."We prefer to be called birders."

Ted said, "It might explain why Bob embezzled. I'm going out on a limb by saying that replumbing of the goodies is not included in most company health plans including South Seattle Industries'."

"For sure not for non-relatives. Mary Ann got online and learned that Thailand does them by the carload. Three months ago, Bob said his company was sending him to India on business. They have oodles of titanium there and he had to be there to spot-check if they were shorting SSI on shipments. He made a detour afterward to Bangkok. She thinks the trip was total bullshit and he'd probably told South Seattle Industries that he was home with a nasty case of the flu."

"Bangkok and Thailand are tourist meccas,"Ted said. "Bob explored old temples. Went on a retreat, living like a monk?"

"Uh huh. Right."

"Visited opium dens."

"I'll go along with that one. Remember when the hotel concierge said he didn't think Brenda had traveled much and was afraid of flying?"

"She may've been zonked on tranquilizers the first time. Didn't remember the procedures. The happy couple had to have wanted that operation a lot."

"How is Mary Ann doing in general?"

"She's in good spirits. She said she hadn't prayed since Sunday school, but when she found out about this she prayed for the operation to've been painful and for Bob to've caught malaria."

"The lady has faith in God. She is a spiritual person."

"Since I have the phone out, I should call Mom, see if she's okay."

Beth's phone did another robin redbreast chirp.

"Wow, we're telepathic. Hi Mom."

"No Mom, I'm sorry. I won't be coming home for a little bit. We've had some things come up."

"You know, different situations. It's complicated."

150

"We're at the Portland airport."

"In Oregon, yes."

"We? Yeah, it's Ted, not Fred, and he's with me."

"Does Portland have a soccer team? I think they do. No, he doesn't play for them. Maybe they'll sign him next season. You never know. Good soccer players don't grow on trees."

"You sound different. Is everything okay?"

"Good. But you hesitated."

"Billy Bob has a drinking problem? That's a bulletin, Mom. He's not being rough with you, is he?"

"A big softy. Oh good. So what's the big deal?"

"He oversleeps, huh? Is he in hot water with the towing company he works for?"

"If he won't say he is or he isn't, yeah, he is. With your bad back and carpal tunnel, I don't blame you for not wanting to go back to work as a grocery checker."

"Try this. Put an alarm clock on the pillow next to him."

"No, not next to you and him. On the other side. If he's passed out, set it on high."

"His eardrum? Not to worry. He has one in the other ear."

"Mom, gotta go. They're calling our flight. Love you too."

"Our flight's not for an hour," Ted said after Beth hung up.

She leaned back and closed her eyes.

He said, "Okay. Enough said."

27

Old Dogs, No New Tricks

The flight to Atlanta was smooth and uneventful, although it left from Baltimore, not Portland, Baltimore being the last leg of their zigzag see-America-without-seeing-America route.

From Sea-Tac, they had flown to Kansas City, went through the terminal, collected their bags, went to the ticket desk of another airline, bought seats to Minneapolis-St. Paul because it was leaving in less than an hour, and repeated the process from there to Charlotte, when a long layover stuck them there for hours, sleeping upright in rock-hard airport seats, heads together, then on to Baltimore and Atlanta. Every single TSA agent looked at them but didn't see them, the norm.

Their luggage accompanied them throughout, promptly dropped onto the carousels undamaged.

"A miracle on the scope of Lourdes," Ted said as they collected their bags at Atlanta.

In spite of flying business class to keep from becoming cripples, the process was exhausting and took a substantial bite out of Birdwatcher Bob's payout, but it should shake the Fellas and Tony Whack Job, should they be nipping at the cloven hooves of their Judas goat. Ted knew he'd have to resume earning sooner than he liked.

They rented a subcompact and headed north on Interstate-75,

which became I-85, in traffic as ugly as anywhere. Atlanta's sleek skyline jolted Ted's naive concept of the Deep South, of cotton fields and dusty rural roads and locals in overalls playing harmonicas on front porches as they drank moonshine out of mason jars, and he said so.

Beth said, "The *Gone With the Wind* mansion where Clark Gable got laid, what was it called?"

Ted yawned. "I forget. Not Graceland. That I know."

As they drove by an endless mall, Beth yawned and said, "Whatever it was, it's gone now, buried under that Wal-Mart."

It was after dark, and they were tired and hungry. Business-class meals were filling, but similar, and booze was plentiful, giving them a series of half-hangovers.

Beth wondered if they'd broken the Guinness record for number of hangovers in multiple time zones inside of two days.

About forty miles from the airport, they took the Hamilton Mill exit, which put them in Dacula (pronounced *duh-kyoo-luh*), a whitebread community where Ted had installed Henry Green ne Jack Bavard. His thinking was that while it was a small town, there were numerous small towns and burbs scattered in the Atlanta vicinity. If anybody tracked him as far as Atlanta, it'd be the end of the line, unless the freshly-minted Henry Green did something outrageously stupid.

Ted had intercepted him in an Austin, Texas hotel room as he was sprucing up to give his Ponzi pitch in its banquet room. Terrified by threats, a hard yank on a half-knotted tie, and a face slap to capture his full attention, the new Henry Green swore to Ted that he would find a quiet neighborhood sports bar with twenty TVs to manage. He was a "people person" and liked the interaction. He'd eagerly go to Atlanta where Ted's new identity had placed him, wear Falcons garb, learn to like boiled peanuts as a bar snack, and develop an accent, like he was a native.

Ted told him to be careful, to pretend he was a human being, to suppress his God-given tendency to be a greedy, sociopathic asshole. Henry Green raised his hand, as if taking a solemn oath, "swearing on his mother's grave" that he'd behave and live a quiet life.

Ted recalled that Jack Bavard-Henry Green had raised his left hand and that matronly Mrs. Bavard and her bleached-blond hair and drooping, silicone-enhanced breasts was living in Coral Gables with her fourth husband. Old dogs in the Bavard family, no new tricks.

During their convoluted journey, Beth had played video games on the laptop.

She pounded on a sticky key and said, "I don't know why we can't do without computers."

Ted smiled. "I've had the same thought. Inspiration."

"You and your Remington that's as old as Mom. What else did you knock out?"

"You know where my chapbook is. Give *The Pied Piper of Sunnyvale* a try. It's my epic poem."

"What's an epic poem?"

"It's a poem that's *way* too long. I ran through a case of Super Bock writing it."

"Oh."

"You asked for it and there's time to kill before we land."

Beth sighed, found it in his carry-on, and read:

THE PIED PIPER OF SUNNYVALE

Sunnyvale is in Silicon Valley,
A state of mind that runs wide and clean,
On streets paved with banknote green,
We are talking an avaricious sheen.
But alas, though, less than a year ago,
A hotshot corporation did suffer so.
In the clutches of electronic vermin,
Viruses and glitches and bugs,

Subatomic critters in semiconductor nook and
  cranny,
Knocking every anti-virus effort on its fanny.
Gumming up servers and routers and switches,
Giving hard drives and software the twitches.

From whence had they suddenly come?
Of programming excruciatingly dumb?
Or a sociopathic teen's conscience gone numb?
Even Ganymedian aliens made the list,
Little green men flexing a technological fist.
Regardless of origin, they had to go,
Customers and stockholders demanded so.
Consultants were flown in day and night,
Though they were a pestilence in their own right.
They fiddled and shrugged and billed,
The problem is insoluble, they helplessly trilled,
Leaving nothing but despair and invoices.
Employees were sounding their voices,
This dastardly invasion, they cried,
If we cannot imminently foil it,
Our 401(k)'s are in the toilet!

The CEO, CFO, COO and chief tech guru,
They knew not what else to do,
As software entrepreneurs too,
They were nigh through.
On the Worldwide Web for help they must try,
Their strangling bandwidth, soon to die,
Too thin to pass through a needle's eye,
So online time they would have to buy.
Bound for an Internet café, they were halted in
  the lobby,

Gary Alexander

By a fellow to whom color clashing surely was a hobby.
In checks and stripes of raggedy polyester,
The man was either a car salesman or a jester.
Shocks of hair yellow and gray,
Spiking wildly like dry hay.
Eyes of blue, nose of red,
A neck much too small for his head.
Dork, doofus, freak and geek,
Each thought, biting a cheek,
The pots calling the kettle black.

Hoo-hah, said the piebald stranger,
I can save your outfit from further danger.
He thrust aloft a black box by its cable,
Your creepy-crawlies, with this I disable,
By piping in a patent-pending charm,
I shall scourge that which does you harm.
The desperate execs exchanged looks,
Deep down they had the instincts of crooks.
In a whispered powwow they decided what the hell,
A piper pied or pie-eyed, not mentally well,
The dweeb is harmless and you never can tell.
They inquired how much his service would cost,
Knowing he knew their enterprise was as good
  as lost.
He replied that since the dot-com fizzle and the '08
meltdown,
His income had declined to a drizzle.
He worked cheap, a paltry few thousand bucks,
They retorted that if he didn't produce, this
  really sucks,
And he countered that if he failed, they don't pay,
  a no-brainer,

And they pinned him down, not even a retainer?
I, sirs, am a magician, not an attorney,
May my device and I begin our electronic journey?
The CFO winked at his colleagues and said
   commence,
Do a spiffy job and I'll add my Porsche to your
   recompense.
Head 'em up, move 'em out, shouted the CEO,
We'll lasso some shares into your portfolio.

A terminal, any terminal with a USB port will suffice,
In Windows 8.1 or OS 10.4, my medicine is as cool
   as ice.
Led to a machine, he connected his box,
Fed a disk into it and said we'll cure your pox.
Thus began snappin', crackin' and poppin',
On the screen multihued pixels were a boppin'.
Then came a metronomic thrum,
Followed by a hypnotic melodic hum.
He pushed his fingers into a latex glove,
A grudging chore done without love.
He made a face as he removed the disk,
Warning that contamination was a risk,
He dropped it in the nearest wastebasket,
And proclaimed the system pristine, just ask it!

The bosses ran every check and protocol and test,
Everything was performing with speed and zest,
Amazed and elated, they lauded the weirdo as
   the best.
My stock and my moolah, he requested, please,
Also, to that gorgeous 911 Carrera, the keys.
On paper, we're zillionaires, they chimed,

However, a cash money demand is ill-timed.
In our pockets, we don't carry a bunch,
And by the looks of you we have a hunch,
You'll settle for us simply buying you lunch.
The Piper's face slumped,
On a table a fist he thumped.
You'll be sorry you demurred,
A fatal exception has occurred!
Whoa, don't be rude and crude, dude,
Summoning security is a choice,
We'd hoped to have eschewed.
But the Piper was no candidate for intimidation,
He said, expressing even greater consternation,
You have performed an illegal operation!

One step ahead of a rent-a-cop fuss,
He retreated to his scabrous Volkswagen bus.
On laptop with wireless modem, he hooked up
  his hocus-pocus.
Into the network his mesmerizing tones beamed,
Shortly, out of the corporate campus they streamed,
Engineers and developers and programmers a plenty,
Support reps and program managers, runnin'
  and joggin',
In toto numbering two hundred and twenty,
The firm's entire inventory of high-tech noggin,
Hustling into their Benzes, Lexii and Z4's,
Into their restored muscle cars and SUVs.
The V Dub pumped noxious smoke as it lurched forth,
The Piper leading a joyous, horn-honking parade,
To Cupertino and San Jose and north.
Turning eastward over the Sierra's grade,
Such a serpentine path they did take,

Cruising Pocatello, Billings and Salt Lake,
Ten miles out of Roswell, for a night they alighted,
Come dawn, nevermore were they sighted.

The CEO, CFO, COO and chief tech guru,
To themselves, they had been reduced to,
Pacing and wringing hands and oh so blue,
Knew from now on what they would do,
From nobody would they ever, ever steal,
For a deal was a deal was a deal.

"You sent the good guys off into the sunset and the bad guys into the dumpster," she said.

"I did."

"You rhymed as you kicked ass."

"I did."

"Roswell? Meaning UFOs?"

"If you like. Reader's choice."

"That sounds literary, but I still love it. You've finally told a meaningful story with one of your poems and rhymed like poems are supposed to. It's more down to earth than the Mars one you won the poet slammer on too."

"Thanks, I think."

At their exit, she said, "There are a dozen bars in and around Dacula and they're all sports bars, which ninety-nine percent of all bars are nowadays. Let's check into the next motel we see and start our Henry hunt. I'm famished and my tongue's swollen from lack of moisture."

"Hair of the pooch," Ted said. "Onward."

They did so, checking in at an antiseptic chain motel, dumping their bags, and finding a suitable eatery across the highway. They split a mountain of nachos and drank cold beer. They could scratch off this bar. The bartender was a trim, energetic young woman who in no way resembled the middle-aged Jack Bavard, who was handsome in a lounge lizard kind of way. A nametag identified her as HI, MY NAME IS AMBER.

At this hour, business was slow. There were a few dedicated drunks at the bar, one or two beers from needing seat belts, and a table of college kids with pitchers and University of Georgia jerseys and/or caps on. The televisions were replaying one sport or another, predominantly football.

Beth said, "Say, I just thought of this. You don't carry a photo of your assignments, do you?"

Ted shook his head. "No. Too incriminating if I'm nabbed, like if I'd been pulled over for a burned-out taillight after Birdwatcher Bob was gunned down, I'd be dead meat."

"Amber's not busy," Beth said. "Should we?"

"Turn your thespian talent loose, girl."

"Excuse me," Beth said. "I'm looking for a bartender who works around here, the last I heard. He's new to the area."

"Why?" she asked, suspicious of Beth and her Yankee accent.

"The dirty son of a bitch stiffed me for child support for going on two years, pardon my French. The last I talked to him, he laughed at me and said to prove paternity." She hesitated, fighting pseudo-tears. "We have an eight-year-old daughter who's as pretty as he is, so pretty it's spooky, and I don't think the rancid piece of shit gives a damn if she's dead or alive. My big brother here, if we can ever catch up to him, he'll put the fear of God into the no-account bastard."

Big brother? Ted smiled and nodded.

Beth was playing the dirtiest of pool, but she was speaking the bartender's language. They instantaneously bonded.

Amber leaned forward on the bar and said. "I'm so sorry, hon. We have no shortage of them in these parts either. I think I was married to his twin brother. There oughta be open huntin' season on 'em. What's his name?"

"Henry Green. He's a walking sugar-talking son of a dildo,

too handsome for his own good and he could sell refrigerators to Eskimos."

He actually had, Ted thought. Before his last Ponzi operation, while on the run from angry investors, Jack Bavard had been sales manager in a Fairbanks appliance store until he'd been caught with his hands in the cash register and on the owner's wife.

"Oh yeah, that name doesn't ring a bell, but I'm damn near sure I know who you mean. I'd heard through the grapevine that he'd been fired from a couple of places when he came in here. He was barhopping with some people I didn't know. It was an engagement party for him."

"When?"

"Ten days ago or so. Wait a sec. I can tell you exactly when." She went to a drawer on the backbar and returned with an envelope. "Jimbo, my boss, he's a soft touch."

She thumbed through it, saying, "These are NSF checks. Here's his for three-hundred-and thirteen bucks. He ordered this wine I had to wipe the dust off of the bottle. It was made in France, wine we sell like once in a coon's age for an anniversary or a job promotion. A small bar like this, that stings.

"Jimbo works days here and was on then. Jimbo went by the bastard's apartment. See the unit number on the check, four-oh-three? The building has only three floors."

The name on the check was Henri Vert, French for Henry Green, pronounced *on-ray ver*. Clever, Ted thought. Too cute for words.

"Who's the lucky bride?" Beth asked.

"It was more like a going away party for him, the scum."

"For them you mean?" Beth asked.

"No. *Him.* She wasn't at the party too, so I should've smelled a rat. Henri hauled ass on her. From what I hear, Danielle's super bummed. I say it's a blessing in disguise, but I'm not gonna tell her that."

"She *has* to be too nice for him," Beth said.

"You got that right. Danielle's as sweet as they come. She's younger than him, but pushing thirty-five. I think she didn't want to end up as a spinster. He caught her vulnerable and cranked on the charm. Danielle's a brain too where math and computers and stuff is concerned. Her guy IQ, though, it's way down there as far as it can go."

The bartender rubbed thumb and forefinger together. "She has this software job down in Atlanta that pays like you cannot believe. If Vert didn't clean her out, lock, stock and barrel, I'll faint from shock."

"I'd like to meet her before we leave," Beth said. "Compare notes and give her a big hug."

"She sure could use one, hon," the bartender said, writing directions on a napkin. "I know she's taking some time off work get her head back on straight. Tell her Amber said to drop on by and give her a hug from me too, y' hear."

"Oh yes, I sure will."

"It you catch up to him, what do you plan to do?"

Beth smiled sweetly. "Cut off his nuts with a rusty can opener, then turn over the remains to Big Bro here."

Amber smiled sweetly and slapped palms with Beth.

"That's my girl."

28

Billy Bob Blamey

I never said I was extra perfect.

I mean, who the hell is?

Are you?

Pardon me all to hell, but I don't think so. Everybody got their little hang-ups.

Glad' ain't perfect neither, although sometimes you can't tell her that, and she knew what she was getting into when we said our vows. I was married once before a long time ago. It was an unnatural disaster for every reason you can think of. Glad's nothing like her, but marriage being marriage, I have these backflashes of what it'd been like, which give me the willies where marriage as an institute is concerned.

Glad', she's lately been on my ass about my drinking, like she never had a taste. I oversleep once or twice and she panicking about my job. I tell her like I'm telling you, Leamy, my boss, me and him go back to when Christ was a corporal. Now and again, if I sleep in and report to work with a hugely gigantical hangover, Leamy's cool. He keeps coffee pot on twenty-four and seven.

Leamy knows I'm there for him when the chips are down. Like that tornado that blowed through five miles west of here. We don't get tornadoes often in Butte, but we get 'em, yes sir we do. It dug a groove wherever it felt like it and I don't mean just trailer parks. I worked like an eighteen-hour shift towing off sedans made into convertibles by downed poles and trees.

So what does Glad' do after her latest drinking lecture? She sets an alarm clock on my pillow on the opposite side of her. The fucking thing rings right through my skull and sets my other ear throbbing.

I'd bet dollars to doughnuts Glad' got that bright idea from that little girl of hers who run off with the soccer player. Beth's a cutie pie, but she sure can be a wise-ass with an attitude. She's been around the block too, an unruly streak in her, married before to a gangster. Her wildness, it's a turn-on if truth be known, but that's just between me and you.

Me and Glad', she's getting all organized for our honeymoon, packing and going over these brochures she'd mailed off for. We had our honeymoon in advance if you know what I mean, and a road trip to Branson, Missouri will cost a bundle, but Glad' has got her mind made up.

I say we oughta think it over and not go off half-cocked and she gets all pissed off. She said I promised Branson before we tied the knot.

I could of promised but I don't remember. I may of had a drink or two, so does that count?

I'm mulling this stuff over in my head while I set a hook to a Ford Explorer that skidded into a ditch. It ain't even icy yet. I'd hate to be with this dumb-ass driver when it is.

There's this old saying that comes to mind in regards to me and Glad' and her honeymoon plans: If you hold my feet to the fire, I'll get cold feet.

29

Alphabetical Cats

The next day, in late morning, as Ted drove and Beth watched for street signs, she asked, "So tell me again why is it that we want to save this scumbag from the pinky rings and our friend without the pinky ring?"

"You pose the same old moral dilemma. Are they worth saving? Nope. They are unredeemable scumbags, but they're my scumbags, living and breathing scumbags that the Fellas aren't gonna buy as rising from the dead any more than they bought Birdwatcher Bob Chance doing a Houdini number from the deep blue."

"Good answer, desperado of mine, but that's not all there is to it."

"Other than saving our asses too? Isn't that enough?"

"The rest, please."

"Professional pride."

"Heavy sigh," she said.

"Besides, I can't retire yet. The piggy bank's not full, and I have no pension plan."

"Even heavier sigh."

Ted pointed at a Union 76. "This is the gas station Amber told us about?"

"It is. Make a left at the light. I really do want to give Danielle a hug. Didn't Slime Boy have any money left when you disappeared him?"

"I know he did. He complained that my fee almost cleaned him out, but his first words as a fetus at his mother's bridal shower were a lie and complaint about money. I make sure they're not destitute. Poverty is a disincentive to good behavior."

"Wow. We're talking bucks here," she said as they approached the gate of a townhouse condo complex, where the units were three stories of brick. The parking lot was like a luxury car dealership's.

"Back a few blocks, did you notice those mansions with mile-long porches? Three of them have blue tarps on their roofs."

"Damned if I know. They may've gotten a deal on roof replacement, three for the price of one."

Beth got on the call box. After receiving a reluctant-sounding "hello," she said, "Danielle, I'm Beth. Amber at the bar said it'd be okay for us to drop by to see you for a minute. We're sorry about what happened and I have some issues with Henry Henri too."

"I'm in H-102. Take two lefts and I'm next to the end," she said without hesitation as the gate swung open.

Danielle opened her door cautiously. She looked to Beth the part of the six-digit-per-year nerdess: thick glasses, stringy hair, jeans and T-shirt that did not accent what figure she had, poor girl. In high school, gals like her did the cheerleaders' homework to be halfassedly accepted. The woman being no slave to fashion, Beth had to admire her for that. She did things her way.

To Ted, she looked whipped, beaten down, Hollywood's notion of a gigolo victim, the last girl asked to dance at the hop. He, like Beth, very much wanted to get his hands on Jack Bavard, onto the body parts that'd cause the most pain.

Danielle stepped back and asked them in far enough to close the door.

Her living room had abstract expressionist works on the walls, probably originals and hyper-expensive, and a desk and computer with the biggest monitor Ted had ever seen. There were other machines and folders stacked every which way, like she'd done a hasty sprucing up for them. He imagined a high-tech start-up that had started up five minutes ago.

At second glance, the paintings were prints, microchips magnified a million times, silicon road maps.

Beth saw them too and classified the decor as Microsoft Gothic. Definitely not a girly girl's home.

The chairs and sofa were leather, a concession to wealth and fashion. A gray cat was curled up on the couch. Another streaked up the stairs.

Danielle said, "That's Andrew. He's first of my alphabet gang. He rules the roost wherever he wants to roost. Betty ran up the steps. She's shy. Charlie and Donna are upstairs somewhere. Please tell me if you're allergic to cats. We can go out to the patio if you are."

"We're fine," Beth said. "I'm Beth and he's Ted. Ted's a cat person."

Ted smiled. "Yes I am."

"Henri said he was a cat person too, but they were all afraid of him. Cats *know*. My kitties sure as heck did. I should have paid attention to my sweeties."

They were standing in the foyer, awkwardly. Danielle didn't invite them in to have a seat and they didn't want to sit. For her sake, Ted thought, they needed to keep this brief.

"We understand Henri's gone," Beth said.

"Him and my 401(k)," Danielle said. "I won't go into details how. It's so mortifying."

"Again, I'm so sorry," Beth said.

Ted kept his reaction to himself. Andrew ran over and rubbed against his legs. Betty had reappeared and was rubbing his other leg, purring loudly.

Beth nudged Ted and said, "Every morning, my man rolls around on catnip."

Wide-eyed, Danielle smiled and said, "Gosh, where are my manners? Come all the way in and have a seat."

"We really can't stay," Beth said.

"No problem. I'm cool. Please don't feel sorry for me. I'm young and make good money. I'll build my nest egg back up in no time."

Ted cracked his knuckles for a tough-guy effect that was ignored by both women and said, "Any idea where we might find Mr. Vert and congratulate him on his windfall?"

"Québec City."

"Why Canada?" Beth asked.

"Well, because of his name. He'd said he had Quebecois roots, a lie I discovered after Henri—left me—that he'd bought a first class ticket on my computer, then deleted the transaction after payment was made."

"How'd you find out?" Ted said.

She pointed at one of the three laptops in the room and adjoining dining room.

"Duh," Ted said.

"Did he make a hotel reservation or anything else traceable?" Beth said.

"Yes he did. A suite at the Le Château de Frontenac. He must have thought he wiped that out too. I Googled the hotel. The place is gigantic and beautiful. It's a French Canadian landmark."

They waited for her to continue.

"Okay, I know. I could bring the law down on him and everything, but I'd rather just have him out of my life forever. Does that make any sense?"

"It does. Listen, we'll get out of your hair," Beth said, going to Danielle and giving her a hug.

Ted wanted to give her a hug too, but her body language said *don't bother*, him a male of the species, cat person or not.

At the door, Beth said, "Why the blue tarps on those houses we saw coming here? It's funny they have to have new shingles at the same time."

"It's not a coincidence. A tornado came through here last week.""

"Oh."

"There's a KKK chapter seventy miles from here. They still have cross-burning parties."

"Oh."

Danielle almost laughed. "Welcome to the Deep South."

Back in the car, Beth said, "She's too sweet to turn into a crazy cat lady."

"She is. I'm hoping her alphabet stops at 'D'. She doesn't qualify as a crazy cat lady until she hits 'E' or higher."

"Well, you are an authority on the subject."

"I am."

Beth said, "A nice guy'll come along for her, a nerd, not a pussy hound with no conscience. Pardon the pussy pun."

"I'll pardon the alliteration too."

"You being a cat person too, after meeting her, seriously, I think that's sweet for a guy. You made her day less crummy."

Ted said, "You once told me that three guys in the entire state of Montana are cat people and that for the rest a house pet's not a house pet if it can't chew through a chain-link fence."

"That was the honest-to-God truth. It's up to five or six guys now, and they don't have to come out like gays do. The state's getting more liberal in general. Guys can hug and cry now in public without being deported to California."

"I'm touched."

"It's a big step. As far as I'm concerned, cats are like those demented, inbred, little muffy dogs that deranged people carry around with them in shopping malls, sometimes in baby carriages."

"An incorrect comparison, lady. Try that with a cat and there'd be life-threatening blood loss. Cats don't ride well in pickup trucks either," Ted said. "They won't hang their heads out the windows. Speaking of cats."

"Are we doing our clairvoyant thing? That two-headed Clarkson kitty?"

"Yep. The exotic Clarkson medium-hair."

"Why would they now?"

"For a progress report. If they're on our trail and we gave them the slip, they're annoyed at their Judas goat."

They fired up the laptop and, bingo, today's *Chicago Tribune* had a beauty available for $499.

"The last one was $599," Ted said, starting the car.

"An inbreeding discount," Beth said.

30

His Nose Was Growing

At Atlanta's Hartsfield-Jackson International Airport, into one of his phones, with the area code for Murmansk, Russia, like a film noir dick, his chosen persona for the day, Ted Snowe gritted his teeth, thinking of the bad grammar that was to follow, and snarled, "Whadduya want?"

Beth Palmer Brutto covered her mouth, thinking that this is the flippant, wise-ass risk-taker she'd fallen for. The teachers who nagged her about wasting her 121 IQ were usually the ones who caught her outside between classes, smoking. They accused her of having "poor impulse control." So what? Her Ted did too, a fun thing they had in common.

"You been fuckin us over, champ."

"That's what you think. Next time, don't send a disturbed boy to do a disturbed man's job."

"Huh?"

"You playing dumb on me?"

"What're you drinking?"

His snarl degrading into a rasp, a Damon Runyon parody with laryngitis, Ted said, "You know what I'm talking about. Your pretty boy who's in need of your dental plan now, thanks to yours truly. I'll tell you what I told him. I didn't add nothing to my birdwatching list."

"I ain't talking about them. That rat motherfucker with the bonds we set him up in and he stuffed his pockets with, you said you done him and you got paid for doing him, he was spotted in Chi-town recent-like. This is how come we're talking. You know goddamn well who I mean."

Roger Higgins, who he had made over into John Shannon, whose life we'd saved in Portland, the low-grade moron, he'd gone back to his hometown, before settling in Portland. Nothing like a whirlwind tour.

Ted said, "Speak English, why don't ya."

"You gotta be convinced? At these car dealerships in different Midwest spots we got a piece of, he drove outta there last month with a set of wheels he paid cash for under a phony name, Shannon or some shit. A hunnert and fifty G's for a Benz if it cost a fucking dime."

"Mistaken identity is what it is. I do what you pay me to do. This guy who done your spotting, he needs glasses."

"Yeah, you been good to your word in times past. We know."

Ted's nose was growing from him to the other end of the line, but the fella was softening, backing off too easily. Something bad was up, a spider and fly scenario in the making.

Beth was reading his face, not liking what she saw and heard.

"Okay, we gotta sit down and talk. Don't put yourself out. We'll send somebody. We'll have us a sit-down and talk things over."

Ted looked through a terminal window and watched a 747 take off, shiny and majestic and because of its size appearing to be doing 25 MPH.

"Sure, no problem."

Beth made an airplane motion with a hand.

"Where will you be?"

"You're not pissed?"

"Not a bit."

"I'm telling you the honest truth."

"Yeah, we believe you. We just gotta iron some things out."

Like a tire iron and the *thing* being *me*, Ted thought.

"Let me get back to you at your earliest convenience," he said and hung up.

"Aren't they the ones who hang up on you, not vice versa?"

"That's the golden rule."

"You burned some bridges, bunky."

Ted nodded. "Right down to the waterline."

"You look airsick and we haven't left yet," Beth said.

As he related the full conversation, he broke the phone in two.

"The idiot could've bought a two-year-old Ford Focus in Chicago and kept his pinhead under the radar," she said.

"Apparently he didn't. Nature is calling us."

They took their telephone pieces into the restrooms and deposited them in the garbage. Ted wished he could have flushed it down the toilet along with the plug-uglies who hired him, and car-loving Higgins-Shannon.

* * * * *

They had a plane change at Philadelphia and got into old Québec City well after dark. As Danielle said, the hotel was gigantic, no exaggeration. Even at night, the Château Frontenac was high, wide and beyond handsome. Lights played on its spires and gabled rooftops, making it in their fatigued eyes the world's largest wedding cake.

Ted had found an Eastern Canada guidebook at the Philadelphia airport. In it was a claim that the Frontenac was the world's most photographed hotel. He was a believer.

On the plane, before dozing on Beth's shoulder, he read that immediately outside the walled old city where the Frontenac dominated, one of the most important battles in Canadian history was fought. On the adjacent Plains of Abraham, on September 13,

1759, the French under the Marquis de Montcalm and the British commanded by General James Wolfe had themselves a battle royal.

It lasted twenty minutes. The British won and both generals were killed. The bottom line was Queen Elizabeth II appearing on Canadian money, not Charles de Gaulle. Like the sports cliché, it was a game of inches.

In a lobby the size of a shopping mall, they took a single room. It cost $300 a night. They couldn't imagine what Jack/Henry/Henri's suite cost.

Beth and Ted hit the sack without unpacking. That and all other questions could wait until the morning.

31

The Fellas

"Motherfucker gets around, don't he? Too much moving to suit me."

"Yeah. Me too. He's all over the place."

"He calls us from Hobart, Tarzana. Today from up there in Russia."

"Up by the North Pole. Nobody travels that quick."

"What's this earliest convenience of ours when we're being nice to him and he goes and hangs up on us? He's disrespecting us is what he's doing."

"He ain't stupid. He knows we ain't nice."

"Last time anybody accused me of being nice, I was two years old."

"He sounded funny too."

"Like a made guy in the movies, not in real life."

"He been on the sauce maybe."

"This mistaken identity thing, it's bullshit. Our car guy out there in Chi-town, he don't mistake nobody."

"That settles it. Fucker's picking our pocket. We're paying him for doing what he ain't doing."

"Two strikes and he's out is how it gotta be. Chance, now him."

"The guy's a no-good cheat."

"He is."

"I got an idea. You know my cousin with the fucked-up kid?"

"The one who sits in his room all day, him and his computer?"

"That's the one. He even graduated from high school and wanted to go to college till my cousin put his foot down."

"Whadduya do with a kid like that? It's sad."

"What it is they think, it's a birth defect. He was being born and the doc squeezed his head too hard when he was pulling him outta his mother. My cousin, he's ready to kick the kid out on the street if he don't start earning his keep. If nothing else, casing for stick-ups, you know. No jewelry store clerk's gonna look twice at that pencil-neck hanging around."

"Let's put him to work finding this guy."

"Yeah, let's do."

"I don't give a shit what his phone calls say where he is. Nobody gets around that quick."

"The computer kid, he can start with our phone and all these places he really ain't calling us from and go from there."

"Yeah, phones these days, they're computers too. The kid, he can use it like it's the start of a road map."

"I'll go and give my cousin a call, see what we can get done."

"When're we gonna hear from Tony Whack?"

"Yeah, well, we didn't give him a whole helluva lot to go on the blonde and the guy."

"Yeah, well, all he gave us was a rented car and a hotel. Two phony names is what we come up with."

"I ain't sweating Tony Whack. He got those books to go over with a fine-toothed comb too."

"It's what you call your multiple tasking."

"Bookkeeper and the other thing. You got two different skill sets there."

"That's it. Tony Whack works on his own schedule and I ain't messing with it or him."

32

O Canada

Ted awoke from a screaming nightmare: In it, all his disappeareds were seated at Leonardo da Vinci's *The Last Supper*, having crashed the party. Jimmy Brutto was in the middle of the group, a halo above his head. Ted had walked and then ran back and forth in front of it, the diners' eyes relentlessly following him.

Ted, a non-believer, hadn't an inkling what the hell they were doing there in *The Last Supper*. He tried to remember their expressions, but couldn't. His only recollection was Birdwatcher Bob Chance, seated on an end with expensive German binoculars around his neck, focused on him throughout.

Evidently it wasn't an out-loud screamer of a dream, for Ted's lady love was pressed to his side, softly snoring.

On his back, he stared at the ceiling he couldn't see.

Recalling how he came to be Theodore Spangler Snowe Junior.

The nocturnal remembrances came as a remembrance of his telling Beth, early on in their relationship, when they were getting to know each other, his life history.

"Your family?" Beth had asked.

"None immediate. Divorced and unmarried. No kids. My old man split when I was a squirt, five years old. He went out for a pack of

177

cigarettes, Marlboro 100s in the hard pack, on Saturday, September 14, 1985.

"My middle name, Spangler, is my mother's maiden name, but we weren't close even after dear old dad blew town. As I grew older, she saw too much of him in me. After that, she moved into Neptune's orbit. She could look you in the eye and not see you.

"She passed away ten years ago and I didn't know until a second cousin managed to reach me six weeks later. I was an only child. I am an only adult. Adult is a matter of opinion.

"You asked me where my hometown is. I don't have one. When the old man was around, when he wasn't drinking, he worked construction, hanging drywall, following the work."

"You should've run away to join the circus," Beth had teased, trying to lighten things up.

"I thought about it for five minutes. For the same amount of time I wanted to be President."

"Exactly what time of the day did your dad go out for the smokes? You know that too?"

"I do. Right after dinner. Six-thirty. We'd had meatloaf. I loved her meatloaf. The edges were crispy and I had dibs on an end cut. The old man hated her meatloaf. Said she burned it. He hated most of her cooking. Hated everything about her, I came to realize."

"Total recall at that tender age. Amazing," Beth had said.

"Yeah, I agree it's weird that I remember those fine details. I think it's because the old man paid a lot of attention to me. We had a bond that in retrospect was a device. Him doting on me was his method of ignoring my mother."

"Ever find out what happened to him?"

"About five years ago, I heard from a shirttail relative that he'd married a much younger woman and died in his sleep. There's doubt whether he'd been sleeping."

"Guys at the bar say that's the way they want to go. In the saddle. I don't get it."

"What's not to get?"

The reminiscence ended there as did his perspiration-drenched ceiling-staring.

* * * * *

In the morning, Beth's first words were, "This poetry thing. Are you thinking that you want to be a poet when you grow up?"

"Why are we on poetry again?"

"I had a dream last night that you grew a goatee, wore a beret, and devoted the rest of your life to poetry. Did I wake up screaming?"

"Nope and have no fear. The average *published* poet earns as much in his or her entire working career as I did in my sixth-grade paper route."

"Good," she said, putting her arms around him. "I like you better as a criminal in a high tax bracket, owing taxes you don't pay."

"Alleged criminal."

After they had each other, they went downstairs and had breakfast. Beth proposed a plan, to which Ted posed no argument.

She went to the desk and spoke to a young woman. Each wiped a tear and Beth returned to their table with a rule violation that could get the clerk fired if it leaked out, a guest's room number.

In the elevator, Beth said, "Don't ask what I told her. We'll be crying like babies. This asshole's on an upper floor. A suite."

"I wonder what he's paying for it."

Beth said, "Same as you'll have made as a poet by the year three thousand."

"With Danielle's money," Ted said. "Money is no object."

"Room service," he said at the suite door after a polite knock.

It opened a sliver. "I didn't order anything."

"Ah, it eez a free breakfast, *Monsieur*, compliments of the house, with champagne."

The guidebook said that Québec was bilingual, French coming first, with many in the province in favor of separatism from Canada. He was doing his damndest to sound the English-as-a-second-language part.

"Champagne?"

"*Oui*. It eez French champagne, *Monsieur.*"

The door opened wider, far enough for Ted to see Jack Bavard's eyes and to kick it in before he could close it. He stumbled backward, but kept his feet. Bavard was naked. He looked like a leading man in a low-budget porn flick.

To be sure he had his attention, Ted buried a fist in a gut that was softer than it looked, thinking *this one's for Danielle*. Bavard/Vert made a wheezing noise and slumped to the floor.

In the bedroom, a naked, curvaceous, amply tattooed brunette sat up in bed and mumbled something to herself in French.

She hopped to the floor and reached for her dress and purse.

Beth asked her, "Isn't he irresistible?"

"I am putting my clothes on and getting my money. This dispute of yours is none of my business."

A pack of cigarettes and a container of pepper spray fell out of her purse.

"I'll take these. They're hazardous to your health," Beth said, kicking the smokes and pepper spray aside.

"My money? Who is paying me?"

"I have a feeling that you earned every penny. Where's Romeo's wallet?"

She put the dress on over her head. If she arrived with underwear, Beth didn't see it.

"Over there by his pants. Lover boy jumped me before he had his shoes off."

"Smooth. Suave. What's your name, honey?"

"Mary Anna Trench. I go by it because—"

"That's way too much info."

"My mother must never know what I do."

"Mothers can be that way."

"Do not look down on me. You and your husband or lover who has an income and supports you, how are we so different? It is sex for money."

"Okay, we're one and the same, except I don't have all those ugly tattoos. Now scoot."

"My money."

Beth found Bavard's wallet in his trousers and gave her a wad of cash. "This is for keeping your mouth shut in French and English."

"With all this, I will. *Au revoir.*"

"Have a nice day, Mary Anna," Beth said as the hooker quietly shut the door behind her.

Ted had yanked Bavard to his feet by an armpit and pushed him into a chair, where he was trying to catch his breath.

"I'd love to play Gestapo with him," Beth said, holding the pepper spray. "Pretty please."

"I yield the floor," Ted said, stepping back.

"How'd you find me?"

Beth said, "Like bread crumbs, we followed the trail of Danielle's money, you no-good pile of shit. Where is it?"

"I don't know anything about her money."

Beth looked at the pepper spray. "I love these little guys, but mine's at home. You can't get them through airport security."

Thinking that oven cleaner, available anywhere, might be a promising substitute, she gave him Bavard/Vert a shot in the belly button. He winced.

"The next one's going farther south."

"Please," he said to Ted, who shrugged.

Beth said, "Her money? Don't make me go on like a broken record."

He pressed his knees together. "The cat-crazy bitch won't miss it. She makes big bucks."

Beth gave him a squirt where promised. "That's for her and her four kitties. We're running low on spray. I can run out for some oven cleaner for the next zap. If it can clean up that caked-on gunk, imagine what it can do with his family jewels."

Ted said, "Why oven cleaner? Have you ever cleaned an oven?"

"That's beside the point. I know it contains lye."

"Works for me. Maybe they sell it at the gift shop. If not, it's on our next grocery list."

"Please."

Beth gave him another small squirt.

When he was done groaning and begging, Ted stepped in and explained why they were so anxious to track him down.

Bavard said, "Somebody believes I'm still alive and wants to kill me?"

"Hard to believe, isn't it? We're not here for you, meathead. The heads up is for me, for us."

Beth was rummaging through his suitcase, flinging the contents every which way. "Where's your laptop?"

"What laptop?"

Ted rubbed his hands and cocked a fist. "This may hurt a little."

"Okay, okay. In my carry-on, in the closet by the window."

"Fantastic view," Beth said, before taking the computer out. "The suite's worth every penny."

Ted said, "You're going to reverse the flow of Danielle's 401(k) and every other red cent you stole from her."

"I didn't."

Ted slapped his face.

Beth *slapped* the laptop onto his bare lap.

"Wanna make a bet on that?"

Jack Bavard/Henri Vert flinched and did as instructed, typing for several minutes, and gave Ted the computer. The transfer was for $300,000 minus the price of an economy car. Ted had been behind Bavard, watching the process. He nodded his approval. Even if he was hanging onto a few bucks, that was above the amount above they figured he'd taken from her.

"Is that it?" he said. "Satisfied?"

"Don't you feel like a better person now?" Beth said.

"Can't I keep a little more?"

"I'd venture a guess that I didn't take everything when I disappeared you."

"I have expenses."

Beth said, "Clip coupons."

"You're going to keep your head down?"

"I promise."

"When's the last time you kept a promise?" Ted said.

"May I shower and get dressed? My nuts are killing me."

Beth laughed.

Ted said, "Stick your head out of your burrow again and I'll do you for real. That is a promise."

33

Danielle

Seated at a computer, my alphabet babies are in the room providing support. I know where the bogus Henri Vert is and what he's up to. As hard as it is for me, I'm letting you in on it too. I cannot stand anyone feeling sorry for me.

Five minutes ago, Henri transferred a paltry amount of my money back to me, playing a numbers game, tacking on a couple of zeroes on that end that didn't make it to my end. Unless you know what you're doing, it looks like you move much more money than you actually do. How generous of him to repay me $3000.

My new wonderful friends, Ted and Beth, I know by the transfer that they caught up to him and tried to make him do the right thing. But whoever Henri really is, he's slippery on many levels, computer literate far above the average, but far below me.

Beth was so compassionate and I know Ted can take care of himself. Their compassion for me wasn't phony.

And Ted. I may not be such a good judge of men, but Andrew and Betty sure are. Beth is lucky to have him.

I'd love to know what they did to Henri when they connected with him and made him pretend to repay me.

Ever the confidence man.

Regardless of what they did to him, I can fix his little red wagon for good and I will!

Andrew, Betty, Charlie and Donna purr their approval.

Henri has a mile-high ego, so he cannot stay incognito. I shall do it for him whether he likes it or not. Under his names, I've made certain now that he's on all social media, every photograph of his manly physique and handsome face too in the event he'll be operating under a new alias.

Click click click.

His old Ponzi-esque website is shut down, so let's give him a new one.

Click click click.

For me, admittedly an ugly duckling, an old maid in the making, who knows her way around a microchip, this is child's play.

Click click click.

Let me give you new interests, my erstwhile Don Juan. Child pornography is repellent to me, but it is there regardless. To make my man an avid viewer and purveyor—*click click click.*

I've done some homework on the criminal justice system and the violent internal politics of those incarcerated. You see, there's a pecking order among penitentiary inmates. Those with "Short Eyes" are the lowest of the low. An individual with Short Eyes is a convicted pedophile. One is convicted of multiple kiddy porn offenses; ergo, one suffered the assumption that one is also the director and producer of the videos. For me to fantasize a bisexual, 300-pound drug dealer for Henri's cellmate is not too outlandish and cruel, is it?

As I *click click click* my vengeance to completion, I dab tears. I am not normally this mean-spirited and vindictive; I hardly know myself.

Oh, one more thing. The money. *Click click click.*

I will distribute the recovered money to offshore accounts in the event I'm smitten again, love and lust overriding brain cells.

I don't know if Canada has public defenders. If they do, that will be all the lawyering he can afford now. If not, oh well.

To steal my heart and my money is one thing.

To take my virginity under false pretenses is unforgivable.
Isn't it?
He will pay and pay and pay for his conquest.

34

A Nicotine Nazi

B eth and Ted were at Quebec City's Jean Lesage International
Airport. This morning, Ted had called one of his investigators.
John D. Dole was still in Seattle, a bit of a surprise. They were
awaiting their first hop to Toronto. From there, they were to be
treated to plane changes to Vancouver and Seattle. A long day
beckoned.

"I see you ditched the pepper spray."

Beth said, "It was a friend indeed. I really am going next for oven
spray. It's available everywhere and easy to replace."

"But not the cigarettes."

"Oh, there they are in the bottom of my purse. An oversight on
my part."

"Now," Ted said.

She sighed. "Nicotine Nazi."

Beth arced the pack into a garbage can.

"Good girl. Nothing but net."

"You probably told me, but I forgot. Did you ever smoke?"

"No."

"Never ever?"

"No."

"Not even in the eighth grade, lighting up a weed swiped from your folks' pack, out in the alley behind the garage, then turning green and puking your guts out?"

"Nope."

"God, I hate you," she said, pinching his midriff.

"I'll work harder on developing some bad habits. I promise," he said.

"Seattle's a big city, but we're maybe headed back to a shitstorm, you know. Tony Whack Job auditing his little heart out and who knows what."

Ted said, "Don't I know. My sources are working on it, but I'm guessing that John D. Dole may not be cleaning toilets."

"Really?"

"But there are thousands of toilets to clean, so my people may come up dry. Whatever they find or don't find, it'll be in my P.O. box."

"How many post office boxes do you have?"

"As many as there are cities where I ordered my disappeareds to go. It's not cheap, but it's one of the mandatory costs of doing business."

"I like that you stuck him in Seattle. You did for good reasons. I was checking the laptop. They have a bunch of educated people who read and are a helluva lot younger on the average than Florida, where their average age is two hundred, with arteries to the brain seriously clogged. That's good, but if our boy's up to the same old no-good?"

"If he is—" Ted stopped.

"Would you?" she said, sitting closer, wrapping an arm around his.

"Do him for real?"

"Mind reader. Would you? Him or any of your others? Ever. For any reason?"

Ted looked outside. "Think it'll rain?"

"This dickwad cleaning toilets, you know. I'm having trouble picturing him scrubbing and behaving."

"I know, I know."

She got up. "I'm gonna find a trashy magazine so I can check on celebrities diddling who they're not supposed to be diddling while the ones they're not diddling have moved on out of their diddle-free zones too."

While she was at the newsstand, Ted checked out current Seattle news on the laptop.

A headline story changed everything.

35

Time Travel

Ted minimized the headline, saving it as a surprise for Beth. He showed it to her after they were airborne: DRIVE-BY VICTIM'S SEX CHANGE A FACTOR? Members Of A Little-Understood Subculture?

The medical examiner had completed the autopsy late yesterday on Brenda Lee Smith, revealing that she was legally a male named Brent Lee Smith.

"She walked out of the beauty parlor where she worked and hasn't been seen ever since. Ms. Smith worked for a short time at that salon. We've received other reports of Brent Lee Smith's hairdresser career. High turnover isn't unusual in that profession," said a lead detective. "We're continuing to delve into the murders with the cooperation of the gang units and the local medical community regarding the transgender process. Smith's sex change is a new wrinkle in the case."

"Does your best gal pal have access to a time machine?"

"That has to be it, stud muffin," she said. "Mary Ann Chance called me with the news tomorrow, not a few days ago."

"We're in some kind of space-time-continuum vortex," Ted said. "A black hole."

"In a science class I took in high school, the teacher said that

Albert Einstein stated that the only reason for time is so everything doesn't happen at once."

Ted looked at her. "Do you believe it?"

"Don't ask me. I got a C-minus in the class."

"I think we have proof he was right. Unless Mary Ann was playing games with you."

Beth said, "I'll take Mary Ann over Albert on that one. How many days ago was it when she called me about the autopsy on her dearly departed that hadn't been done yet?"

"Too many."

Ted opened a new Word document.

"A blank screen. It looks so innocent and unspoiled," Beth said.

He said, "While we're on the subject, let's kill some time by laying out what we know and don't know. Where we're going and why. A game plan."

"On the computer?"

"Yes ma'am. Me and my magic fingers."

"When you type, it's gotta be a poem, doesn't it? Remington or no Remington."

"I change the font to old-timey typewriter style, so it's okay."

"This isn't being done like a love poem, I hope. It's not very romantic up here even if we could recline the seats to a romantic setting."

"Just organizing my thoughts, and since you insist, I'll put my thoughts into verse."

Beth dug an in-flight magazine out of the seat-back pocket. "Knock yourself out."

36

Roses Aren't Red?

"Herewith for your perusal," Ted said, after their plane change and the pilot told them that if you looked out you could see Winnipeg directly to their north.

He said he'd be happy to accept Beth's input so long as it didn't include a finger in her throat at each sappy rhyme:

She shrugged. "Okay. It's this or Winnipeg."

"Read."

She read:

> Roses are not necessarily red,
> Birdwatcher Bob was not blue,
> He happily deserted his wife and responsibilities too.
> His hands in the cookie jar were deep,
> Yet at night he could sleep.
> A man who cares not wrong from right.
> Titanium is strong and oh so light,
> Not as good as gold on a ring finger,
> Though Bob's tweaking of its books did linger.
> Impelling those who drove by to end the love,
> Sending him and Brenda probably to not above.
> Into an endless sleep,

A bird count he can no longer keep.
Killers and the resplendent quetzal,
Their quest unfulfilled at all.

Beth cleared her throat. "Done?"

"No."

"Oh goody."

"You can't run and hide on this flying machine. You're my captive poetry-slam audience."

He scrolled and she read:

Fate gave unto us bad guys galore,
Tony Whack Job and ample more,
A beating he gave and took,
The simplicity of our pursuers forsook.
Blamed as I was by Tony for clipping Chance,
He revealed that he knew not who gave them
A bullet-ridden last dance.
Three of four disappeareds accounted for,
A nouveau janitor the last, had best be sweeping
  a floor,
Or risk unemployment for ever more.
Into a maw of peril we ride,
To unknown scoundrels we face,
A Whack Job redux or a kiddy drive-by,
Russians or Martians or a generic bad guy,
Ours is to keep our heads down as we reason why
A sexual switcheroo prophet
Had us flabbergasted and upset.

"This is so awful, I adore it," Beth said.

"Thank you."

"That reminds me, your forehead looks less forsook. You're almost back to normal."

"Thank you."

"Didn't you say you were drinking when you wrote the poems you wrote in Portugal?"

"I may've had a few."

"That much, huh?"

"Yeah."

"This Al Selkirk creep will be the last butthead we warn. Then what?"

Ted kissed her cheek.

She squeezed his arm as hard as a blood pressure cuff. "Then there's us, huh?"

37

Cash Flow

"Anonymity is the name of my game," Ted said. "Shortly, you will be getting a demo of how I follow up on my disappeareds."

"Cool. We've been telepathing again," Beth said. "I've been wanting to see the nuts and bolts of your scam, not just a summary and the end result."

"A life-changing and -saving project, not a scam, my sweet."

Late in the afternoon, they arrived at Sea-Tac, collected their luggage, rented a car, and drove to a private mailbox service he used. It was southeast of Seattle, in a strip mall anchored by a big box store. They parked in a slot close to the mega-monstrosity, an asphalt vista offering a view of the mailbox store.

"In case we were trailed."

"How will we know?"

"Damned if I know."

Beth watched him watching for whatever he was watching for, eyes darting to small birds that swooped nearby, thinking that he needed her even more than she needed him. One way or another, she had to snap him out of his Birdwatcher Bob guilt trip before he made a fatal mistake. Fatal for both of them.

"Why not a post office box? There're more post offices than these."

"I don't know if using a United States Postal Service box for my business is a federal beef if I'm nailed, but I have chosen not to risk twenty years to life finding out," Ted said.

"Sensible. Who are you here?"

"Thomas Neale signed up and paid two years in advance."

"Who's he? Is he real?"

"You mean who was he. In 1691, the British appointed Tom as the equivalent of postmaster general of the Colonies."

"Did he look like your average mailman?"

"Not at all. I saw a picture. Neale wore the white wig of the period and a fancy suit. He looked serious and focused."

"Unless an employee expects a white-wigged dude opening your box, your anonymity is safe."

Beth went to the front of the store, bought the morning paper out of a machine, and browsed it while Ted went inside.

A thicker than usual envelope was in his box, #338. Ted had exchanged it for cash.

"*Nada*," Beth said, folding the paper and laying it on the back seat. "Not a word on the Chances or Smith."

"Odd," he said, opening the envelope. "Old news, I guess."

Inside was a DVD and a note with an address.

They inserted the disc into the laptop and watched Al Selkirk/ John D. Dole extolling the cash flow magic in his system of buying real estate for no money down. Seated next to him was a washed-up celebrity they couldn't quite place. It obeyed the infomercial formula in which the luminary would be the emcee and/or be giving a glowing testimonial.

Al Selkirk stood like a televangelist, arms spread, sincerity and hope on his made-over face. There was a scene of a South Seas island behind him, the reward for those who called his 800-number and forked over their credit card info and their common sense.

The original Al was a young forty-five, chubby with a red perm that went with his freckles and sincere blue eyes. He looked like a character Mark Twain would have come up with, an aging eager beaver, at worst a tad mischievous.

Ted had given Al Selkirk a picture ID of one John D. Dole, an unsmiling man with a shaved head and thick-framed glasses, a dropout and loser with no ambition beyond the janitorial. This new and unimproved Al Selkirk was captioned as a Wealth Manager. He had tweaked Ted's makeover with a gray brushcut and a cardigan sweater, what passed in his greedy little mind as avuncular.

"A slicky boy if I ever saw one. He'll manage your wealth from you to his own wallet," Beth said.

Ted didn't reply. He drove out of the lot faster than he should, white-knuckling the wheel when he wasn't pounding it.

Beth continued watching the path to financial freedom. Judging by Ted's red face, the Wealth Manager was not going to be in the clover much longer. Next stop, deep shit.

"His present name is Jerry Smith," she said.

"An all-American boy's name," Ted said. "The stupid asshole's promoted himself from seminars to TV, multiplying the number of people who can see him."

"But they have to set the alarm for three a.m. to catch his act."

Ted's phone rang.

"Thanks. A pleasure doing business with you," said the co-holder of box #338.

"You too. Interesting."

"He's doing a shoot as we speak?"

"Wouldn't miss it. Thanks again."

Ted hung up.

"Your people?" Beth said.

"Yep."

"Our boy's janitorial career's on hold, huh?"

"It is."

"Area code of this phone?"

"São Paulo, Brazil. You can't be too careful. Like the Fellas, they're used to my world travel. If the money's there, they couldn't care less."

"You've never told me any of this. I *love* it."

"I didn't want the Fellas or anybody else to torture it out of you."

"That's sweet."

" Care to see show biz in action?" Ted said, accelerating under a yellow light. "It's not far from here."

"I already have stars in my eyes."

* * * * *

Al Selkirk/John Dole/Jerry Smith's version of a glamorous Hollywood studio was a flat gray building in a rear corner of a business park in the south Seattle suburbs. Its neighbors included a motorcycle repair shop, a beauty school, AVAILABLE, FOR LEASE, payday loans, and ATTRACTIVE TERMS.

The studio was unmarked, the door unnumbered and unlocked. They walked into a boiler room, to tightly-packed prefab cubicles dense with chatter and cigarette smoke.

"I need your answer *now*. The special offer ends in five minutes!"

"I can give you names of fifty people who are millionaires thanks to the Magical Cash-Flow System!"

"—your address and credit card number. We'll handle the rest!"

"With our help, you can change your life now!"

"Classy. If this was a porn shoot," Beth said. "We'd be at a Motel 3, livestock and all."

Ignored by everyone, they marched along the hallway and opened the studio door. There was Al and that same vaguely-familiar ex-celeb, a man in his fifties with a jut jaw, sagging jowls, and a rug. They were seated at a jury-rigged podium that might've been salvaged from a condemned cocktail bar, and another guy aiming a tripod-mounted camcorder.

Al fronted a screen frilled with graphs, arrows and dollar signs. His companion wore a forced smile and an aura of defeat.

"What the fuck?" Al said, seeing the intruders, going pale at the sight of Ted.

Ted knocked over the camera and told the cameraman to take a break.

The cameraman was short and pasty. Without a word of protest, he left his camera as is and hurried out to take a break.

"Didn't you used to be somebody?" Beth asked the onstage stooge.

The faded star was on his feet. "This brouhaha isn't my concern. My contract calls for union scale."

"The check's in the mail, sweetie," Beth said.

Ted was going for Al Selkirk. After a half revolution around the furniture, he caught the wealth manager by the collar and pulled him back from the side door he had one foot through.

"What the hell are you thinking, Al? That the bad guys aren't insomniacs who won't catch your hustle?"

"It's my life," he said with halitosis-fumed bluster.

"It's *my* life too. You no longer exist."

"It's my life."

Ted slammed him against a wall, lifting him to his toes by his shirt. "You have the life I gave you."

"I'm no janitor."

"You are if I say you are. A custodial engineer if that sounds better to you. You're alive only because I made you a custodial engineer."

"So you say."

"If you're not swamping out urinals in seventy-two hours as John D. Dole, I'll do you for real."

Ted completed his bluff with a fist to the gut that had the cash flow swami on his knees, gagging.

"Want a second helping?"

Al Selkirk shook his head.

"I'm serious. I'll be aiming lower next. You'll be eligible to try out for the Vienna Boys Choir."

"Okay, okay. I get the message."

Ted had serious doubts, but left him as a baritone.

On the way to the car, Beth said, "I got his autograph."

"Who is he? Who was he?"

"I don't know. He was too shook up to say, but he used to be somebody. I can barely read it. It's like a doctor's on a prescription, you know. Lance Ensley, it looks like."

"He could've played a doctor on TV."

"He could've," Beth said, punching buttons on her phone. "I'll call Mom. She watches junk TV twenty-five hours a day. I have to check in on her anyway."

"Hi Mom."

"No, nothing's wrong."

"Mom, I *don't* always call you unless something's wrong."

"Yeah, I'm hanging with the soccer player."

"No, he didn't sign with Portland. He'll try out elsewhere."

"Yeah, it's serious. He has a name and it's not Fred."

"Right. Ted. Ted, not Fred."

"Besides his soccer career, we're traveling around, having a good time. No, nothing special, just seeing the sights, seeing America."

"No, I'm not lying. Speaking of travel, you and Billy Bob. When are you leaving for Branson for your honeymoon?"

"Billy Bob has found a fill-in at the tow company. Good deal. You're packing now. Super!"

"I have a question for you, Mom. Is there a movie or TV star named Lance Ensley? He used to be studly with a jaw out to there, but not so much now."

"Yeah, was, not is."

"A soap opera. Uh huh. Uh huh. Uh huh. Okay, thanks Mom. I'll stay in touch. Love you. Bye."

Beth put her phone away and said, "You're right. He did play a doctor on a soap opera. It was so long ago, she can't remember the name of the soap. He was killed off by a nurse who was a friend of his wife who didn't like him banging this other nurse when he was banging her too."

"How about the wife? Did she like him banging nurses?"

"The wife did not like him banging the nurse she was friends with, even though the wife was banging this other doctor. Get it?"

"Got it. I think."

"Poor guy's past multiple-banging age, so that's why he's through on the soaps."

"He's unemployed as a scammer shill too. All in all, not a good day for Lance."

38

The Gospel According to Tony

In the afterlife, if indeed there is an afterlife, I reckon that rigid rules apply. Whether in a religious or in a secular venue, who can say?

You have your ideas, I have mine. Yours are doubtlessly wrong, but you're welcome to them.

Regarding mine. Let us surmise the former, a sharply-defined heaven and hell.

It would be wise to plug in purgatory, that in-processing netherworld where for a thousand years or so the bosses mull over which elevator button one pushes, the up-arrow or the down.

You can bet your *bottom* dollar that Hitler, Stalin, bin Laden, et al, rule the roost in the overheated basement.

For smaller fry like Ted Bundy and at a later time, me (though I'm not yet at Ted's level of achievement) and others who fit the Italian-American gangster stereotype, indefinite purgatory seems more logical. If we take for granted the Bible's extreme cruelty, included will be an auto-da-fé, burning at the stake, softening us up for eternal heatstroke.

I'm in no rush for verification, though, so why am I sorting out possibilities?

Post-orgasmic torpor is the culprit. Too much time to linger, too much time for nonsensical daydreaming.

Snap out of it, I tell myself as I dress.

Pat pat pat. Fresh cologne on my face.

An imperative kiss to my team-building partner's cheek and, hi ho, hi ho, it's off to work I go!

Mock-titanium and forensic accounting awaits.

Good times with my ice pick and garrote (lovingly constructed of pencil ends and dental floss, identical to my father's sentimental gift) and vampire choppers will surely come later.

39

Woman's Intuition

Well after dark, Beth and Ted took a room at the first hotel they came to, registering as Mr. and Mrs. John Coe. The motel was L-shaped, two-story, clean enough, and nondescript. They were flanked by chain restaurants and gas stations. Ted forgot the name of the place before he put the key card in the door.

Close your eyes and open them, and you could be virtually anywhere but North Korea. They were staying nowhere, near nothing extraordinary, the way they liked it.

Beth tried Mary Ann Chance's number. No answer.

"Mary Ann, hey girlfriend."

She hung up and said, "It went to message."

"What was her message?"

"There was no message."

Ted was in his skivvies, in bed, stretched out. "Ah. First-class legroom. What am I laying my head on?"

Beth ate the chocolate on her pillow, saying, "Don't forget to shampoo when you get up."

* * * * *

In the morning, after a late breakfast, they swung by Mary Ann's, saw that all drapes and blinds were pulled. They parked in the empty driveway and knocked.

"What do we say?" Ted said.

Beth said, "I don't know. We happened to be in the neighborhood. Concerned about her. Play dumb."

"Playing dumb. Not a problem."

Mary Ann peeked out a window and let them in. "Hurry. The media has been driving me crazy about Bob and his circus-freak lady friend. I've been trying to keep under the radar."

She invited them to have a seat in the living room and asked if they'd like coffee or a drink. They said no thank you, though both smelled liquor on her and her hair was uncombed. Could be she'd had a few when she had jumped the gun and called Beth with the news. They had never *not* smelled alcohol on Mary Ann Chance.

This was their first good look at the interior of Casa Chance. On their last visit, they were concentrating on the outside and the cell phone photos of an anchorman-esque homicidal mobster. The Chance furniture was sturdy middle-class, wood, glass and leather. Both judged the decor as neutral, inoffensive, a DMZ of interior design.

There were lighter squares and rectangles where hangings had been on beige walls.

Birdwatcher Bob Chance's birds, Beth wondered?

Resplendent quetzals on velvet, Ted wondered?

Beth said, "We're flattered."

"Pardon me?"

"For breaking the news to us first about your late husband's lover. It must've been devastating."

She was set to spring up and offer a sisterly hug, but, arms tightly folded, Mary Ann didn't move from the kitchen doorway.

"I put two and two together. Woman's intuition or whatever. I needed to vent, to let it out, to blow off steam. I didn't know about the embezzling at first, but I came to know that he was fooling around. Control freak that he was, Bob paid the bills and took care of all household finances. I work at a bank. At least I think I still do. So I'm not a complete dummy where money's concerned. I did some digging and saw that he was getting his hair done twice a week. Please. He was a walking comb-over. Want to guess who his stylist was?"

Beth raised her hand like a teacher's pet. "Brent Lee Smith?"

Mary Ann smiled. "Good for you. Are you sure I can't get you guys coffee or a drink?"

She was fidgety, definitely in need of lubrication to keep talking. Before Ted could say "Sure, whatever you're having if it's not too much trouble," Beth said, "Sure, whatever you're having if it's not too much trouble."

Mary Ann wasted no time getting to the kitchen. She brought the mimosas in champagne flutes, then one for herself. "I have a pitcher made if you want more."

They touched glasses in toast.

"To better times," Ted said.

"Has that monster SUV been back?" Beth asked.

"No, thank goodness, but I've had nightmares about it. Him. That guy."

Ted didn't have nightmares, but had flashbacks wherever he touched his forehead. Odd that Mary Ann didn't mention or even seem to notice his battle scars.

"Any leads on the murder?" Beth said.

"Not that they've revealed to me," Mary Ann said, as if commenting on the weather.

"Your late husband is suspected of embezzling a sizable amount from South Seattle Industries. Know how much or where it went?"

Mary Ann laughed and, bottoms up, finished her drink. "This is old news. I only know that I don't have a penny of it. For all this, the situation, Bob grabbed more than pocket change."

"South Seattle Industries, is it a big outfit?" Ted asked. "Did we see the tip of the iceberg?"

"Anybody ready for a refill?"

So not to be impolite, they drained our glasses too.

"Smooth and tasty," Beth said.

"Chock-full of Vitamin C," Ted said. "No danger of scurvy."

After her trip to the kitchen, she said, "No. Actually it's fairly small. Robert never said how many worked there. The no-good bastard, never said much else about South Seattle Industries. I went with him to last year's Christmas party at a downtown restaurant, not too long after he started there. Twenty or thirty attended, including spouses and guests. I found it weird that they didn't talk shop. At most office parties, that's all they do. If somebody started on titanium, somebody else jumped in and changed the subject."

"What did they talk about?" Beth asked.

"Weather, football, soccer, all the things that make parties a bore."

"Tami, the gal at the front desk, was she there?"

"If she was, I don't remember her. The employees were mostly guys, some with accents I couldn't place."

"I guess Robert had his reasons for clamming up," Beth said.

"Money talks," Mary Ann Chance said. "Or money keeps mum."

"Titanium must be a moneymaker," Ted said. "Who did they sell to?"

"Robert was closemouthed on this job and his twenty-year non-career, citing confidentially. Like I'd let it slip at coffee klatches the fine details of bookkeeping, as thrilling and exciting as it is. He was really mum about South Seattle Industries and their titanium, though, except that they export it. Or import it. I don't remember which. I do know that they don't store it there. I was given the impression that they're a clearinghouse or a brokerage."

Conversation degraded to Mary Ann's nosy neighbors and how they kept bringing over cookies and sympathy.

"That house on the end to your left, the split-level with the blue trim, when you come into the cul-de-sac, she's sweet, but she'd have her Bible with her and those pamphlets they hand out."

"I hate that too," Beth said. "Why can't they mind their own business?"

"She wanted to sit with me and pray for Bob Chance's immortal soul," Mary Ann said. "The last time, I told her that he doesn't have one of the fucking things to pray for. She hasn't been back since."

Beth said, "Your non-prayer was answered."

40

Fluffy, the Wonder Cat

When they left Mary Ann Chance and her mimosas, they figured that as Judas goats, they'd temporarily ditched their flock, and relaxed a bit. They meandered around yupscale suburbia. There was a depressing sameness to the competitive lawns and three-car garages.

"Think you'll ever want this?" Ted probed.

Beth said, "This and three kids with braces and a mortgage and a dog and PTA meetings and chocolate chip cookies right out of the oven?"

"That's the complete package. Less a cat."

Was Ted fishing? Beth made it abundantly clear by jabbing a finger in her mouth.

"Good answer," Ted said, meaning it.

They headed toward a main drag and an entrance to I-405. Their plan, such as it was, was to get a room at the fateful hotel. They'd sniff around again, though they knew they'd probably come up with zilch.

Beth's phone filled the car with a *dee-dee-dee.*

"You changed it to a black-capped chickadee," Ted said.

"You're getting pretty good at recognizing bird calls."

"We heard that one at the very start of the field trip. Bob IDed it for us."

"Hi Mom. Long time, no hear."

She increased the volume so Ted could listen in.

"Honey, the worst damn thing happened."

"Oh God, what?"

"There's no honeymoon. It's off."

"No Branson, Missouri? I thought you'd be on the road by now."

"I am not. We are not. We were all set to go, but Billy Bob had to work a double shift. Horace was down sick with the whiskey flu. That's okay, extra money to take along, but that's when he found the goddamn cat."

"Cat?"

"Fluffy. That's what Billy Bob named it. Filthy grungy mangy is a better name."

"Cat?"

"Billy Bob found it in this abandoned car he was sent out to tow. It was up this dirt road out in the middle of nowhere blocking this farmer's access to his road. Billy Bob said he couldn't just leave the cat there. He has a point there, I guess, and it's cute in its own disgusting way."

"He brought it home?"

"And he feeds it. Leftovers and real cat food he bought a twenty-pound bag of. The thing eats like there's no tomorrow, which there almost wasn't for him. Fluffy drinks beer out of a saucer too. Laps it up like milk. That won Billy Bob over for sure. Fluffy the Wonder Cat he's named it. He said Fluffy may've been a human in a past life, who hung out in taverns and played shuffleboard. God help me!"

"So what are you gonna do, Mom?"

"I'm asking you, Elizabeth."

"Mom, you use my formal name on special occasions, like when you're blotto drunk or pissed at me or have a big problem."

"Mom, please don't cry. I don't know what to tell you to do, I honestly don't. A Montana tow truck driver who adopted a cat. Wow. Call the Guinness people. And, oh yeah, keep the damn thing out of my room, it and Billy Bob."

"Don't you worry, honey. The door's closed and your window's latched. Nothing and nobody's going in or out of there."

"Thanks, Mom. What about Branson?"

"It's on hold. I'd ask Adele Johnson to take care of Fluffy, but I know she's allergic to cats. Billy Bob says he'll arrange with someone, but he hasn't done it yet."

"What's that word? Proactive. I think leaving things up to Billy Bob, you'd best be proactive. Is there a bulletin board in the trailer park office?"

"Good idea. You're still off gallivanting with that soccer player?"

"You know I am."

"You and him, you could come home and cat-sit."

"He's a cat person, but no, sorry, we can't. Not for the time being. We have an agenda we're trying to wrap up."

"You be careful, girl. Those pro athletes they all have those groupies, you know, those loose women. Even soccer players. There was a special report on this show I watch."

"Cut back on the tabloid TV, please, Mom, okay? That stuff rots your brain from the inside out."

"Stop it now. They're the ones that tell the news like it is."

"I'll be on the lookout for the groupies, Mom. If those sluts get too close to my soccer star, I'll give them radical mastectomies on the spot."

"Good girl. Stay in touch. Hear?"

Beth stuffed the phone in her purse, leaned back, closed her eyes, and said, "Mom can be exhausting. You know what?"

"What?"

"Billy Bob's stalling on Branson, making an excuse, don't you think? If I was the suspicious type, I'd think the timing of Fluffy's rescue is fishy."

Ted said, "Branson, Missouri or a cat, it wouldn't be a tough choice for me."

"I don't think I ever asked. Did you have groupies?"

"No, you never asked me that, not for the last twenty-four hours. Same answer."

"Did you?"

"Sure. Hundreds of them," Ted said. "But minor-league jock groupies have more tattoos than teeth. They outweigh us too."

"That's what you say. NBA players get the babes. You had the leftovers, sort of sexy older women who want to mother you after another loss, they were your groupies, weren't they? They can massage your aching knees too."

"We've been all over this before, woman of my dreams."

"It's been so long ago. Refresh me," Beth said, half-teasing, half-insecure, an insecurity that would not go away.

"Those clouds ahead of us look ominous, don't they."

"The subject isn't closed, mister."

* * * * *

They packed and left Motel Anonymity without checking out and took a room at the airport hotel, registering as Mr. and Mrs. Chick Addey, and had sweet rolls and coffee at the hotel bar, a cure for morning-mimosa cotton mouth.

The racist bartender was on duty. He didn't remember them.

People came and went.

Nobody queried anybody about the double murder.

"It's not old news, it's ancient news," Ted said as they settled up.

Beth said, "I hope we are too."

"We can't quit, you know."

"I know. We have to find out who did Bob and him-her, before somebody else does us."

41

Nature Abhors a Coincidence

Beth and Ted mulled over their remaining option before skipping town, a follow-up reconnoiter of South Seattle Industries in an attempt to get a rise out of somebody.

"Us playing Sherlock and Agatha, how realistic is that, really?" Beth said.

"Only in novels inhabited by steely-eyed crime fighters," Ted said.

"Which we're not," Beth said. "We're real life, flesh and blood semi-criminals."

"All four recent disappeareds are accounted for, dead and alive," Ted said.

"Make that six; their sleazy asses plus ours," Beth said.

"The world's full of unsolved crimes."

"The world hasn't come to an end because of it."

"So is it home to Butte?" Ted said, hoping she's say *just long enough to pack for anywhere else in the world.*

But she didn't.

"Do you want to drive to Butte?"

Ted shook his head.

"Me neither. The earliest flight that'd get us there will be this evening, don't you think?"

Ted nodded.

"We have oodles of time to goof around and get ourselves in another jam, but why are we considering this?"

Boring/boredom/bored, variations of the b-word. A word he feared as much as the m-word. At this point in time, inoculation against the b-word was unnecessary recklessness. There were no alternatives.

"Are we being clairvoyant again?" he asked.

"Hurry up and finish your coffee."

* * * * *

At South Seattle Industries, there were only sixteen cars in the employees-only back lot. South Seattle Industries was no Boeing. They saw no delivery trucks either, importing or exporting titanium, just as Mary Ann Chance had said.

Ted saw it first. "Bandits at three o'clock."

"What?"

"Next to the green SUV."

"Holy shit."

It was a small white car with Washington plates that began with 994.

"It has to be the same one, driven by Tony Whack Job."

"Has to be," Ted said. "Nature abhors a coincidence."

"Where the hell did that come from?"

"A high school physics class."

Beth said, "It'd make a great name for a poem."

* * * * *

It was a pleasantly-brisk autumn day for a walk. They parked across the highway at a dead teriyaki café with brown paper covering its windows and took one, keeping their eyes on South Seattle Industries as they did. Around 11:15, they sat in their car and waited.

At 11:45, lunchtime, the little white car left, front-desk Tami behind the wheel.

"An SSI pool car?" Beth said.

"If we can, we'll ask her."

They followed her to a neighborhood restaurant, a small diner, and waited outside for five minutes.

Tami was alone at a booth. They sat uninvited across from her as she began eating a club sandwich.

"They get the food up fast here," Ted said. "Is it any good?"

"I am begging your pardon. Who are you?" Tami said. "There are empty booths and there are spaces at the counter."

"I'm not old enough to have a teenage daughter," Beth said. "He is, but I'm not."

"Oh yes, you are the lady who said your daughter is interested in studying engineering."

"She's a figment," Ted said. "Like South Seattle Industries is. How much titanium volume do you do?"

"That is proprietary. Am I going to have to call the police?" Tami said.

Beth said, "Who does your little white car belong to?"

Tami said nothing.

Beth said, "The last person at the wheel was a gorgeous hunk of man-flesh, a charmer who can chop folks up in tiny pieces while balancing the books, although he should leave that off if he's answering a questionnaire on an online dating site."

"I have a strict lunch hour," Tami said before taking another bite. "I can be fired if I am late."

"Speaking of late, the late Bob Chance," Ted said. "How much did he steal and whose money was it? Really. The Mafia's?"

Tami chewed slowly. "All right, since you think you know so much. I do not know if they have determined that of Robert Chance. Watch the news programs, read the newspapers. That is all anyone knows."

If she'd mourned him, she had recovered nicely, Beth thought.

She said, "Him and his sort-of-gal pal being gunned down by punk gangsters in a drive-by at a fancy hotel, people aren't safe anywhere, are they?"

No answer.

"Not in this country. I doubt if Russia's any safer." Ted paused. "Is it?"

She looked at him. "Why do you ask me?"

"Who would know how much Chance embezzled? They say it's a large amount to lift from a small company."

"It is common knowledge that we have auditors in to learn the stolen amount."

"External auditors, like the aforementioned Tony Whack Job?"

"You speak nonsense. I am not told such information. I am not a boss. I am on the front desk."

Beth said, "Your fiancé, the machinist. During pillow talk, doesn't the subject ever come up?"

She glared at Beth. "He and I are none of your business."

"Touchy touchy," Beth said.

"Did Bob Chance have any close friends in the office?"

No comment.

"It's my experience that guys will open up more before sex than after," Beth said, leaning forward and winking. "They'll say damn near anything. They'll bark like seals if you tell them to."

"She's right," Ted said.

Tami looked out the window as she munched on a pickle.

So much for girl-to-girl talk.

So much for conversation, period.

They gave up when Tami bit into her last potato chip as she gazed into some middle distance known but to her.

42

Making a Molehill Out of a Mountain

"She's one cool customer," Beth said.

"A cold customer too, but I think I saw her pulse jump a notch when I said 'Russia'," Ted said. "That's all I picked upon. No slang, contractions or accents in her speech today either, so she could well be a Russki who had a crash course in English."

"Why do you think' Russia' upset her?"

"Siberia? The camps didn't go away when the commies did."

"Seriously?"

"Beats the hell out of me. I know she's not American."

"Does that make any difference?"

"Damned if I know."

They sat in the car waiting until Tami finished her lunch. She went to the little white car without giving them a glance.

They followed her back to South Seattle Industries at an indiscreet distance. She parked in the employee lot and went in a rear entrance.

"Good girl," Beth said. "Exactly forty-five minutes."

"I can't get the encounter with Mr. Whack Job out of my mind," Ted said.

Beth stroked his forehead. "I don't blame you. The swelling's almost gone, but you might have a little scar. That and nightmares."

"I mean him not believing I didn't kill Birdwatcher Bob."

"He didn't say so."

"He growled skeptically."

Beth sighed. "I know, I know. There has to be a third player."

"Like the second shooter on the grassy knoll. If there was one."

"It'd be a lot simpler if you'd given Tony Whack a short-term memory problem so he'd ride off into the sunset."

"So he'd've thought he made a molehill out of a mountain."

"I have an idea," Beth said.

43

Tami

If it is any of your concern, my full name is Tamara Ludmilla Larrionov. I am not in actuality a front desk clerk at South Seattle Industries. This is a ruse for visitors, expected or unexpected, welcome or unwelcome. I am the general manager. South Seattle Industries is owned by Vladimir Ilyich Larrionov, my father, my Daddy.

You may recognize my father's name. Vladimir Ilyich Larrionov owns a prominent European football club, oil and mineral refining, technology companies, and skyscrapers in four nations. In your terminology, and the negative connotations it brings, Daddy is an "oligarch." At last tally, Daddy is the eighty-fourth richest person in the world.

My fiancé I spoke of to those two busybodies is not my fiancé, and my "engagement ring" is also a smoke screen. My ring is made of platinum, not titanium. I do not adorn myself with base metals.

My fiancé is not a machinist. He is my chief security official who poses as a worker, a technician and general laborer. I mistrust electronic security in America. It entails outsiders. My "fiancé" has an apartment in a rear corner of South Seattle Industries. If a person breaks in at night, the intruder is in for a painful surprise.

He is with Russia's Federal Security Service. FSS is the successor to the KGB. The official line is that the FSS is kinder and gentler than the KGB, but it remains headquartered at Lubyanka Square and "Siberia" remains a dreaded word to those brought in for questioning and are not candid.

When I ask him if the FSS has retired the KGB's thumbscrews and meat hooks or not, he smiles. He has the prettiest smile and he worships President Putin. He is excessively loyal to each of us. I may make him my genuine fiancé if I have a need for sexual fulfillment. If marital engagement is my choice, he knows better than to resist my charms.

Antonio Benito Spazento has a pretty smile too. He thinks he is God's gift to the fairer sex. He is smart too, so consequently he does not test his masculine charm on me. He *knows*. I joke to him that he is a Triple Threat, this a term borrowed from American football journalists.

He can pass for a televised news star, he is a maddened dog killer, and he is a skilled forensic accountant who can get to the bottom of criminal activity. He smiles and chuckles, but I know he hates me and would kill me in a minute if he did not value his own life.

Antonio Spazento is with us to assess the financial damage done by the late Robert Chance and to perform other tasks within his expertise as they may apply. We had preposterously and foolishly hired Robert Chance to get us caught up, a long-term temporary worker basically, who could pass security checks required by federal government agencies.

I thought Moscow was greedy and careless with money. They have nothing on Washington D.C.

SSI and its titanium is in your jargon and slang a "pickled herring." On our computers and telephones, we launder money: $, ¥,£,€. If you have hard currency that you want to keep secret from rivals and the taxation officials, we can perhaps do business, yes?

It is our own fault for making the process so complex, a collaborative among Mother Russia, the American government, the Brighton

Beach outlaws, and the Mulberry Street Italians. Chance picked our pockets to the tune of—how much? My stab in the darkness is $1.5 million, but that may be exceedingly low.

Chance was an ordinary law-abiding bookkeeper with the mediocre professional credentials to be our front man. One prior employment, fine references, an unspoken bitterness when he interviewed with me. Robert Chance gave us an exterior layer of polish. He was our harmless barrier to outside suspicion.

Upon financial review, Robert Chance was adroit at his craft, superior to our estimation of and control over him. His duplicate, triplicate and overlapping system was brilliant. His strange romantic difficulty, if we had known, we would have been more alert to ungainly grabbing at money.

Because of complex timing and laundering, the Italians took the biggest loss and sent someone (Spazento) to pinpoint the loss amount and the person culpable and for Chance.

The money is missing and Robert Chance can no longer reveal where it is. My fiancé speaks yearningly of interrogation techniques he would use on Chance if he had the opportunity.

Triple Threat Tony is on the job, in what complete capacity and progress, I believe he is keeping this to himself. If he is close to a resolution on Chance's looting and where the money has gone, he is not saying. He is making vague promises with his false charm.

The meddling pair that disturbed my lunch break, warning me off, I cannot take them seriously, though they know more than they should. The saucy woman, making suggestive comments about my sexual life, she was audaciously rude. Her man, I believe, contains more secrets of himself than Chance did.

Triple Threat Tony is on the job regarding those two too. If he has discovered their purpose, he is close-mouthed. Literally. He speaks at a murmur, saying he has an abscessed tooth. The vacuous television smile gone, he looks like an overgrown infant waiting for his pabulum.

As I sit at my desk after an unsatisfying lunch, I watch him from the corner of an eye, but I am seeing an illusion. He is not working at his desk, focused on his computer. This is bad. He comes and goes without my permission, missing more work than I like.

Antonio Benito Spazento is here with the highest recommendations from serious people, so I will let him be. If he desires to play murder detective and seek the Robert Chance and sexually-altered killers, however, I prefer that he does so on his own time. The man is dead and gone, but our money lives.

Is that a mistake?

I should consult Daddy?

Dah?

Nyet?

44

Breaking and Entering

"We were bird-dogging the wrong gal, teddy bear. Tami's not exactly pure as the driven snow, but she's not our vital mystery clue."

"That's your idea?"

"Whatever time it is, where we're going, it's cocktail hour."

Beth had directed him to head back to Mary Ann Chance's.

"I can't disagree, but I think she may be snoring off her latest ration of mimosas."

"I don't know why I have the idea. Mary Ann and time travel? We shall see."

"More woman's intuition?"

"Is that a sexist oink-oink remark?"

"Yeah, it is."

Ted turned into the subdivision.

"Okay, it is woman's intuition. So what?"

"I know when to shut up, so I am."

They saw the black Caddy Escalade before they pulled into Mary Ann Chance's cul-de-sac.

"Her kids must be getting out of school soon. Whatever's happening with Tony Whack, this is cutting it close."

"Let's take a little stroll," Ted said. "Have your phone ready for nine-one-one if he's hurting her."

"If she's still in one piece."

"For the nosy neighbors, we'll be realtors," Ted said. "Licensed to snoop."

"This little car isn't gross enough to be a realtor's car."

"Good point."

There was a small park and a playground a quarter mile away. They parked and rummaged in the glove box, coming up with an owner's manual. That and a pen would have to do as a realtor's notepad. They walked as fast as they could to Mary Ann Chance's without attracting attention.

Beth said, "I'm not keen on ringing her doorbell."

Ted said, "Let's go around a side and check for warped siding and crabgrass."

They picked the side with the taller neighboring fence. The Chance's back yard was all grass and dandelions that could use a trimming.

Ted said in a low voice, "There's no plants or garden, no kids' toys, no outbuildings like a kiddy clubhouse."

"We're only playing realtors. Hurry!"

The patio was a concrete slab dotted with green mold. Above sliders were a half-dozen hooks that may have held Bob's discarded bird feeders. He'd spoken of them, how anybody could be a birder by simply looking outside: goldfinches, red-breasted nuthatches, and others Ted couldn't remember. Whenever Ted saw a bird, it was an ongoing eulogy to Bob.

A window adjacent the sliding glass doors was half open, as was one on the second floor.

"That noise."

"Shh."

They listened to squeaking bed springs and feminine moaning.

"Oh my God," Beth said.

"Are we hearing what your woman's intuition is telling us we're hearing? She's not being drawn and quartered. Not yet."

"He may be a monster, but he is so cute," Beth said, touching the opened window sill. "Can you?"

"Break and enter?"

"Without breaking anything."

"Can do."

Ted hoisted himself up and through the window. He was directly above the kitchen sink and counter. Thankfully, Mary Ann was tidy. There were no dishes, dirty or clean, to fall onto and make a racket.

He reached the floor on tiptoes and let Beth in. The upstairs passion hadn't abated.

Beth whispered, "What do we do? Why did we do this?"

To neutralize the b-word, Ted didn't say. He opened the fridge, and got out two beers. Mary Ann's beer was behind a pitcher of orange juice, a half-used six-pack of lemon-lime soda pop, and three bottles of cheap champagne. There was food in there too, but not much.

They drank the beer, looking at each other.

"There are millions of black SUVs in the world, right?" Beth said.

"Sure. Yes, there are," Ted agreed. *Nature abhors a coincidence.*

"There's no law saying that milkmen can't drive black SUVs," Beth said.

"Sure. You can sell tons of cottage cheese out of them."

The upstairs action intensified, then ceased.

Like a couple of cats waiting to be killed by curiosity, they stood there.

They hadn't long to wait, just long enough to wonder why they were waiting.

Mary Ann came downstairs and into the kitchen, wearing a short robe.

Her mouth fell open, her eyes widened, as much satiated as shocked.

Behind her, wearing boxer shorts, stood Tony Whack Job.

225

45

Mount Vesuvius

Antonio (Tony Whack Job) Spazento was an eyeful, Beth thought. With nary a tattoo, he looked like Michelangelo's *David*, except with better hair. The marble was tarnished (i.e.— bruised) in spots.

But for the dental damage, he came out of our skirmish better than I had, Ted thought. All that bedroom thrashing had not moved a single strand of his anchormen hair out of place.

Lips clenched, Tony moved around Mary Ann toward Ted. Beth had her oven cleaner out of her purse, aimed at Tony's shorts, freezing him in mid-step.

"Believe the warning on the can, hon," she said. "It contains lye."

"Let's talk about this like adults," Ted said.

Unsteadily and oddly unperturbed about the break-in, Mary Ann kissed Tony gently on the neck and pushed him back. "Easy, sugar. Easy."

"Down boy, down," Beth said.

Mary Ann said, "I can imagine how this looks."

"I can imagine how this looks, us being in your kitchen," Beth said. "Why don't we sit at the dinette, okay? We're close and we have a little barrier between us too. No screaming, no nine-one-one."

"Some other time. I don't mean to be impolite, but the kids will be home from school shortly. I need everybody out of here. You are trespassing. I could have you arrested."

Ted said, "There are no kids."

Mary Ann had no response.

She seemed absolutely sober, Beth observed. The girl could hold her mimosas and her temper.

Ted said, "No pictures on the wall. No kid things in the back yard. No food for the youngsters in the fridge unless you count orange juice."

Mary Ann's eyes puddled. "When we did have sex once every other blue moon, Bob was shooting blanks, a billion tadpoles short, and he wouldn't go in and see anybody about it, the selfish bastard."

"The bronzed baby shoes?" Ted said.

"I bought them in a thrift shop. I thought it was so sad that they were there. Why I hung on to them, I don't know. A shrink might say it was a slap in Bob's face without slapping him."

Beth squeezed her forearms, a long-distance sisterly hug. "I am so sorry."

Mary Ann sniffled. "It's for the best now. Anyone for a drinkypoo?"

"We have our beers," Beth said. "But thanks for asking."

Tony shook his head, eyes on the blonde. He licked his uppers, channeling his inner Bundy. Oh what fun she will be!

Mary Ann was out and back in thirty seconds with a mimosa.

Ted offered Tony his hand. "How about it, Mr. Soprano, I mean Mr. Spazento. No hard feelings. I think we're on the same page. In a way."

Tony Whack Job responded with a cold stare, lowering the room temperature ten degrees.

Mary Ann touched his leg or something else under the table. "Relax, baby. Hear them out."

He nodded. A single, violent nod.

Beth said, "Mary Ann, you knew about the Brenda and Brent and the Thai crotch mechanics before anybody else. You knew about

Bob's embezzling at South Seattle Industries too, didn't you? Maybe he'd had a few and spilled the beans. Maybe he talked in his sleep. Whatever."

"Whoever you really are, why do you *really* care?"

Ted said, "You really don't want to know."

"That's a stupid answer."

Ted shrugged. "It's best I can or will do."

Beth said, "The ballpark guess is that Bob embezzled three quarters of a million dollars."

Mary Ann laughed. "They're a million too low. That we know of."

"So Mr. Spazento here was dispatched to tally up the numbers, hunt for the deficit, and generally clean up the mess," Ted said.

"We know your gorgeous hunk here didn't gun down your husband," Beth said. "We didn't either. We don't even have gun permits. Me from Montana no less."

"I'm terrified of firearms," Ted said. "That's a personal confession. It's somebody else's turn to join in and spill their guts."

"Of course Tony didn't do it," Mary Ann said. "He came here after the murders and he's here to trace the money Robert embezzled. Nothing else. He came here to ask me about Robert, you know, if I had any knowledge of the money. I didn't, but one thing led to another."

Ted said, "How much money is left?"

"This is confidential, but as near as anyone can determine, hardly anything. Another secret my beloved husband had was a gambling problem. Video poker online. He lost it trying to fill inside straights as fast as he stole it."

Ted tried to read Tony's opaque non-expression, but couldn't, and said, "Well, it was nice to clear the air. We should be running along."

"You too, doll," Mary Ann said to Tony as she slid out of the dinette. "I have a couple of things to do and I need a nap. I'll call you later."

Tony obeyed automaton-like, went upstairs, came back down dressed, and slammed the front door behind him in three minutes.

"If it's fine with you, Mary Ann," Beth said. "We'll finish our beers first. Seeing Tony outside, well, it'd be kind of awkward. We'll lock the door behind us."

Mary Ann yawned. "Sure. Help yourself to all the beer you want. It was Robert's and it's bad for the waistline. I'll be upstairs having a siesta."

So they did, standing in the kitchen, enjoying their second brew.

"What's your take on Mr. Whack Job?" Ted asked Beth. "He's playing it too normal, kind of like a human being, doing what his gal pal says."

"Yeah. Pussywhipped even. I felt like we were in Pompeii, having an orgy or something, minding our own business, waiting for their volcano to blow its stack."

"Vesuvius."

"That's the one."

Mary Ann Chance screamed.

46

Tony Spazento,
Mild-Mannered Auditor

They hustled up the steps, taking them two at a time. On the upper landing, hand on his chest, Beth ordered Ted to wait in the hall in case Mary Ann was showing an excess of Mary Ann.

Beth went inside and after a moment of whispering, peeked back out, and curled a finger.

Ted went in to darkness and let his eyes adjust. Beth was sitting at the edge of the bed, her arm around the weeping widow Chance. She cocked her head to a side.

Ted saw teddy bears and other stuffed animals on the floor, and on dressers and end tables. Cute fuzzy things for children that never were.

It was a big bedroom full of nail holes where wall hangings had been. Piled in a corner were framed photos of birds, a resplendent quetzal on top, possessions of Birdwatcher Bob that hadn't made it to the dump, his presence not completely obliterated.

Beth said, "Ted, I mean look what she found under the mattress while she was tucking the blanket in."

From the pillow beside her, she delicately picked up an ice pick by the point as if it were a poisonous insect. Beside it was a hacksaw and a pair of boning shears.

"Uh oh."

"Yeah. All you guys have mood swings, but this is over and above."

Mary Ann said, "He'd been snooping in my pantry. I asked why. He went, oh, I was looking for trash bags so I can take out the garbage for you and earn my keep. I put an unopened box on an upper shelf for him. It was the big black ones with the red drawstrings. They'd been on sale. He had this funny smile I haven't seen since. His teeth were spooky too, like, you know, a vampire. I don't like dentists either, but *please*."

Ted sat in an armchair by the window. "Mary Ann, there is unaccounted-for embezzled money, isn't there? Money no auditor will ever find."

"I think there is. Robert was clever with numbers. I have to hand him that."

"Bob didn't really have a video poker habit, did he?" Ted said.

"Are you calling me a liar?"

"I am too," Beth said, giving her a hug. "That's two against one."

"He could've, him and his secrets, the goddamn motherfucking pervert! If he did, how would you know he wasn't a video poker addict?"

"Man's intuition," Ted said.

"Easy, girl. It'll be all right," Beth said, holding her tighter.

"The money," Ted coaxed. "Can you show us the money?"

"You know, you two keep turning up on my doorstep with money on the brain. You breaking in to my kitchen, you went too far."

"We may've saved your life, dear."

"Well, there's that," Mary Ann said.

"I know, we're bad pennies," Beth said. "But, listen, you've been encouraging us, beginning with the cell phone pic of lover boy."

"This, you, the situation, it's fishy. Let's be honest. You want so much from me, so let's open up. Who *are* you? You weren't just on a stupid bird hunting field trip with Bob."

Beth and Ted exchanged telepathic nods.

He began, telling all, mostly all, omitting their last names, Beth interrupting him to edit.

Mary Ann laughed hysterically and said, "Let me get this straight. You make your living as a hired killer who isn't."

"I save lives. I perform a community service."

"You disappeared Bob to keep him alive, but he rose from the dead only to get gunned down for real, and these gangsters you cheat by not actually killing people they want killed blamed you and sent Tony to kill you?"

"You got it."

Beth said, "Bob transferred $150,000 into Ted's offshore account. So it logically follows that there's more. A shitload more."

"After expenses, it was only $84,533 to me. But with unanticipated costs on this trip, my net's only going to be—"

"Only?" Mary Ann said. "Poor baby. That's a pretty big 'only'. It's tax free too."

"Yeah, well, I can live with that so long as I'm not audited."

Beth said, "Let's get back to your strong silent type with the ice pick, hacksaw and boning shears. You're damn lucky we broke and entered when we did."

Mary Ann said, "Tony came to me as a mild-manned auditor, a CPA who looked like he went to college to play football, not an accounting major, simply trying to find the money for South Seattle Industries' parent company. I'm wrong on many counts, aren't I?"

Ted stopped himself from saying *dead* wrong.

"Dear," Beth said softly. "Their parent company is whoever they're laundering the money for."

Ted told Mary Ann what they omitted when they told almost all, most of it anyway, relating what they knew about Tony, his affection for ice picks, and their scrum in the parking garage.

Beth brushed his forehead.

"Tony's bruises and his busted teeth. He said he'd had a recent car accident." Mary Ann beseeched the ceiling. "God, how could I be so stupid?"

"It's your hormones that're at fault, not you," Beth said. "It's happened to me too. Many times."

Ted said, "Why'd you show us his picture in the SUV, alerting us, and act like you were afraid of him?"

"I don't know. I wanted somebody else's reaction to him, a back-up opinion."

"Woman's intuition," Ted said.

"You got what you wanted. He was and is bad news, dear," Beth said.

"He was leaving after him and I, you know. I also wanted to have another look at you. I knew you weren't Robert's birdwatching friends."

"Birding friends," Beth said.

"I thought you might be private eyes after the money or undercover cops who weren't convinced I didn't kill the bastard. And Tony. Why would a dreamboat like that put a move on me? I. Am. So. Fucking. Stupid."

"Stop that," Beth said. "You have a lot going for you. Pardon us for overhearing from your kitchen, but he was rocking and rolling upstairs too."

"Mary Ann, who do you think killed Bob?"

"Why are you asking me again and again?"

"When you said he had a video poker problem, may we please drop that?"

Mary Ann said, "Why couldn't he have a video poker problem, him and all his secrets? Anything's possible with him and his embezzling and that creature he tried to run off with."

"Except that he didn't have a video poker problem," Ted said. "There'd be no money to pay me, not to mention mounds of loose cash."

"I already said there's money. Somewhere. Well, he'd get offline when I walked in on him, so I assumed."

"Could be he was surfing porn," Ted said. "I do that until Beth walks in on me. I minimize and pop up dirty pics I've taken of her."

"My man's joking or he's as good as dead," Beth said.

Mary Ann looked at them. "I envy you two. Robert and I never talked to each other like that. That lovingly jesting stuff. We never had anything like that between us. Not from day one."

"Where do Russians fit in?" Ted asked quickly to forestall her tears.

"That's a new one on me," Mary Ann said. "He didn't even talk in his sleep about them. The man was afraid of his own shadow. Live Russians on the scene would've given him a heart attack."

Beth said, "Pack a bag, Mary Ann. You're gonna stay with us a few days at our hotel. The Whackster will be back to finish the job. Count on it. Thanks to our rude arrival, you're a liability."

"I can't," she said. "I just can't."

"We'll trade our room for a suite, Ted said. "You'll have privacy."

Beth said, "We're at, you know, that hotel. We can move to another if it bothers you."

"*That* hotel?"

"Yeah."

"Then what are we waiting for? Give me a little time to pack."

47

Poetry Isn't His Fault

"You really are staying here?" Mary Ann Chance said. "At this hotel? The same hotel?"

"We said we were," Beth said. "We wouldn't kid about something like that."

"I thought you were testing me."

"How do you mean testing?"

"I don't know. You don't trust me any further than I trust you."

"Lighten up, girl."

Ted was parking in the circle at the hotel entrance. It had taken Mary Ann a while to pack, but, surprisingly, she hadn't argued with them. It gave Beth and Ted time to throw together a goofy plan.

"Bad memories?" Beth said.

"It's memories after it happened, flashbacks of the police grilling me like I was a criminal. That's the worst memory."

"Not Bob's demise?" Beth said.

"You know how I feel about that. If I get my job back at the bank or any bank, which is unlikely, I'll never have a position of trust."

A mountain range of goose bumps on his arms, Ted stared at her.

"It'll be for a few days, to give Mr. Whack Job time to think you flew the coop for good. Then you can go home, go back to work at the bank thinking smiley-face thoughts, and find yourself another stud, one that doesn't have an ice pick fetish," Beth said.

Ted went inside to make room-to-suite arrangements. He knew Beth was no more convinced of her happily-ever-after pitch to Mary Ann than she was. It was important to get her the hell out of the house for everybody's peace of mind.

They were done settling in at dusk and invited Mary Ann downstairs for dinner and drinks on them.

"We could call room service," she said.

Beth said, "Come on. We'll be safe. They have a nice bar here. You'll like it."

Mary Ann waited a minute for them to change our minds, then said, "Okay. If you let me pay, we're on."

They gave in and headed downstairs. Mary Ann should be red-eyed and hung over from the earlier mimosas, but she wasn't even drowsy. A hollow leg?

They had burgers again and Mary Ann had the chicken-and-pasta special. The drinks kept coming, beer for Beth and Ted at a ratio of one to every two mimosas for Mary Ann, who was beginning to get tipsy.

Per the plan, Ted had brought down his chapbook. He'd laid it on the chair beside him, but now put it on the table.

"What's that?" Mary Ann said. "Did a kid leave it here on a high chair?"

Beth said, "Ted's a poet. This is gonna be his life's work after he retires from the disappearing profession."

"You're kidding."

"It's not his fault," Beth said, giving his hand a sympathetic squeeze. "He was an English major in college. He's sick and can't help himself. They brainwashed him with that sugary Browning doo-doo."

He opened the chapbook and gave it to Mary Ann.

"Read this and tell me if I'm a poet or not. Be blunt. I can take it. I think."

She looked at him, then Beth, shrugged, and read aloud:

ARSENIC

Arsenic's chemical symbol is *AS*,
the beginning of a word for people
who misuse it.
But who knew way back when?
In Victorian times, women applied
arsenic compounds to their faces and arms
to improve their complexion
and iron out the wrinkles.
The price of vanity was
through the ceiling.
Centuries before that,
in the good old Renaissance times,
arsenic was known as
inheritance powder,
baked into cakes.
Who knew that homicide
could be so tasty?

Mary Ann closed the chapbook quickly so, Ted thought, he wouldn't be tempted to ask her to read another.

"Well, it's a little twisted and it doesn't rhyme."

Ted bowed his head. "That'd be a high compliment at a poetry slam. Thank you."

"Mary had a little lamb. Now that's a poem," Beth said, segueing to the point. "By the way, speaking of arsenic and murder. Obviously you didn't use poison on Bob."

Ted asked, "Who did you hire to gun them down?"

Mary Ann shook her head so violently that her mimosa lapped over the rim. "You're nuts."

"No we aren't. Do we have to remind you that you knew about the hairdresser's genital remake ahead of everybody else, so it logi—"

"– cally follows," Mary Ann interrupted with a groan.

"That you hired gangbangers to do the job. How'd you manage it? You live in different circles," Ted said.

"But I'd think the little scamps do work cheap," Beth said. "Strictly for cash and a helluva lot less than Tony Whackster asks. No paperwork, no strain on the budget."

"That took guts," Ted said. "Your IT expertise must've helped bleed Bob's embezzled loot from him to you. You said you wrote code, whatever code is, writing rings around the pimply nerds. You can do everything on a computer anybody can do on a computer."

Beth said, "If the homicidal little rascals don't have websites, you could leapfrog from others and connect."

"South Seattle Industries could use you," Ted said. "No glass ceiling there, no glass above the titanium that's not there."

"How many beers have you had?" Mary Ann asked Ted.

"Little Miss Misdirection," Beth said. "I have to hand it to you. You raved about wanting him dead so much that they couldn't believe you'd actually hired it done. That and a flimsy alibi and you were home free."

Mary Ann sniffed her glass and stood up. "The o.j. smells like it turned. Between these mimosas and your bullshit, I think I may be sick. Excuse me."

They watched closely as she went into a restroom, hand over her mouth. They resumed drinking beer. There wasn't much to say until Mary Ann returned. The next move was hers.

After ten minutes, Beth said, "I'd better go check on her."

She was in and out of the can fast, waving an arm at Ted.

Ted went to her.

"She slipped out on us."

"Upstairs?"

"We can try."

The elevator they waited for arrived.

Mary Ann Chance came out rolling her suitcase.

She glanced at her watch and said, "Let's not let our drinks go to waste. I have time before I have to catch my plane."

48

Getting The Hell Out of Dodge

"You have the floor, tootsie," Beth told Mary Ann.

Mary Ann led off with a smile. "Well, the cops didn't say not to leave town, like they do in the movies, so I'm leaving town."

A super-bitch smile, thought Beth.

Coquettish, Ted thought, thanks maybe to the full-strength mimosas, undiluted with soda pop from her home fridge, to give the illusion that she was a marginally-functioning alcoholic.

"Your passport's conveniently with you?" Ted said.

Mary Ann's smile hadn't wavered. "Never leave home without it."

Ted said, "When we first met, you said you'd been eliminated as a suspect. You had an alibi, getting yourself ready for work, your car in the driveway, et cetera. They ruled you out hiring the job. You had made no big withdrawals and professed ignorance of any dirty money. Who did the Boy Scout uniform you packed belong to? Was it something you picked up at a thrift store to fatten the happy nuclear family image?"

She finished her mimosa and waved the glass for a fresh one. "My, you have a good eye and memory. Like I told you, it was Bob's."

"Did he make it to Eagle Scout?"

"He didn't, but he was still my hero. Bob refused to toss out anything of his. He had a merit badge for birdwatching, you know."

"With your IT skills, glass ceiling or no glass ceiling, you'd pilfered the dirty money from Bob's dirty money, socking it away for a rainy day, to spend it where it never rains, a rainy day like today."

"Not in a rain forest country chock-full of exotic birds, though," Ted said. "Bob's dream destination."

"You two are so repetitious."

"Yeah. Broken records," Beth said.

"You repeat your questions and statements like the cops did, hoping I'll flub and change my story."

Ted said, "Let's see. Did we ask this? How did you hire Bob's drive-by shooters?"

"Prove it," Mary Ann said, smiling.

"You really are too good for that bank job. You know more IT and its secret code and coding than your boss and his boss," Beth said.

"Flattery will get you a smile. That's it. Again I say, prove it."

"Ever hear of gratitude?" Beth said. "We whisked you the hell out of your house before you had your last horizontal dance with the Whack Man."

"Proving it isn't our job either," Ted said. "Hell, I don't know what our job is with you. I was too late to shove Bob's head back into his burrow. We took care of the three others. I think. Not that it was necessary after all, a waste of time and money."

"Whip a hypothetical on us, geek girl," Beth said. "How you'd jiggle and wiggle and fondle the computers and peek under a rock and find Bob's embezzled bucks? I am dazzled by your skill. Really."

Mary Ann sipped her mimosa. "Hypothetically. Think of a corn maze. The rustic at the county fair gets lost and you have to go in and lead him out. Not too hard if you designed the maze or saw how it was made. Okay?"

"Okay."

"Let's make the maze three-dimensional. By the time you've built it, you've forgotten how complicated it is. What you do, you fabricate templates, puzzle parts, and link them. Understand?"

"I understand that you and Bob were sharp enough to pull it off," Beth said. "Each on his-her own. You weren't only estranged in bed. You were on the keyboard too."

Ted said, "Bob transferred everything to his home computer. You got into it and his password, kicking the virtual door in. He didn't know you had gotten into the money and his relationship with Hairdresser Smith."

Mary Ann said, "If you're thinking of being sterling citizens and calling the police with your far-out story, I'll lie and tell them my version of the truth, whole truth, and nothing but the truth. I'm taking a vacation to decompress and try to pick up the pieces of my life. I'll be crying like a baby when I do. My beloved husband dead, him and his lover girl or boy."

"May we ask where you're going?" Beth said.

Mary Ann's smile broadened. "You may ask."

Ted wanted to ask Mary Ann Chance if she realized how much trouble she caused them by having her hubby killed for real. His knuckle-dragging employers had been on his case like they were when Jimmy Brutto resurrected himself from the dead. At no small risk and expense, they had gotten to the three disappeareds he'd done after resumption of his career.

All he'd accomplish by spilling his business woes would be to widen her smile from ear to ear.

Mary Ann's purse beeped. She fished out her phone and looked at the screen.

"I have an intruder at the house. My security system's linked to this little goodie. There, that'll do it."

"What'll do what?" Beth said.

"It called nine-one-one and sent a robo message. The police are on their way. God, I love technology."

"The man of your dreams?" Beth asked.

"Methinks."

Ted said, "Will he have time to throw a tantrum and tear your happy home apart with his ice pick like he did our rental car before he's arrested? You should've seen it."

"Did he tell you that story?" Beth asked.

She avoided the question with a yawn. "He does have a temper. I'll hire a realtor to have it fixed up and put on the market."

"Beth, what is it you do when you're not running around the world and playing games with your man?"

"Tend bar."

"Talk about glass ceilings."

"I can deal with it. I have no management aspirations. My glass ceiling is the top shelf where the spendy tequila and vodka are. But you and Tony. How will you sleep at night without him on the pillow next to you and his work tools under it?"

Smile remaining in place, daubing a nonexistent tear, she said, "I'll cry myself to sleep. I have so many reasons to. Or not. I have money. Acquiring lovers will be no problem."

"If they manage to throw a net over Tony Whack, depending on what they unearth and what he says, they'll want to chat with you."

"Good point," she said, wasting not a drop of her mimosa as she stood. "I can wait for my plane at the gate as well as here. It's been real, guys."

She was out the door and in an airport shuttle van before it dawned on Beth and Ted that she had stiffed them with the check.

Beth's phone chirped.

"Mom, hi. What's wrong?"

"You're not serious."

"When?"

"Billy Bob had the afternoon off and you were in your chair snoozing between your talk shows and your soaps. Okay."

"With my bedroom door wide open, he had his face all over them? Mom, throw *every* pair of my panties out or, no, burn them, every last one."

"Snoring doesn't mean you're not a light sleeper. Well, that's one lesson the son of a bitch learned."

"You have him on probation? That's generous of you, Mom. Only because you're getting kind of attached to Fluffy. Okay, yeah, we're going by your way. We'll see you soon. Love and kisses."

Beth flipped her phone shut, looked at Ted, and said, "I make a motion that we saddle up and get the hell out of Dodge too."

"Giddyap," Ted said.

49

Whither Tony

When they stepped out of the elevator on their floor, Ted said, "True love has its limits. It's tragic."

"Yeah. Whack Boy in the can, Mary Ann in the sun."

Ted inserted the key card in their room door. As it blinked green, he said, "Hey, Beth. Did you see Mary Ann's key card on the table?"

"No, I didn't."

He was wrenched inside, an arm around his neck, then two arms, then one.

Beth had reached for Ted and was inside too, blouse half torn off, the door kicked shut behind her.

The arm around Ted was replaced by a thin wire or cable around his neck. Ted barely got his hands under it before it tightened. Not wire. Something softer.

His natural impulse was to push forward, but that tightened the pressure.

Ted surprised his attacker by shoving backward against him. They collided against the dresser and the TV atop it. The television came down, hanging by its cables.

The pain was worsening.

Beth was in front of them, trembling, shaking her fists. Her purse had gone flying, so she had no oven cleaner. Nor a beer bottle handy to clobber a sweet spot. Spazento was going to decapitate Ted with that thread thing around his neck.

Ted wanted to tell her to run for help, but he couldn't rasp out a syllable. He kicked against the dresser sending them onto the bed.

Tony watched the blonde throughout. When he and his dental-floss masterpiece were done with business, he'd grab her, the blond bitch frozen with fear. He'd take her down and go for the neck, biting, sinking in, through skin, fat, muscle, blood, all the way to bone.

After she bled out, he'd begin seducing her. Gently, caringly, expertly.

He was aroused. Mr. Bundy and him, they would prevail. Ted coaxing from beyond, mentoring.

Tony tightened his grip. He had to work fast. With two of them he knew he had his hands full and he was in a time crunch.

Ted turned over, moving Tony on top, hoping to rotate onto the floor, the impact stunning the Whackster.

Tony anticipated it and spread his legs, digging his toes in to the bedding.

That was when he felt the hand moving between his legs.

The blond whore was on him, crying and grabbing.

"A boner," she said, hand on his erection. "You sick fuck."

She squeezed and twisted and yanked.

Tony screamed, released Ted, and knocked Beth loose with a forearm.

Limping, he was out the door and gone.

Beth got on her knees and to her feet. She turned on lights, hooked the safety chain, and looked at Ted. "Poor baby. Your neck."

Flat on his back, seeing a constellation of stars, he said, "I'll be fine."

She applied ointment from her kit and lay on the bed beside him.

"You'll have a red mark. To go with your forehead, if you aren't Frankenstein with a head sewn on, I don't know who is."

"My damsel, me in distress," he said, gasping. "We have this perils-of-thing assbackwards again."

"He had a hard-on, honey. That is *so* sick. Was he getting off on doing you or what he was gonna do to me? We're damn lucky he gave up and scrammed."

"Who did set off Mary Ann's home alarm? My money's on the Bible lady. They don't give up when there are souls to save. Her trying to jam a pamphlet under the door tripped the alarm."

"Mary Ann's soul could use saving."

"And I sure could use a drink." She sat up. "We knocked the fridge and TV over. It's a mess."

"Did the little bottles fall out?"

"They did and the little guys didn't break. Praise the Lord."

"We'll have to pay for them anyway."

"Hey, who are we this time? I wasn't paying attention when we checked in."

"Mr. and Mrs. Dejavoo. If they ask, I'm East Indian on my father's side."

Beth got out of bed. "Why do you think he split before killing us? Sore pecker or no sore pecker, I was no match for him. How did we get so lucky?"

Ted said, "He has a plane to catch."

50

Unfluffy Fluffy

Beth and Ted left the hotel at pre-dawn, when Mary Ann and Tony were likely approaching the torrid zone. They believed that the happy couple would land where the sky was blue topaz, the beach sand was as fine and white as granulated sugar, where palapa bars served mimosas with umbrellas and fruit, where young copper-skinned men were on the lookout for plain, moneyed women twice their age.

"She'd be easy pickings without her chaperone," Beth said.

"Tony's not leaving her side. His mission was to locate the Fellas' money and he has."

Wanting to waste no time arranging a flight to Butte, they drove. Their skies were not blue topaz, but dishwater gray. Eastbound on Interstate-90, they crested Snoqualmie Pass, which was not impeded by ice or snow, but as they passed into Idaho there was a brutal crosswind pushing at them from the north, threatening to sweep their little rental car off the road like sagebrush.

They took an exit at a shopping area that featured a big box store. After lunch and Beth buying undies as Ted served as a technical consultant on lacy and sheer products, they drove straight through to Butte.

Throughout, they had telepathed silence on the subject of their future. Together. As a couple. Was she going to stay with Gladys and Fluffy and Billy Bob (?) while Ted moved on? Or not.

When they arrived at Beth's mother's trailer, snowflakes the size of quarters were beginning to fall.

Inside, as usual, thanks to cigarettes and fried food cookery, the smog level was that of Shanghai's.

"Mom, Fluffy isn't fluffy," said a horrified Beth. "Fluffy's gross."

The cat had short dirty white fur, saw-toothed ears from innumerable battle campaigns, and an attitude. Fluffy sat defiantly in a corner of the kitchenette by a plate of leftover meatloaf and a saucer of beer, one green eye and one blue eye never wavering from the new arrivals. A Clarkson medium-hair if there ever was one.

Gladys Marshak Palmer Wiley Johnstone Higgins Dickey Blamey lit a cigarette and said, "According to Billy Bob, it'd gone feral from being on its own. How it got in that car is anybody's guess, unless Billy Bob was fibbing where he found it. It won't have nothing to do with people, and it scratched Billy Bob half to death getting it from there to here."

"Mom," Beth said. "You told me it was cute."

"I said it was cute for a cat. It looks more like a pit bull than a cat is what makes it cute. Keep your distance or it'll claw you to ribbons. We thought the beer would relax it some, but Fluffy's a mean-ass drunk and when he's hungover, he's as dangerous as all get-out."

Ted patted his lap. Fluffy came to him and hopped on it. He petted the animal and scratched under his chin. Fluffy began purring and drooling.

Ted picked Fluffy up, rested him on a shoulder, and patted its back. "His gut is as hard as a rock."

The cat belched loudly.

"I'll be go to hell," Beth's mom said as cigarette ashes fell on her housecoat.

Beth said, "Am I hallucinating or did you just burp it like a baby?"

Ted put Fluffy down. "He was bloated from the beer. He should mellow out."

Beth said, "My man's got a cat-person gene. There's nothing he can do about it. Say, we'd better be getting to the motel. The weather's turning rotten, fouler by the minute."

"Yeah. The temperature's dropped twenty degrees in the last two hours. In Montana, you know, you can have snow any time after Labor Day. Eighty degrees one day, a blizzard the next. Billy Bob and the rest of the tow company crew are on duty, ready for the worst," Beth's mom said. "You can stay here in your room if you behave yourselves."

"We already have a motel room, Mom. Thanks for asking."

"Not in one of those hot sheet dumps?"

"The room's okay. It doesn't stink too much."

"Well, your room here's the way you left it, stuffed animals and everything."

"Thanks, Mom. Did you get rid of my panties?"

"Every single pair. I told Billy Bob that if I caught him pawing in the trash I'd jam him in it and wave bye-bye when the garbage men came. Like I said, he's on probation. Second strike and he's out."

"Snow's falling like out of a shaken snow globe, Mom," Beth said, looking out a window. "We have to go while we can."

"Where're you gonna be playing soccer and what happened to your neck?" Gladys said when they were at the door.

Fluffy was rubbing against his legs and meowing.

Ted said, "Soccer's a rough game, Gladys. I'm considering retirement."

Beth said, "He has a birthday coming up. If he goes back to soccer, he'll have to get in his walker and be a coach."

They stopped at a department store-supermarket combo for sandwiches and drink to sustain them if stranded, which Ted secretly hoped they were. He had a brainstorm of sorts, and put a dart set and a map of the world in the cart.

As they stood in a long line with locals stocking up on food and beverages too, Beth asked, "What's with that stuff?"

"In case we're bored."

* * * * *

They weren't bored. They fishtailed to a sideways stop at the motel, skipped dinner, got semi-drunk, and made love with a ferocity unusual even for them, banging the headboard against the wall like a pile driver.

Buried under the covers, Ted whispered, "I love you."

"I love you too."

"I can't live without you."

"Me neither. There's one thing, though."

"Okay."

"We don't ruin what we have with, you know, the m-word."

Ted said, "I'm with you. Nothing kills a passionate romance faster than the m-word. It's an automatic, guaranteed method of boring each other to death, the b-word."

"The i-word too."

"Insecurity?"

"Insecurity. Yeah, you tie the m-word knot because of the i-word, you wind up with the b-word."

"This telepathy we have, it's eerie," Ted said. "Thanks to your sm-therapy, I'm cured of the i-word and b-word."

"What's that? Sadomasochism? No way."

"Sex maniac therapy. Are you? Cured too?"

"Oh yeah and I'll never b-word you to death until death do us part and I'll go wherever you want to go."

"Portugal's out."

"Agreed."

"I will miss the times we had."

Beth said, "Me too, but I'll never try doing it in salt water again, like by that beach near Milfontes. Fresh water okay, salt water no. It smarted in spots."

"I'll miss my old Remington."

"Hey, how about an English major poem? Do you have one in your chatter book?"

"If I find one, will you lay off about the English major thing?"

"I will. Maybe."

"It's an epic poem."

"C'mon. You already did an epic."

"There's no limit on epic poems."

She sighed. "How long is it?"

"Long."

"I'll take my chances."

He went for his chapbook and let her read:

THE EIGHT PARTS OF SPEECH

On the First Day,
Noun descended from the Heavens.
Hot to trot, but stuck in place.
What to do?

On the Second Day,
Adjective descended from the Heavens.
Lascivious, lonely, luscious.
Everything Noun wanted.
But stuck in place, always to his left.
They joined at the hip and elsewhere,
but could not move.

On the Third Day,
Verb descended from the Heavens.
Noun secured Verb to its right.
Spooled up to full power and ran.
Tap danced and sang.

On the Fourth Day,
Adverb descended from the Heavens.
Not so fast, said Adverb!
As Verb's modifier,
I have a say in this.
So they throttled back
and smelled the roses.

On the Fifth Day,
Pronoun descended from the Heavens,
and scolded Noun.
I am anonymous, said Pronoun.
If you cannot behave,
use me.

On the Sixth Day,
Preposition descended from the Heavens.
To, from and of,
doing wonders for
everybody's lateral mobility.

On the Seventh Day,
Conjunction descended from the Heavens.
Kind of like a marriage counselor or
a computer dating service,
Conjunction got everybody together,
including the same from
faraway lands.

On the Eighth day,
Interjection descended from the Heavens.
There's no Eighth Day, you say?
Who the hell cares!

With Interjection on board,
it's always party time!

"I can dig the blasphemy. It's kind of dirty too, Conjunction hosting an orgy. You can read all kinds of stuff between the lines if you have a filthy mind like I do," Beth said. "This is your best poem I've seen. There's a smartassedness to it that's spiritual."

"Hey, thanks."

They snuggled and kissed and groped.

Beth said, "Time out for a minute. If not Portugal, where to?"

"That's why the darts and map. If I was the praying kind of guy I would've prayed you'd be okay that we'd toss a dart and go where it hit."

"A-fucking-men."

Beth threw back the covers and asked what they were waiting for.

Ted opened the world map and folded it at the Tropic of Cancer and Tropic of Capricorn.

"Unless you're interested in Baffin Island or Tierra del Fuego."

"Pass. On Baffin Island you can have a polar bear, but you can't have a cat."

Ted pinned it to a wall with darts. They sat on the bed, staring at the tropical and subtropical planet, and got beyond semi-drunk.

"Let's do it. No, not that," she said, slapping his hand away. "Let's leave it to chance."

"Chance, not capitalized," Ted said, standing unsteadily.

Beth blindfolded him with her bra and hugged him from behind to keep them both from falling on their inebriated butts.

Ted flung a dart and hit a cheesy print of the Rockies hanging above a rickety desk.

"Nice shot, deadeye. Try again."

"Much better," she said, clapping.

Bra/blindfold off, Ted squinted. The dart had landed toward the top of the map, just below the Tropic of Cancer: San Juan, Puerto Rico.

"Works for me," he said.

"Me too. We'll go out for sunscreen in the morning," Beth said.

51

The Fellas

"The dough he makes off of us, he could live better than he is. This little Portugal town, it's a hole in the wall in a country that's a hole in the wall."

"He got his dough offshore in a piggy bank is what I think. Saving for a rainy day."

"He was living kinda offshore right here. Down near the shore, looking out at the Atlantic Ocean. The little white houses and the beaches, it's peaceful here if you like peaceful."

"Yeah, saving for a rainy day. No wife or nothing. I don't see no pictures on the walls except for this here framed paper. There ain't nothing with his right name on it, even this."

"Your cousin's computer kid, he come through for us."

"He did. He found his hideout here, but he couldn't find his right name."

"He found four names for the slippery motherfucker."

"Which is worse than no name at all. Hell, we don't even know what he looks like."

"On the wall here, it's an award for what they call here a poetry slam. It's wrote in English and Portugal-eze too. He won himself ten Euros and the dumb fuck, he's framed it."

"Smash it."

"Here goes. Careful of the glass."

"We'll buy us a couple of drinks with this money."

"A drink, it'd hit the spot. I got jet lag like I can't fuckin believe."

"It's like eleven bucks, this bill. These Euros, they look like play money and they're worth more than real money is."

"The local yokels, they say our mysterious guy, he does okay with the ladies. So he's not, you know, double-gaited. Not like the broad with Chance who wasn't no broad."

"Wasn't that something?"

"Yeah, she had too much of both and not enough of neither. Medical science, they do all that shit and they can't cure the common cold."

"What's this?"

"I don't know. Look it this here he wrote down all typed out."

"I'm reading it."

"You're moving your lips."

"Fuck you."

"Fuck you too. Read it out loud."

YELLOW

Have we not seen these dimwits in a museum or a gallery?

Signs say: *cameras yes, flash no.*

There are pictograms for the illiterate.

Flash does harm, especially to old-timey yellow oils.

Yet, *flash flash flash.*

Help yourself to this fantasy:

A knucklehead shutterbug faces Goya's *The Third of May 1808,*

the firing squad one,

the most famed of his horrors-of-war period.

Flash, flash, flash.

A hand reaches out from the masterpiece

and yanks him into it.

Señor, do you desire a blindfold?

Sí?

No?

Bang bang bang."

"That's a pome?"

"Don't ask me. It don't even rhyme."

"A guy at the end of this yellow pome, he gets clipped at the end so it ain't all bad."

"What're you looking around for?"

"A litter box. Guy who writes pomes, the homo, he gotta have a cat."

"That there Remington typewriter, huh, he typed the pome on that?"

"I stole me a Remington like this in the ninth grade."

"That the year you dropped out?"

"Fuck you. They tossed me out in the tenth after that thing with the lady teacher. The Remington, I pawned it for ten bucks."

"I dunno, our guy, he got this basketball hoop set-up in his yard, maybe he landed on his head from too much dribbling."

"He writes pomes, so he gotta be a faggot, don't he? Just like, you work in a museum unless you're sending pitchers out the back door. This guy, he's the type who'd have a cat."

"That guy down the street who told us where he was, he said he used to have this blond babe, a hot number."

"He switch-hits?"

"Don't ask me. This place is as clean as a whistle. Any guy who keeps house like that, if he ain't queer I'll eat my hat."

"His visibleness too, going to these poetry slam-dunks with all them fruits and twinks and fairies and weirdoes? That ain't no low profile."

"You see his name wrote down anywheres or papers or anything?"

"Nah, but it's him."

"He's gone cuckoo for sure."

"Too bad Tony Whack's tied up bean-counting and the other. He ain't been seen for a few days so maybe he's closing in on him."

"Yeah, I can't hardly wait till Tony Whack plants his pieces like it's a petunia patch."

"Jesus, what a no-good crooked motherfucker he is. Bavard. Him and his Ponzi. Our people seeing him on a street corner up in Quebec Canada and a cardboard sign. God Bless, Please Help Me. That's what our boys up there saw."

"Yeah. Eyeballs about fell outta their heads. Him, they're saying he got the hots for kiddies. They saw it on their computers. The cops are looking into it."

"Fucking short eyes."

"Should we have him whacked?"

"Yeah, our service to society. Our guy up there in Quebec City who works for the Montreal crew, he says he'll do it for half price just to wipe him off the face of the earth. Gives French-speaking Canada a bad name, he says. I'll make the call."

"Our boy here, Chance and Higgins and now Bavard. How many others he said he disappeared that he didn't?"

"You gotta wonder, the sleazebag crook."

"All those area codes of his. He could be on the fucking moon."

"This Remington, my uncle, many years ago he wrote a ransom note on an old typewriter like this."

"They matched up the keys to the note, didn't they, when they busted in and searched his room?"

"He wasn't the brightest guy in the family. You can't do that now with this word processing thing they got."

"Your uncle, he doing life without no parole?"

"Yeah. Still is, till the day he dies."

"This boy of ours here who flew the coop, all we can do is lay out some more bait and talk nice to him and hope he swallows the hook, you know, in case he gets by Tony."

"Yeah, nobody's perfect, not even Tony Whack."

"This is why we got to handle business ourselves, you know."

"Yeah, I know."

"Get up personal and close to the motherfucker."

"We do."

"This ten Euros?"

"Yeah."

"Let's go get that drink."

"Let's go do it. It's all the dough we're maybe gonna see outta this."

52

Billy Bob to the Rescue

They weren't going out anywhere in the morning.

It had stopped snowing and the skies were blue, but there were drifts above the mirrors on some cars and completely covering their little rental unit.

Looking between the curtains, Beth described it.

Ted said, "Makes you homesick?"

"Are you serious?"

They had breakfast in bed, the sandwiches they hadn't gotten around to eating for dinner.

Beth checked her phone messages.

"Five. All from guess who," she said, putting the phone to an ear.

"Hi Mom."

"Yeah, we're fine. We're at our motel and—"

"No, Mom. If there are hookers and dope dealers here, we haven't seen them. They're indoors too. I don't think you can peddle much dope in a blizzard."

"Yeah, we are trying to get out of town."

"No, we haven't decided where, but it'll be where they haven't seen snow since the last Ice Age. If we can ever get out of here, that is."

"I promise, cross my heart and hope to die, I'll call and write regularly."

"Don't go away? From here right now? Don't worry, Mom."

"Be packed? Sure, Mom. Yes, Mom, for once in my life, I'll do what you say. Okay, Mom."

"Heaven knows why, but let's do what she says," Beth said.

Ten minutes later, they heard noises out front and a horn honking. Beth peeked out. "It's Billy Bob. Let's go."

Awaiting was a tow truck with a snow plow mounted on front. They crowded into the front seat with Billy Bob Blamey, Beth shoving Ted in first.

He was as Ted pictured, a big man with a big gut, rheumy red eyes, and a crimson schnoz.

Introductions were made. Billy Bob was a man of few words beyond answering Beth's question, that, yes, he had been working all night, clearing roads and pulling dumb-asses out of ditches who should've been home eating popcorn and drinking toddies.

Beth said that he must've been living on coffee.

"Beth, I just wanted to say that—"

"Don't go there."

"You got it. All I was wanting to say, you hear of guys with a thing for gals' shoes. *That's* sick. They collect these shoe catalogs."

"Get the wax out of your ears. Do. Not. Go. There."

"Loud and clear." Billy Bob popped a pill in his mouth and said, "This here's my caffeine all bundled up small-like."

That put an end to the conversation. Billy Bob cracked his window every couple of minutes to spit out tobacco juice. Ted supposed that if Gladys kept the trailer on smog alert with her smoking, in all fairness she could tolerate her husband's chaw and his cat. Postponement or cancelation of the Branson, Missouri honeymoon, well, that was between them.

Billy Bob dropped them off at the airport terminal door.

"Thanks and have a nice day," Ted said.

"Tell Mom and Fluffy to have a nice day," Beth said.

The Butte airport wasn't JFK, but it was warm inside. It was barren of people and services, so they drank coffee and watched TV until a flight was able to make it in from Salt Lake City.

A Seattle-area news bulletin came on, the audio in closed captions. Yellow police tape surrounded an old car on the fifth floor in the Seattle-Tacoma International Airport parking garage.

It was a stolen 1996 Honda Accord. Items of interest found inside were spent pistol cartridges on the floor and, in the glove compartment, photos of Robert Chance and Brenda Lee Smith, victims of unsolved homicides.

"Well," Ted said.

"Well well," Beth said.

53

Tamara Ludmilla Larrionov

Daddy has ordered me to close down South Seattle Industries to mitigate and cut our losses.

When he tells me to close down, he tells me to stop throwing a tantrum.

I tell him it is not a tantrum. I am yelling because of the bad connection between my logic and his brain.

He has ordered me to shut down South Seattle Industries instantly before it fires back in our faces, so this is what I must do.

Triple Threat Tony is our reddened flag, our precautionary tale.

Not only has Tony (I think) located the remnants of the Bob Chance embezzlement, he has vanished. Without a word, without a trace. I was stupid for letting him be as is. If my boss was not my father, my future would be in mortal peril with Russians and Italians.

Tony is a madman dog killer, a skilled forensic accountant. But in reality a traitor who has zeroed onto the money and taken it away from us. I have no evidence of this and I have no evidence that he has not other than he is vanished, which is plentiful evidence for me.

He will be so sorry. Nobody can hide from Daddy forever, nobody.

My "fiancé," my security chief, my Federal Security Service agent, is in charge of dismantling incriminating evidence.

I yell at him to work faster.

He yells at his crew to work faster, wiping clean each and every pixel, then smashing the computers and hammering the hard drives into balls of tinfoil. Paper has been shredded and reshredded until it is lint, the ethereal titanium alongside with it.

South Seattle Industries was my brainstormer. Thanks to its failure, Daddy's losses have plunged him from being the eighty-fourth richest man in the world way on down to being the eighty-seventh richest man in the world. I can feel his embarrassment from here to Moscow. I feel his shame.

Daddy wants me to come home and stay with him at his mansion on the Black Sea. It is like him sending me to my room.

I lie and say I will obey when my work is done.

I cannot keep my eyes off my security chief. He is a commanding presence.

Gleaming in sweating muscles, he is physically powerful. He is frustrated that some of our frail, pimple-pocked computer experts do not work fast enough, and lifts the machines high over his head and flings them against a wall.

I like this. His violent streak excites me.

Him and I, we can be engaged for real?

I have money Daddy is not cognitive about.

My new to-be fiancé and I will not go home to Mother Russia and Daddy.

We will go somewhere warmer than the Black Sea. We will be wintering where there is no winter.

Dah?

Nyet?

Dah!

54

No Passport Required

Mary Ann Chance, wherever you are, eat your heart out, Beth Palmer Brutto thought, walking hand-in-hand with Theodore Spangler Snowe Junior.

Old San Juan was all they could ask for and more. The history, the cobblestones, the walls and battlements, the food and drink, the friendly people, the cleanliness of the town, the Spanish-flavored architecture, ad infinitum.

Beth and Ted were on Old San Juan's northernmost *avenida*, at the cruise ship docks. Three ships were in, the streets awash with mismatching outfits and ample waistlines. They enjoyed the eighty-plus degree weather and sunny skies most when Old San Juan was inundated with tourists, safety from observation being in numbers. They conjectured too that the Fellas didn't take cruises unless they brought along a stiff in a steamer trunk they wanted to commit to the deep without ceremony, in the middle of the night, in the Bermuda Triangle.

When anyone tried to cozy up to them, tourists or shopkeepers, Ted took Beth's hand and said, "We have to get back to the ship before it sails."

Enjoying the view of the Atlantic, Ted said, "We can't live on our good looks alone, you know."

They had been in Puerto Rico for two weeks and this was the first mention of practicalities.

"We're running low on money?" Beth said.

"Not so low that we don't have options. Not so low that we have to be ultra-paranoid," Ted said. "Not yet."

"You are on their ten most-wanted list, toots."

"I'm honored."

"Better paranoid than dead," Beth said. "A good title for a poem."

"I'm on poetry hiatus," he said.

"How about birding?"

"We may have to find a field guide to Puerto Rican birds. All I've seen is pelicans and gulls. We can rent a car and drive around the island after we decide that the heat, if there is any, is off."

Whenever that might be, Beth thought.

They stopped at a viewpoint. While Ted looked for waterfowl, Beth checked on their newly-purchased tablet for Clarkson medium-hairs.

"Hey, *The Los Angeles Times* has one for $199," she said. "For that price, it has to be as scraggly as Fluffy."

"Take a chance?"

"Why not? We have nothing to lose but our lives."

"I heard that line in a war movie."

"How'd it end?"

"They lost their lives."

They carried a few phones in Ted's backpack. Beth dug one out.

"Fuchsia. It's the prettiest colored one you have. It'll bring us luck."

"Area and country code: Perth, Australia," Ted said.

He went through the procedure of hearing a message saying the cat had been sold, punching #35, and waiting.

"Where you been, fuckhead?"

"And a good day to you too, sir."

"I asked you a question."

"On the move, but always available for an assignment, sir."

"You gonna clean up your act?"

"I made one little mistake, of which I will forever regret."

"One too many."

"I'm so very sorry. Discretion got the better part of me that time and remorse is eating me up. The people in question, they were five minutes from flying away. I had to stop them by any means possible. Chance's underwater Houdini skills, who knew?"

"After you told us you done him."

Any answer would be wrong, so Ted said nothing.

"Chi-town. Make that two mistakes."

"No sir. I beg to differ. Chicago is a big city. It was mistaken identity."

"If we give you another shot, you gonna do what we pay you to do?"

Ted paused and looked at Beth.

She winked.

"Yes sir."

"You gonna stop being so trigger-happy?"

"I promise," Ted said. "I learned my lesson. I simply had to right a wrong on my part, an unintentional error."

"You do good work when you do it like you're spose to. We're gonna give you one last chance."

"I really do appreciate that, sir."

"Shut the fuck up and listen. This'll be harder. This guy, see, he does what you do, but he ain't checked in for a coupla weeks. We got no address on the guy, so we'll give you a bonus for hunting him down."

"You have no idea where he is?"

"We got some clues."

"Vital mystery clues?"

"Huh?"

"Never mind."

"This guy, he took a powder. He knows a shitload of stuff about us. This is bad."

"That's ironic," Ted said.

"That's iron what?"

"Sorry. Never mind."

"Him and you, you maybe, you know, crossed paths."

"I can't imagine who you're talking about, but go ahead," Ted said.

"Lemme put it this way. If you was lying to us about the swim the bookkeeper took and the Chi-town thing, we don't take it personal. You cut some corners. We all have. It's just business and it's in the past."

"No hard feelings by you. That is so generous," Ted said. "I am so grateful."

"You'll have the specificals waiting, same deal."

"I'll get right on it."

"This is different. We gotta have a sit-down in person to lay out the problem. Like I say, this guy is different, a special case."

"I understand. You name the time and place."

"Where you at now?"

"I'm taking a little vacation, here and there, working on my tan."

"You still in the U.S.?"

"I am."

"So when can we have this meet?"

"I'll be available real soon."

"Don't take forever."

"I won't. In fact, I'm cutting my vacation short and changing airline reservations now."

"Whadduya mean by soon?"

"Soon."

"You're flying to where?"

Ted gave the phone a long toss into beautiful warm blue water.

"They were playing kissy-face with you, tossing their hook out for a second time."

"That isn't the Fellas I know and distrust with my life."

"They were talking Tony Whack as an assignment?" Beth asked.

"Might be they were."

269

"You'd have to go after him, but if they clue you in where he is or could be, what're the odds that they're setting a trap for you?"

Ted said, "If I say even odds, I'm being optimistic. If Tony can't find us, we go to him. Or to them."

"I wonder if he has a valid passport."

"When you tended bar in Queens, was there any scuttlebutt at all about him having a record, something that'd deny him a passport?"

"No. None."

"Well, as we know, it doesn't matter. Puerto Rico is a U.S. commonwealth. No passport required to enter."

"The Fellas will be putting out an APB on you to every goombah they know."

"Yep."

Beth said, "I can't worry on an empty stomach."

He took her hand, heading toward the closest restaurants.

She pulled on him, saying. "I know just the joint. We've been there. They have the best mofongo in Old San Juan."

They entered a small bar three blocks from their hotel on Calle Fortaleza. There must've been twenty jewelry shops on Fortaleza, many offering discounts to cruisers, so they did not have the bar to themselves.

A moment after they sat, the bartender brought enormous, top-heavy fruit drinks. Atop Ted's was a candle.

He placed the drink in front of Ted, lit the candle, and said, "*Feliz cumpleaños, Senor.*"

"*¡Ay caramba!*" Beth said. "*Cuarenta años.* Blow out the candle if you muster the breath."

The forty-year-old disappearer blew out the candle and feigned a wheeze.

Mofongo was a favorite Puerto Rican dish: smashed plantains with olive oil and garlic, and sides of meat, fish or vegetables. The natural accompaniment was the mojito. As traditional on the island as mofongo, the mojito was made of rum, lime juice, and mulled mint leaves. But the mint was often so heavy-handed that it tasted to Beth and Ted like grass clippings.

"After we eat, we'll go museum-hop if you like. And I know you like."

"*Museo de Arte de Puerto Rico?*"

The Puerto Rican Museum of Art was an absolute jewel, a ten-minute taxi ride to the Santurce district.

"My favorite too. We can bet money that the Fellas don't do museums. Ted?"

"Yeah?"

"Think we should buy a new map and dart kit?"

Ted said, "We should. Staying in one place too long. Not good. We had fun doing the dart throw."

She squeezed his thigh. "We did. While we're waiting for our food, whip a poem on me."

"Sorry, I'm fresh out."

"One that pops into your head. Stream of consciousness."

"Like a fifties beatnik in a coffeehouse."

"Like, that's it, man."

Ted thought for a minute. Okay. Here goes.

> **Tourist gringos.**
> **Full of bewilderment and hard currency.**
> **Not us, not Beth and me.**
> **In enclaves, living by our wits.**
> **I love you.**

"Cool. Your best ever."

Their food came. They ate lunch and sought to live happy ever after.

55

Me and My TonyPoo

We walk on the beach, stepping over and around shells and coral that are sharp and hazardous to bare feet, but collectible at home, not that I'll ever return, with or without shells. Because of the heat, I feel overdressed in shorts and sleeveless blouse.

Tony, who is overdressed in long pants and a wifebeater, has been coaxing me to wear a bikini.

"My little bikini girl," he mumbles and whispers.

Let's be honest. I look in the mirror with my eyes wide open and without rose-colored glasses on. I never did have an hourglass figure and it's too late to develop one. I am Missy Plain Jane.

I know he's patronizing me with his flattery. He has his reasons for being with me as I have my reasons for being with him.

For me it's excitement and great sex with an incredible hunk of manhood, to spend my money with in tropical paradise. I am, however, waiting for that great sex. He complains of pain but is vague where and he won't allow me to see him undressed.

My Tony Poo walks with a limp, so I know his discomfort is connected to his ambush of the busybodies in our hotel suite. He will say nothing of it except that the problem has been resolved. Tony said he had "to teach them a lesson." All my instincts tell me not to press for details. *Hear no evil* is wise of me, don't you agree?

Therefore, I do not bug him about his limp, but I know the confrontation didn't go as scripted. He barely made it to the airport in time.

We're here, though. That's good enough for me.

For my TonyPoo, a name he despises that I bestowed on him during one of our non-sleeping siestas, at which I asked him to satisfy me by other means (don't ask for details!) that he did without much enthusiasm, who knows. Oh well. I guess there's no such thing as paradise even in paradise.

It bears repeating that he's with me strictly for the money. If he discovers the source and how I transfer it, I'm as good as dead. A piece of me will be buried under every palm tree from here to the village.

Thanks to Bob's ill-gotten gains that are now my ill-gotten gains, Tony is a hired killer on sabbatical, pure and simple. He has no scruples, no conscience, but my password system and series of offshore accounts would take a roomful of hackers to enter. I may've been under a glass ceiling at the bank, ladies and gentlemen, but I knew my IT biz. The nosey parkers were right on the money regarding my ability to find the money.

Call me nuts, but being with this living, breathing time bomb is half of the excitement.

The sequence of there to here was extemporaneous from the very start. I had no endgame until the discovery of that pair in my kitchen. What a saw and ice pick were doing in my bedroom under Tony's pillow, the Pollyanna in me chooses to believe that he had to keep his tools somewhere in the event he was arrested.

"Lunch?" he mumbles in my ear.

My vain, vain TonyPoo. Poor man, his front teeth are as cracked and broken as a hockey player's. He can have crowns done here. Dental care is cheap and I'd be paying anyway. I'm not bringing it up, though. It would be a reminder of his fight in that hotel garage. It might set him off, my TonyPoo, my lovey-dovey time bomb.

My lovey-dovey who mutters "case study" and "networking" and "Ted" in his sleep. My Tony Poo is a complex man.

I am parched and could go for an ice-cold mimosa. A full-strength mimosa. No longer do I have to dilute them with soda pop, to play a day-and-night drunk, unhinged by my husband's violent death.

I think more clearly after two or three mimosas. Hiring homicidal street punks was an easy task at home. It's been even easier here, where the poverty rate is Third-World high. Walk into a bad neighborhood and be accosted, simply say that you can rip me off for the little money I'm carrying or listen to a proposal and make more than you'll make in ten years robbing tourists.

They listen. Guaranteed.

How do I know that?

Because I already have Pedro and Juan on retainer:)

They may not be necessary, hopefully not in the near future. My Tony Poo has asked me to dye my hair blond, my pubic hair too. If this turns him on so he performs and not like a machine, what's the harm?

I take Tony Poo's hand without asking his opinion on food and drink options, and we go to lunch.

56

In a Central American Cloud Forest

Those on the ground are unnaturally quiet.
    Motionless.
Staring up at me with large glass eyes.
Me: a long, sleek colorful body with tail feathers twice as long.
They are in awe.
I am unafraid of them. I have no two-legged predators.
Let them stare.
I love the attention.

About the Author

Gary Alexander is the author of sixteen novels. *Disappeared*, first in the Buster Hightower series, has been optioned to Universal Studios.

He's also written 150+ short stories and sold travel articles to six major dailies.

One story appeared in *Best American Mystery Stories 2010*, and another in *Mystery Writers of America Presents Ice Cold: Tales of Intrigue from the Cold War* anthology.

On his last visit to Lisbon in 2015, Alexander walked where Harry Antonelli had in 1940, although somewhat less recklessly.

His website is www.garyralexander.net

What's Next for Beth and Ted?

RAISING CHICKENS ON MARS is.

It's the name of the fable and of a Pollock-esque abstract expressionist painting that was auctioned for a record $325 million just before it was stolen in a brutal robbery.

Two years later, Ted disappears the painting's unlawful owner and RAISING CHICKENS is part of his double-dip fee, a multi-million dollar albatross, the mother of all white elephants.